Bookends

Ella M. Hayes

Valenza Publishing

Valenza Publishing
Hadley, NY 12835

First published in 2023

ISBN: 979-8-9891368-8-9

More by Valenza Publishing

Praise for Bookends

"A tribute to the romance genre and a candid exploration of the trials of upholding one's essence in an ever-changing society. Crafted with charm and depth by Ella M. Hayes, the novel is a compelling invitation to anyone at the crossroads of following their heart or conforming to societal expectations."

-Chris Jones, Overly Honest Reviews

"...an exceptionally cute and fun read... This book had a good bit of a twist in it and overall, I highly recommend. Especially if you are looking for a refreshing and fun read. This book pairs well with a cup of tea, a comfy chair, and a free afternoon."

-Jade Nimoa, author of "Fate's Tether"

"The gamete of emotions felt through this story from one chapter to the next had me craving more, and not being able to put this book down."

-Inkitt Review

"A compelling easy read that book lovers, including us binge readers will truly appreciate. A uniquely written tale...."

-Inkitt Review

"So engrossing."

-Inkitt Review

Dedication:

To my incredible fiancée. You're the only celebrity I need in my life!

The Playlist

Wolf Alice:

Lipstick on Glass
Delicious Things
Your Love's Whore
In the Bleak Midwinter
Feeling Myself
The Last Man on Earth
How Can I Make It Okay

Other:

California Friends - The Regrettes
I Dare You - The Regrettes
Maps - Yeah Yeah Yeahs
You're So Fucking Pretty - The Regrettes
Proof - Paramore
Still Into You - Paramore
Eighteen - Pale Waves
Easy - Pale Waves

1

I am in love with a man I will never meet. From my backstreet book-store in my hometown, I sell the words of this love to all who share my passion for the works of Daniel Cassidy.

Bookends is everything I've ever dreamed of. My store is small, prac-tically in the basement of a jewelry store on Phila Street in Saratoga Springs, but it's cozy. My own private heaven. Part of this heaven was peace and quiet, which almost bittersweetly, I have plenty to spare here.

Just two blocks down the road is a chain store. They had prime real estate on Broadway, and licensing with all the major publishers. Working on trade-ins and buy-backs, I really just can't compete. I'm lucky to get a dozen customers on any given day, or fifty in the sum-mer when Saratoga is hot with horse racing. When people do come in though, it is rarely to buy.

My store is an attraction. People like to look at the ancient books locked in glass cases, and comment "If I had enough mon-ey…" What people *do* buy are old books from their childhood, or Daniel Cassidy's books. But other than his, I can't bring myself to bring in all these new paperbacks fresh off the print. On top of the fact that too many books today are just the lowest-common-denominator smut, with what looks like the same graphic designer doing the work on

EVERY.

SINGLE.

ROMANCE book, I believe a book has so much more meaning when it's shared. When I pick up a book that looks like it's been read through a hundred times, I know it has a history to it. Someone loved it before me and now I get to share in that. It's even better when it comes directly from a friend, giving you their copy to read because they just *had* to share it with someone. That's the kind of feeling I want to foster in my store. I want you to come in and share in an emotional journey with someone. You don't get that in a corporate bookstore or in a digital copy. At that point, it's just words. Other people may have read it, but it's not like holding something physical that has passed through the hands of people who connected with it. Sure, this becomes a problem when the back room of the store is brimming with hundred-year-old books that I just *can not* let the owner sell. Do I get a little too attached? Sure. But at least I'm aware of my problem and that makes it okay, right?

Even though I just made that rant, I do have one exception to my rule you might have guessed.

There are not enough copies of Daniel Cassidy's books in the world for everyone to get to, and patience can go right out the window waiting for someone to finish their copy that you can borrow. No, you need to read day one. Be the first at the store and read it five times on that first day. He will CHANGE YOUR LIFE! So, I do my part, and provide you with his art. You're welcome!

But I guess my story isn't about Daniel Cassidy. Maybe one day I'd see the writer on one of his book tours, which would ironically be at the store right up the block from me. But for now, at this very moment, there are two men in my life. The first is the UPS guy that will be delivering the stock of Cassidy's latest book, and the other is the one I'm stuck with, and trying desperately to get rid of.

At least once a week *Harry* comes around. And every week, it's the same old lean-on-my-counter-with-a-book-he-might-have-heard-me-mention-in-passing-one-time trick. Sometimes he tries to play it off like he was visiting his sister, Nyx, who owns Witch's Brew next door, but I know better.

"What is it this week, Harry?" I ask.

What attracted me to Harry in the first place was how naturally cool he is.

Was.

We'd known each other for a while through a mutual friend/ roommate, Aria, but didn't formally meet for the longest time. Then one evening about, what, four years ago(?), Aria had convinced me to go out to one of the bars on Caroline Street with her. I'm not really one for partying or bars, but I figured 'what the hell' and went out anyway just to try something new. Not even an hour into the night, Aria was off with some other guy and ditched me to find my own way home. I tried to make my way out of the bar through the suffocating crowd, but every inch of the place was filled with groups of rowdy drunk girls singing way too loud together, or guys desperate to find a girl they could buy a drink for. At every step I took I was either being tossed around or blocked off by someone who "just wanted to dance." It wasn't until Harry, who had noticed me from across the dimly lit room, forced his way through the crowd and escorted me to the exit. When he first touched my hand, I thought he was trying to kidnap me, but the softness of his hold somehow convinced me it was okay. I couldn't see his face, only heard him shout at people to "make room! She's gonna throw up!" That sure did the trick. In seconds we were out of there and he let go of my hand. Now able to breathe again, I was able to take in who it was that got me out of there. Harry's warm, kind smile softened my beating heart. When he spoke, it was more friendly than anything else and did a great deal to put me at ease. From there, the night seriously turned around.

In hindsight, I should have realized he should only ever have been a friend.

"Good afternoon to you too," he always says with a flirty smile. "I heard this one was a good read." This week, Harry slides over a battered, spineless copy of *The Princess Bride*.

I can't believe this guy. How long has it been since we broke up? Two, maybe three months?

Yet, he shows his resilience with as much charm as he can muster. "Never heard of the writer though, S. Morgenstern? What else did he write?"

"He didn't. The guy's not real. But I appreciate the effort."

Look, I don't hate the guy. We dated for a reason, and I guess it's partially my fault he still hangs around. Like every other couple, we said we could stay friends after the break-up. "Not the right time" and all. We kept on texting a little here and there, just making sure we were both okay and when he asked to hang out, I didn't want to hurt him more and say no. And now here we are. Two or three months later I see him regularly. The biggest issue is I know I'll never want him again, but he'll never move on.

Shit, I hope that doesn't make me sound like a bitch.

"Wait if the guy's not real, who wrote the book?" He asks, now genuinely (I think) curious.

I can't help but smile lightly at him. "It was just a joke by the real writer, William Goldman. The book messes with the audience by starting with a note by Goldman saying that what you're reading is just his abridged version of the original book." I reach over the counter and begin to flip through the author's note to show him.

He leans in closer as well, but I know it's not so he can get a better view of the book.

Sometimes I wish moments like that would spark something in me again. I want a moment in my life like in one of Cassidy's books. I can't stand enemies-to-lovers tropes but, like a taboo, I do think about it happening to me sometimes. I want to feel that tension in the air. That raw sexual urge to grab each other and devour his face... but with Harry, it's just not there.

I pull back from the counter and my eyes drift to a woman wandering around in the next room over. She's been browsing for a while and is starting to come off as the kind of person who will touch everything in the store but never buy anything. Right now, I feel like letting my mind escape to people-watch, rather than giving in to this conversation with Harry, but he also hasn't crossed any lines into annoyance yet.

"That's an old copy. It's a bit beat up but still goes for quite a bit."

He straightened up, but his smile never faltered. "How much is quite a bit?"

"Enough that you might wanna wait for our Black Friday Sale. Half off everything used!" I joke, trying to keep the atmosphere light.

"Oh, come on, for this?" He holds it up, lack-of-spine side to me. "How much could this go for?"

Without thinking, I reach closer and tap the small yellow price sticker on the top left corner that reads "$150."

"You should see how much people will pay with the spine still on."

He stares down at it, unbelieving, but I know exactly what's going on in his head. "Well, you know me…" and he laughs uncomfortably. "Just want to support the local business. Gotta keep this place afloat somehow right?"

See, *this* is why he pisses me off sometimes. He's not a bad guy, he's just not *my* guy. He can't just *not* be nice once in a while. He had no problem with it when we were dating. And with this case in particular, with my store… God, it doesn't even matter. It's not like I'll be here much longer anyway.

I didn't realize how long I took to respond, and before I knew it, he had his wallet out, card slid my way.

"I insist. It's the least I can do."

He knows, doesn't he?

I ring him up and offer him a bag which he doesn't accept.

Now comes the part I dread the most every week when he asks me out and I have to-

"Take care, Silvia!" He's walking out the door!

My head shoots around as he leaves, confused, and honestly slightly disappointed. I raise my hand to give a polite wave, but my face doesn't betray the confusion.

He leaves me with another small smile.

Now I know what you're thinking. At least, I'll take a guess. *Oh, he isn't that bad, I bet they'll end up together.* No. I promise you; he is not the man for me. If only you'd seen what we had been through, all those delusions for a fairy tale get-back-together would disappear in the blink of an eye. Besides, as I said already, my heart belongs to Daniel Cassidy. And as Harry exits this scene, he bumps into the delivery man with Cassidy's latest novel.

I help the delivery man through the door and tell him to leave the box on the counter, then I rush to sign for the delivery as quickly as possible so I can open it up.

And there it is. Seventy-five brand new copies of *Stargazing into her Eyes* by Daniel Cassidy, the first book in his latest series, a sci-fi romance story about a scientist whose wife was lost in space and he has to travel the universe to find her again. Doesn't that just scream classic romance? I can't wait to read it!

Every fiber of my being is telling me to close shop and hide in my corner in the back room to get started. But thankfully, it's almost my lunch break, and I don't *have* to close.

I shout to the back where my boss is working, "New delivery!"

"Cassidy?" she asks with indifference.

I would think that for being the owner of a store like this, she'd be-

No, just as a person who appreciates *GOOD WRITING!* for Christ's sake, she'd be a little more excited for Daniel Cassidy's books. But no, Eliza May got through the first two chapters of his book *Vanilla + Cherry* and gave up! Crazy, I know. By and large, her taste is good, but everyone has at least one bad opinion, right?

I promise I'm not this snobbish all the time. Tell me honestly, there's something you're passionate about that you get annoyed at others for not understanding right?

"Who else?" I shout back, trying to sound more gleeful than condescending. I really do love Eliza. Cassidy is the one thing we don't see eye to eye on.

She walks in from her office in the back and reads my mind. "Go on dear," she says. "Take your lunch. I know you're dying to get started and I'll dock it from your pay."

Eliza truly is a wonderful old lady. She and her husband opened Bookends nearly fifty years ago, and from the pictures I've seen of the place, it's just as crowded with old books now as it was then. But back in the days of the younger Mr. and Mrs. May, people were more enthusiastic about what they offered. Sometimes I think it was their love for each other, bleeding into their passion for the store that attracted customers. That too would have been a wonderful story.

But that's not the one I'm concerned with right now.

Instead of dwelling on that, I grab a copy of *Stargazing into*

Her Eyes and hold it tightly against my chest.

"Thank you! I'll just be in the back!"

Eliza dismisses me with a wave and I'm off to fall in love with Daniel Cassidy all over again.

The back room used to be much bigger. Eliza's desk is up against the far wall, with the room's one lamp on her desk. There's a short but wide green couch on the right side of the room that's been sitting there since the place opened, and it shows. I don't know how many times Eliza said she would get the thing upholstered, but I also don't blame her for not getting it done. It's like the old hatchet question. If the head breaks off and it gets replaced, is it still the same hatchet? What if the handle gets replaced next? Most of the tears can't be seen though. They're hidden by those old books I mentioned, the ones I'm too attached to. Which I know, bad for business. Those old books line the rest of the walls of the room like books were used to build the place. There isn't even a door for the room. I was feeling silly one day last year and stacked some of the books to make an archway. Eliza wasn't a fan at first, but I think it's cute. And it ties the place together well for a comfy cozy little reading area.

Sitting on the couch, I stare at the artwork on the cover of *Stargazing into her Eyes*. My heart beats fast at the look the main characters are giving each other, with star-filled galaxies backlighting them. It's simple posing, but the level of stylization and attention to detail that went into the art is breathtaking. It's so much richer than those flat, single-shaded characters you see on all the others.

Before opening it, I take a moment to smell the fresh paper, inked with the words I know are bound to send me to a paradise in my head. I then run my finger slowly down the spine. The letters are raised and I love the texture. I then turn the cover of the paperback over, opening the first crease of the spine. Oh, how I love that feeling.

Okay, now we skip ahead.

Forget the legal text.

Forget the contents. I don't want to risk spoilers.

Forget the dedication. To Auburn? No, that should be for me.

Forget the foreward. Honestly, I like going in without context, sometimes.

And here's the prologue.

The last thing Dillon saw of Louise as her pod ejected from their ship were her sparkling sapphire eyes and the tears that flowed from them. Explosions rang out all around the station. Asteroids pelted them with an incredible fury and accuracy that some would call intent.

Dillon had to all but force Louise into the one-man pod, struggling to maintain the appearance of being just *her superior officer, in order to ensure the rest of the crew on the ship wouldn't assume anything about their romantic involvement. That's to say, that he was playing favorites. But Louise said, "To hell with what they think." She drew the line of discretion when danger and death were in the air. No, if she had to leave, he was coming with her.*

"Louise, I won't fit in there! There's no time to argue, I'll find another pod!"

The station rocked as an asteroid hit.

Louise grabbed Dillon's large, calloused hands, "I'm not leaving with-

out you!"

"Don't worry about me, I'll be okay, darling." He tried to sound soft and sweet, then raised her hands to kiss them, but the station shuddered again, more violently than ever before.

Louise fell and slammed the back of her head against the pod's navigation console.

Dillon struggled to maintain his balance but was knocked over by a passing crewmate.

"Captain! We have to leave! There are more pods in the next sector!"

Before Dillon could say anything, the crewmate slammed the ejection button for Louise's pod. The airlock sealed and Louise began to fly out into space.

Dillon jumped to his feet, banging on the airlock.

"Louise! Louise! I'll find you!"

He couldn't hear her voice but saw her screaming back at him with tears in her eyes.

The crewmate tried with all his might to push Dillon down the hall to the next sector.

"Come on, Captain! She's fine but this whole place is comin' apart!"

Dillon, aching heart holding him in place, couldn't say anything but continue to call for Louise. He wanted to believe this wasn't the end, but hadn't even been able to kiss her goodbye for what he hoped was only a brief separation.

Under the terrible banging and crashing of the crumbling space station, Dillon couldn't hear what the crewmate was shouting at him. He also could no longer keep himself planted. Dillon was being half dragged down the hallway, further and further from the only thing in the universe that mattered to him. And the image burned into his mind, the first and last thing he remembered seeing on their first, secret anniversary, were her sad, beautiful, dazzling sapphire eyes.

God, what an opening! Daniel usually does romantic adventure storytelling, but this is his first foray into science fiction, and so far I. AM. DOWN!

I start reading the next line, a time jump back to the beginning of the day but am interrupted by a commotion up front. Eliza has raised her voice to a customer, who I can only assume was the woman who spent the whole morning "browsing."

I try to block out what's going on, it's my break time after all, but am unwillingly dragged into the conversation.

The customer's voice amplifies and asserts itself in a condescending, high-pitched tone. "I really don't see what *your* issue is. The girl that was just here said everything used was half off!"

That's insane! I never spoke to that woman all morning! And Eliza would have no idea about that, she spends most of her time in the office, and when she is up front, she's completely in her own head. I slam the book shut and drop it onto the couch then make my way to the argument.

Eliza rebuttals her as I walk in through the hall, trying to sound polite, but the irritation cannot help but seep through her lips. "I'm sure you must have heard her wrong, she wouldn't have told you that if it wasn't true."

"Well then maybe you just have incompetent workers here, because that's what she said. And if *your* workers are telling *your* customers these things then *you* are obligated to honor them."

At being called incompetent I freeze on the threshold of the storeroom. Already I'm charging in, heated, wanting to diffuse the situation but terrified of confrontation, but now she's throwing insults. Later I'll tell my friend that I was ready to fight this woman, just completely deck her, but in all honesty, I want to go back into the office and hide! My heart's beating so fast and I can barely breathe, but I have to compose myself. Eliza is better at keeping her cool in situations like this but that doesn't stop her from getting walked all over.

I begin to slowly approach the customer, worried I look like I'm about to attack her.

Eliza sees me out of the corner of her eye and tries to wordlessly tell me not to bother, but the woman notices Eliza's focus has shifted and turns towards me.

"It was her," squeals the woman with a shit-eating grin on her sagging face. The woman looks like she wandered out of a hospice ward, depending on excessive makeup and jewelry to hide her obvious age. Either that or she hasn't smoked less than three packs a day for the last fifty years. Her eyes pierce through me like a hunter with its prey caught in their sight, and all I can think of is her use of "incompetent."

"I just heard her say everything used was on sale," the hag continues with a ring-crowded finger pointed at me.

Eliza tries to take the woman's focus back. "Ma'am, this is a *used* bookstore."

The woman turns back to Eliza and holds up a tall stack of books from the arts section. "Then *WHY* would you ring me up so much for this? She *did* say it was on sale." The woman dropped the books back onto the counter with a large thud. The book at the top of the stack, a photo album of the history of Saratoga bounced from the stack and fell to the floor.

"Ex... excuse me?" I try to speak but the words are stuck in my throat. I clear it and step forward slowly. "Ma'am, I think you misheard me earlier?"

She turned and looked at me again with a look of surprise and disgust. "Are you calling me a liar, missy?"

I'm taken aback at the insane escalation she continues to bring to the storeroom. I want to shout and scream and swear at her, mostly because I know Eliza won't. The most vulgar her vocabulary gets is "darn" or "shoot." If she's really in a fit, she'll even use "golly." I think maybe once she's said "shit" when she thinks I'm not around.

"Silvy, go on back," Eliza says to me. "You don't have to deal with this."

I wait for Eliza to scold that horrible woman for the nasty things she's said to me, but nothing comes and the woman continues.

"I can't believe this place. Is this how you treat all your customers?" She looks back and forth between Eliza and me. "I thought these run-down places were supposed to be nicer than this! Now she said these books were on sale, and I am NOT paying full price."

I step forward again nervously, feeling like the woman will infect me with her nasty character if I get too close. My face is feeling red hot, and I know if she yells at me again I might start to cry, but the day will only end worse if people like her are allowed to treat others this way and I'm the one that lets it happen.

"What I said was... it's... everything will be on sale on

Friday." The words come out without conviction, and her response comes swiftly. Exactly what I thought it would be.

"Friday?" She turns to Eliza again. "Well today's Monday and it's going to be on sale anyway, just ring it up!"

Eliza exhaled deeply in defeat, and sighed, "Yes ma'am, I'll get that taken care of. Silvy, can you grab that book?" She pointed to the photo book on the floor.

I can't believe her right now! After all that she just gives in? And on top of it, she lets the woman walk all over both of us, lets her directly insult me, then still wants me to help out this bitch?

My heart is beating heavily in frustration, but I do as she asks me.

The customer gives me another shit-eating grin as I place the book on the counter.

"Silvy, wait in the back, please. You're still on break," Eliza almost whispers the command to me.

I turn fast and walk swiftly back into the office, and I hear one more comment from the counter.

"And the receipt. Just in case, haha."

One of life's biggest questions: just how quickly can the perfect day go to absolute shit?

Before I have a chance to let my emotions take over me, Eliza is coming to the office.

"You really just let her treat you like that?" I ask her as she enters the room.

Eliza raises a hand to me gently as if to say 'It's okay.' Then, "Take the rest of the day off. I'll still pay you for the day, but you need to cool down."

"*I* need to cool down? Ellie, she called me 'incompetent' and a 'liar!' And then you just gave into what she wanted and didn't even put up a fight!" I can feel the tears welling up again. I should have just kept my head down and stayed in the room.

"Silvy, if this was your place, you could run it however you want to. But I've owned this for almost fifty years now. Those books were going to sell today, or never, regardless of a sale. Do you know how long they've been sitting on that shelf?"

I know she's right that they wouldn't have sold, but she still could have gone about it differently.

"Well about the… the umm… store integrity?" I wipe my eyes.

Eliza crosses her arms. "Silvia, what are you talking about?"

I breathe deep and compose myself, but for the life of me, I can't think of anything else to say. I want to defend myself and call her out for not saying anything when the insults were said.

"Silvy, listen," she sits down on the couch and invites me to join her. "Please?"

I sit next to her on the couch and she puts her arm around me like a friend. If this was any other employer, obviously I wouldn't let that slide. But over the years Eliza and I have built up a decent relationship. She can be like a grandmother to me. She always knows when to act like a boss and when to be someone I can turn to for support.

"I'm sorry I didn't say anything to her about the names she called you. I really am. This store can't afford to turn customers away though. After all these years, I think it's finally time to call it. I didn't want to tell you this just yet but… I'm closing up. After this year, it's time to move on."

I straighten myself up. Eliza brings her arm down and lays it in her lap.

"What?"

"Come on, this can't be a huge surprise," she says with a soft smile. "No, she shouldn't have talked to you that way. But right now, we need to get what we can from this place before it closes. With some people, it's really not worth it to argue if a sale is today or a week from today. I get it Silvy, you're just trying to help, but you need to pick your battles a little better. Some things aren't worth fighting over. Some people don't deserve your attention." She lifts my chin gently with her hand. "Some people are just assholes, sweetie," she says with a laugh.

I can't help but laugh too.

"You better watch your tongue," I tell her, finally smiling again. "How many Hail Mary's for that?"

"Oh, I'll check this Sunday. Will I see you?"

"Maybe not this weekend, Ellie," I let her down politely.

Thankfully she never takes my rejections to heart. I will go to church with her every once in a while, but with Black Friday coming up and the start of the Christmas season, it'll be a busy weekend for everyone, and church to me just doesn't scream "relaxing."

"Well, that's all right," she says as she stands back up. "Any who, time to get back to work. And you best be getting on home."

"Oh, Ellie I'm fine."

Bookends

I stand to walk back to the front with her, but she reaches down to grab *Stargazing into her Eyes* and plants it in my hands.

"Take the day. You can think about what I said tomorrow, but right now we both know how desperate you are to get reading. Just don't stay up too late, I need you to make those signs for Black Friday in the morning."

"Sure thing, Eliza." With the book in hand I grab my hat, coat, Vera Bradley bag, and water bottle from the desk, then give Eliza a quick hug as I say goodbye.

In just a little while, I will detox all the negative energy from this day, and be comfy cozy in my apartment with a fantastic (I have no doubts in my mind) new book to get me through the night. Here's to you, Mr. Cassidy!

2

Starting a new book is usually nothing special for me. If I treated everything like a big event, even Daniel Cassidy's books, then I'd *really* have money problems. But if I'm starting a new series, I will make it a big deal. I am potentially starting a years-long commitment to new characters and their emotional journeys. And of course, this won't be a one-time thing. If I know I'm coming up on the end of a series, I always like to re-read the first book before I get to the last one. It's interesting to see with better context, just how much the story has evolved over time.

The first thing I do to prepare is two-fold. When starting a new series, I always get Chinese take-out for my roommate and I. Part of it is a superstition I have. Consistency of this following "ritual" (if you want to call it that) is incredibly important, as the last time I strayed from it, I ended up reading the absolute WORST book series ever. Coincidence? Maybe. But if this new series has the potential to be on par with *A Court of Thorns and Roses*, then I am *not* taking any chances. The second part of this is to bribe Aria to leave me alone for the night. Food certainly is the best way to buy anyone off.

Now today is a little different because I'm off early. It's currently… hold on let me check… 12:57. I still haven't had my lunch so I could get take-out now, but that might throw off the rest of the night if I get it too soon. So, how to kill time until this evening?

It's weird having free time like this. Bookends doesn't pay much, so I usually fill the rest of my week with a "part-time job" working for my parents. Saratoga Springs' typical residents all seem to be doctors or lawyers, and mine fall into the former. Dentists. I hate it, I promise I won't bore you with it. To make it short, I help them with their social media. Two years ago they decided it was the best way to get themselves out there and stay up with the times, but all I do is share photos of them posing next to their patients with the cheek retractor in, and once in a while a half-assed video testimonials. I try getting them to hop on trending audios or make silly stuff but they always outright refuse. It's not fun, and I have no passion to follow in their footsteps, but it pays for rent.

This is not to say there isn't more to me than my love of books. A girl can work a part-time job and not be in love with it. So, here I am, letting myself be myself with this rare free time.

I can think of something to do. There's so much going on in Saratoga all the time!

I could go to one of the museums… but it's not as fun unless you're with someone.

Congress Park is always nice to walk around in… oh, but it's so cold today.

And I don't want to do anything that'll cost me money either, which is incredibly limiting when all of Broadway in Saratoga is

28

either a clothing store or a restaurant. Plus, the rent's due next week.

Nyx, Harry's sister the witch, is sitting outside her shop as I leave Bookends. She's accompanied by her cat, a little silver and black thing, and smoking from a Cabriole. I always wanted to get along with her, but she isn't the easiest person to talk to. Look, I don't get the whole "witchcraft" thing, I'm not into it, but I think it's a cool style. Her tattoos are cool, and she's got a great sense of fashion, but you make one wrong assumption, and good luck getting on her good side again. I mean all I wanted to know was if Nyx was her real name (it's not, it's Whitney, but Nyx is all she will answer to.)

"How's the hopeless romantic today?" Nyx asks after a drag of her smoke. If there's one thing we agree on, or maybe even "bond" over, it's that we wish Harry would give up on me.

"Same as always. Hopeless." I try to say it without conviction. He's still her brother, and I don't want to be rude.

"I could make something up for him. Only costs a small fortune." She strokes her cat.

"You'd drug your own brother, for my sake? That's so sweet of you, Nyx."

She takes another drag. "Just looking out for you, honey. One day you'll come around. Just open your mind up, honey. I think I've got a few things in here that could help."

"Thanks, but I'm okay. Don't need any spells cast on me today."

"Who says I didn't already?" Her curly black hair bounces as she laughs.

Turn, just go the other way. Don't engage Silvia, she just

wants to sell you something.

I walk up the street towards Broadway and put my earphones in to block out whatever it is Nyx is saying now.

Wolf Alice's *Blue Weekend* plays. Fantastic album.

I figure something's got to be going on in town, even if it is a cold Monday afternoon. The first place I pass is the cigar shop on the other side of Phila Street. Glancing past it, my mind almost tricks me into thinking I saw Cassidy sitting in there.

Ridiculous. I mean, everyone knows he's not a smoker.

I turn north onto Broadway and decide to let my feet carry me to wherever, but my feet don't move any further. In all honesty, I could go home now; just as long as I go through my process tonight, I'll be fine. But with every step I take, the more I worry the bookstore is all I really have in my heart.

After the breakup, I found solace in the store, and ever since then, I've committed so much time to it that I never realized how much it's taken over my personality.

Maybe this day and that rotten customer was a wake-up call. Today could be an opportunity to branch out and try something different. Today could start something new. Maybe I'll go into that cigar shop and become a cigar connoisseur or whatever that crowd is called. Or I could run south to the school and volunteer to help with after-school programs. I wasn't too bad on the cheerleading team back in my day, and I'm sure they could use an extra hand. Hell, I could even sign up for a Brazilian jiu-jitsu class in case that woman wants to make trouble again in my store. Why not? Start of something new.

A wave of excitement rushes over me as I realize just how much freedom I truly have right now. Freedom I either didn't have in recent memory or wasn't able to see. As if to balance out my warming heart, a snowflake falls on the tip of my nose. I look up and see a small flurry coming down. The first snow of the season. It might be a nice chance for a walk through the park anyway. Maybe my future is waiting there.

That's what I've decided. To the park it is. I turn heel south and cross Phila Street, but I can't even make it ten feet until, clouding my own thoughts, I crash into a man walking my way.

"Oh, Lord! I'm sorry!" He says as I drop my things and my headphones fall out.

We both drop, he grabs my bag, and I chase after my headphones that bounce away from both of us. When I've retrieved them, I give the headphones a wipe on my coat and put the right pod back in, then I see the man for the first time and the second song on the album begins. It's like a movie scene playing out in front of me. The song matches perfectly as this new character is introduced.

Holding out my bag is this perfect doppelgänger for the one and only, Daniel Cassidy. He's standing in front of me looking like he walked off the about-the-author page with his trademark popped-collar jean jacket and disheveled dark hair. And the way the snow is falling lightly on him only makes this feel more like a fantasy meeting. Of course, he can't be the *real* Cassidy. It's the week of Thanksgiving and he's born and raised in Iowa! So, why would he be here? On top of that, I can smell the hazelnut cigar scent hovering around him. Not a very healthy habit is that, Mr. Cassidy? Still, the likeness is uncanny, and I'm still nervous in front of him. The only thing off about him is there's a pin for, what I can only guess is, a red flower with a black dot in the center. I've never seen that in any of his photos.

"Here you are," he says, holding out my bag with a look of embarrassment. "Sorry, wasn't really looking where I was going."

"That's fine," I say a little too excitedly. For some reason, I'm unable to convince myself of what I already know, and I'm staring at him smiling like a fan girl.

He only looks back at me, embarrassment shifting to confusion.

"Are uh… are you okay? I didn't hit ya too hard, did I?"

I can't help it, but I let out a small laugh. "No!" Was that too loud? God, now I'm the one embarrassed, and I feel my face going red.

"Would you, uh," he glances down quickly at my bag in his hand, "like it back."

My lips purse, trying to hold back my childish smile, like I'm holding back a secret. *Do you know who you look like? You're beautiful and I love you. Can you just pretend with me for a second? What about a picture so I can mess with my friends?*

I can't help but think I've just said all these things to him, then let escape a loud, horribly unattractive HA!

There it is, I've scared him off. He definitely thinks there's something VERY wrong with me. Now I don't care who he is, whether he's the real Daniel Cassidy or not, I just want to be gone.

I quickly grab my bag out of his hand, then high tail it out of there in the direction of the park with a very sudden "Thank you, Dan!"

Shit, did I really just say that out loud? And before I have the chance to hear if he's going to say anything in return, I jam the left earbud into its place. The song playing no longer fits the mood, and I'll probably be stuck with this awkward memory from now on when I hear this song.

In a matter of seconds, I'm at the end of the block and turn left to walk down the road towards the north entrance of Congress Park. By the time I'm there, the snow has started coming down harder, leaving a thin layer on the carousel by the entrance, and erasing the walkway that led to the old casino. It's the kind of snow you hope to wake up to on Christmas morning, and thank God for that, because I need literally anything else on my mind right now than that last encounter.

For the next hour or so, however long the album lasts, I walk around the park with the snow slowly building up around me. I don't mind the cold as much as I thought I would. The fountains are shut off, and one of the two pods in the park is completely drained, but it's all still lovely. I wish it was later in the evening now, because at night, with the lamps turned on around the park, it will look absolutely beautiful. I remember coming here one New Year's Night, not Eve, with Harry when we first started dating. The park had been completely empty. We assumed everyone had their fill of partying the night before. We had just finished dinner with his parents at one of the local high-end restaurants I could never afford on my own in a million years. The snow was falling like it was now, and though I was in nothing but a short Black navy-blue dress and coat that was no-where near appropriate for the weather, I didn't mind the cold at all. Harry and I were in such a comfortable, loving place in our relation-ship that he really was all I needed to stay warm. We walked together along the path from the casino to the carousel, and he surprised me with a private ride. "I thought it was shut down for the season," I said to him, but he told me they opened it up last night, and he was able to convince someone to do him a favor and keep it running for one more day. It doesn't hurt to remember some of our memories together. With the snow falling around us, and Harry pretending to escort the carousel horse and me around, it really did feel magical. He said the way the snow rested in my auburn hair was a moment that should be captured in a painting and displayed for the world. What does hurt now is how quickly the silly lines like that faded from the relationship.

I don't mind walking by the carousel and the memories as-sociated with it. It's the memories that came after I wouldn't mind moving on from.

3

I'm home just before three. Take-out's been taken. I guess it'll just have to be an early dinner tonight, and thank God Aria's home because I do not want any distractions after getting this night started!

Aria and I share a two-bedroom apartment on the outskirts of Saratoga. It's just over 1000 square feet of cramped space. When you walk in, you enter through the kitchen, decorated almost entirely of Crate and Barrel by Aria. How she could afford all of it I will never know. The living space is decently spaced for the apartment, and it's where we have most of our meals. We have a small cabinet along the left wall of the living room where we used to have a TV until we sold it because why have a TV when we can use our laptops, and usable space doesn't come easy in the apartment? Eventually, we replaced it with a record player when Aria decided to make collecting vinyl her new hobby. She never did, and neither did I except for two albums. *Abba Gold*, naturally, and *Blue Weekend*. So, now it just comes off as pretentious. There are two seats in the living room, one a lovely cloud-like couch that my parents got us as a housewarming gift, and a single recliner we got secondhand, which is where I do all my reading when I'm home. Someone left it out on the sidewalk, and it didn't smell bad at all, so we figured why not? Thankfully Aria's then-boyfriend was able to help us move it up to our 5th floor apartment.

My room is on the left side of the apartment. Now you probably think that every inch of my wall is covered by bookshelves. Sorry to disappoint, but there is only one in the corner. It's one of those triangle shelves that can hold maybe 3 things on the bottom two shelves and one or two books on the top shelves. If I had real bookshelves, I wouldn't have any room to walk. Plus, we won't be here forever, so more furniture means more work when we leave. That was at least the mentality when we moved in. Though I don't have the shelves, I have all the books that would have filled them stacked up along the wall, and no space to walk. It's like the floor is lava. But instead of lava, it's an addiction and crippling debt.

Even though there's a balcony, there isn't much of a view, unless you like watching cars go by. Still, it's a cozy place for the time being. Cozy enough to get this night started.

I walk in, hang up my coat in the closet, and kick my shoes off.

Aria is sitting at the kitchen counter, wearing her scrubs and drinking a High Noon. She's on the phone with someone, maybe a co-worker from the hospital. She gives me a nod, which I return as I hold up the take-out bag.

"I don't know what his deal was," Aria says into the phone with serious annoyance in her voice. "Rich was just having one of those days and I wasn't gonna deal with it in front of everyone."

I place the bag down on the counter, then take out my food and find a seat on the couch.

"Seriously, I thought it was clear that it was just a stress thing. We'd both been working back-to-back shifts and needed release. That shit happens and now… RIGHT!"

This conversation might take a while, but I try to ignore it. The next step for the ritual is ambiance. Hopefully, Aria will understand what I'm doing if she hasn't already taken a hint from the food.

I first close the blinds, which I usually don't have to do because I usually start later in the evening. Next, I light a vanilla Woodwick candle.

At this point, Aria understands what's about to go down.

"No, yeah, no… yeah I'll call him in a bit about it." Aria grabs the bag from the counter and the High Noon, and mouths *Thanks! Enjoy!* as she walks to her room and shuts the door.

Thank God I have such an understanding friend.

Just a few more steps and I'll be ready to go. I next take out one of the albums from the cabinet, *Blue Weekend*, because it starts very softly, doing a fantastic job of easing you into the faster, wilder songs. Abba is great but just a little too high-energy pop for right now. With the album playing, I'm just about there.

I turn the rest of the lights off, except for the torchiere floor lamp that sits behind my reading chair. The mood is now set, and it's time to read.

I take my seat in the chair, place my take-out, pork lo mein, in my lap, then reach over to grab *Stargazing into Her Eyes* from my bag and…

My heart almost stops! I jerk closer to my bag, dropping my food onto the floor.

"Shit!" I shout.

From her room, I hear Aria jump to her feet and run to the door. "Everything okay?" She asks through the crack.

No! No, it's not! Where's the book?!

"Yeah!" I lie, nervous that I won't find the book. "I'm fine, just spilled."

Aria gives me a soft okay, then returns to her room.

For a moment I don't even realize the pork lo mein is on the floor. My mind is focused on the book. I know I grabbed it before I left, and I didn't sit down anywhere in the park. I didn't even go inside the Chinese restaurant to get the food, it was brought out to my car. Could it still be in the car? UUUUUUUGGGHH… whatever.

I get to my feet and (God, can this night get worse?) step in the noodles. I step away from it quickly, but the sauce has already been soaked into my socks.

Whatever, it is what it is. I'll change my socks, grab the book out of my car, and get the night back on track.

Never mind, forget the change of socks. Instead, I take them off and toss them into the hamper in my room, then find a pair of slippers. Grab my keys quick, and I'm out the door.

My only thought on the way down to the garage is, *please don't let anyone be walking around right now.* I feel like at this point the smallest thing will set me off for good and there will be no rescuing this night. And *that* means this whole series will potentially be ruined for me. Thankfully, God is having an ounce of pity on me tonight.

No one is in the halls, elevator, or garage.

The garage is freezing, and my car is all the way on the other side. It was the only spot open when I pulled in but for SOME REASON everyone's apparently decided to leave now that I got the worst parking.

Keep your cool Silvia. Things'll pull through.

There sits my car. A 2015 Chevy Sonic. I'll open the passenger door, and there will be the book. My night will begin to turn around.

With every step, the remains of my limited optimism vanish. I don't even have to open the door or search under the seat. The book is not there.

It then hits me where I left it. That goddamn Daniel Cassidy look-alike that bumped into me. Oh, the irony.

The stupid, stupid irony.

In this defeat, I only have one option, and I hate it. But I'm desperate.

When I get back to the apartment, Aria is cleaning up my mess. I think she can guess what's going on because she doesn't say anything and isn't acting annoyed at cleaning up for me.

I tell her with a pout, "I lost it."

"New book?"

I nod and slump back to the couch.

"Cassidy?"

"Mhmm." I fall on the sofa, face first. "An ee sole it too." my words are muffled by the cushion.

Aria sits down next to me and asks, "Someone stole it?"

"Mhmmmm." I lift my head a bit to clarify, "Daniel Cassidy stole my book," then drop my head back down.

Aria laughs at my pain. "Okay come on, I don't think *the* Daniel Cassidy stole anything."

"Except my heart and book," I say and reposition my head on her lap. "Some jerk who looked like him. He bumped into me and I dropped it."

Aria tries to sound sincere, but I hear in her voice that she's not taking this as seriously as I am. "Okay, so he didn't *steal* it."

"He robbed me of my happiness."

Her lack of seriousness for the situation, mixed with the sound of genuine empathy in her voice is working to get me to ease up.

"Well, it was just a mistake, that doesn't make him a jerk."

No, he wasn't, but he *was* the final straw on an already shitty day. That book was the one saving grace I had and now that's gone too. Thinking about all of this, I can only mumble agreement. I know if I get started on the rude customer today, I'll only make myself feel worse.

But Aria persists. "At least it smells good in here, right? That's a positive."

In my mood, I've forgotten all about the burning candle and the music. I shoot up and blow out the scented candle.

"What was that for?" Aria asks, surprised.

"*Vanilla & Cherry* was Daniel Cassidy's fifth book." I don't say it then, but that book was the reason I chose that scent for my ritual.

Aria sighs deeply. "So, what, just gonna stop being a super-fan anymore because of one bad day?"

Why can't she just let me be dramatic? Aria is one of the most carefree, come-what-may, do-what-your-heart-says kind of people I know. I love her, but she only thinks reasonably when it comes to other people. She's like the friend who gives everyone else the best relationship advice but is never in one herself.

She's right though. As much as I hate to admit it, she's right.

I stand there, halfway between the kitchen and the living room, with the candle in my hand. She's staring me down with a half-smile on her face, waiting for a response.

I mumble through a hidden grin, "Noooooo… I still love him."

"That's what I thought. Good talk." She stands and walks to her room.

"But I'm not using vanilla," I make clear to her as she passes into her room.

"That's fine, just keep it quiet during the good parts," she says, then closes her door.

I won't light the vanilla candle again. The ritual is already screwed up, so what's the point? Instead, I'll heat some leftovers (to eat quickly at the counter), grab a White Claw (pineapple), turn off the music, light a nutmeg Woodwick because I still need a nice atmosphere, and then finally get in bed with my heating pad and download a digital copy of *Stargazing into her Eyes*. "Oh, and get in comfies!"

Once again, cozy.

I feel like I've done enough complaining today, so I'm going to down this White Claw, maybe grab a second, and try my best to enjoy this book without getting distracted. It always happens when I read on my iPad, but hopefully, I'll get too sucked into the book.

So, let's continue.

The first chapter is thrilling, in a cheesy way. After the meteor attack in the prologue, we jump back to a few days prior. Dillon, the captain of the space station, and Louise, one of the younger officers, have found themselves in an affair, intoxicatingly drawn to each other. As per regulation, higher-ups aren't allowed to fraternize with their subordinates, so he's risking his career for her. On top of that, the station is receiving strange, aggressive signals from an unknown entity. It's melodramatic as hell, but I love it. The tone reminds me of Daniel's fourth book, *Treasures of the Deep Desert*, and though it wasn't my favorite of his, it's definitely a guilty pleasure for how sappy it is.

The chapter ends with a change of shift. Dillon and Louise escape to his cabin and things get steamy, but not overly explicit.

Really, ever since *Habits*, Cassidy has kept his books pretty PG-13. To be fair, that book nearly ruined him. Critically and mentally, apparently, but the writing during his isolation era because of COVID was so raw and honest. I think he showed too much of himself in those books and it made people uncomfortable. I appreciated them though. Especially *Binds*, but I'll never tell.

Anyway, I'm getting distracted.

So, there they are, things are getting hot and heavy. Leaning more towards hot. At this point, they're both still telling themselves it's only a fling, but it's so cheesily obvious they both feel something greater. On the last page, we cut to the bridge. An asteroid is en route to collide with the station, and everyone's scrambling to find the main crew, but Louise, the Chief Navigations Officer, isn't in her bunk, and Dillon isn't answering his radio. The crew is finally suspecting them right at the worst time. Juicy.

I think I need another White Claw.

The second chapter is almost exclusively action, with a few cheesy lines added here and there for the romantic melodrama. The buzz I'm feeling only adds to the excitement. With every line, I fall deeper and deeper into the story, until I'm reading "Daniel" instead of "Dillon," and "Silvia," instead of "Louise." In the sappy lines, he says to her, I hear it in Daniel's voice. I know everyone wants to insert themselves in the story. Who read *Harry Potter* and didn't want to be in on the magic? But in this, it feels like he wrote about me when creating Louise. From the auburn hair, the medium-large circular glasses resting on her upturned "Scandinavian nose." Even her eyes that Daniel Cassidy loves to mention are described as blue with small specks of green in them. I swear he's talking about me.

I grab a 4th white claw and start the third chapter.

Wait, what time is it? Shit, it's already six! Still early I guess, but how many times have I re-read lines or dazed off into my own fantasy? Maybe I should take a break. But on the other hand…

My heart weeps as the universe rips her away from me…

Chapter 3 is mostly an internal monologue from Dillon's point of view. Duty demands that he ensures the safety of his crew, but he's crippled by having to admit to himself his feelings for

Louise, unable to lie anymore that it was just a fling. Everything is crumbling around him, and his first mate is picking up the slack. Destruction rains down around them. Crew members are killed in explosions, electrical fires, or sucked into space, but the only thing he can think clearly about is Louise. When they finally find an escape pod the situation only gets worse. It turns out that the navigation systems across the station, to include the escape pods, were downed in the initial attack. Dillon realizes two things here. If he and Louise had responded when they were supposed to, this would be an issue. Also, since the system was never restored, Louise is now floating blindly in space.

Dillon is now presented with a choice. Does he help his men fix their pods and ensure they get home safe, or does he go after Louise and fly the pod manually, hoping he can follow her trail?

This obviously doesn't set him up as the best leader, but it's a great opportunity for growth as a character.

The chapter ends with him narrowly escaping in a pod headed after Louise, and he looks back on their final moments together before the first asteroid hit. It's flirty and sensual, with their true intentions hidden deeply beneath. When he talks about her body, it reads like it's her soul he's infatuated with. When he's caressing her breasts, he's only trying to feel the beat of her heart so that he can beat in time with her.

I feel my legs shake with anticipation as if I'm there and it's Daniel's hands on me. I want to keep reading but now I *NEED* a break.

I turn off the tablet, and turn over to open my nightstand...

Interlude:
Summer Snow

Released: March 6th, 2018

Synopsis: For the last 30 years, Sarah Lauder has been a historian at McConnelston High School. Life had always been kind to her until her husband was killed in a hit-and-run three years ago, and instead of moving on, Sarah only buried herself deeper in her work with the school. Now, with the third summer break approaching, her friends and coworkers worry about her mental health and group together to send her on vacation to wherever she wishes in an attempt to help her find a bit of comfort.

Sarah is now booked for three weeks in Iceland, her dream spot, but once she arrives it's hit with historical colds. Alone and unsure of herself in a new country she slowly finds herself not vacationing but becoming ingrained with the people of the town she's staying in and forming a connection with one of the locals, a young wide-eyed man who carries the reflection of her lost husband.

-Page count: 488

Bookends

-Read: Oct 1st – 8th, 2020

       April 3rd – 7th, 2023

-Rating (Goodreads average): 3.9/5 Stars

-Rating (Mine): 4.5/5 Stars

Reviews (SPOILERS): This was an interesting read, and it definitely took a minute to get into, but my patience paid off, and I'm glad I stuck with it. The book is… I wouldn't say *thin* on plot… but it takes a back seat to the main focus of the book, which is a look into the mind of the protagonist, Sarah. It feels like a majority of the book are her reflections on her lost husband and internal monologues trying to make sense of how quickly everything falls apart. It's a slow read because of that, but again, once I got going, I really don't think it hinders it.

       The tone was really the hardest hurdle to overcome for me. This being the third book of his I read, I didn't expect this level of depressing material. I'm sure if I'd read his stuff in release order it would have been very different. And it's really not until the third act that it begins to lighten up. At every moment you think something is going to start to turn around, something else always gets in the way to screw it up. It's like, come on Daniel! Give the lady a break! But, for all the depressing stuff in it, it's used well, always serving to show Sarah these internal strengths she didn't know she had, and I think that's really powerful stuff, which allows the narrative to have its cake and eat it too.

       One of my biggest worries in this, was that at the end of the day, it'd be Emil that "saves the day," so to speak, and is the reason she's able to get over her dead husband. I'm really glad Daniel Cassidy didn't go that route, but still utilized him when necessary, and was able to make an engaging romance where it still respected Sarah's lost husband.

Speaking of Emil, he might be one of my favorite Cassidy characters. Running theme in this book was me thinking, "Hmmmm… I'm not too sure about this," turning into, "Okay, I get it, and I love it." When his character is first introduced, I really thought this was going to be some guy's fantasy of getting with an older woman. Maybe there is a bit of that in there, but I don't know. If I ever meet Daniel Cassidy, I'll ask and let you know. The way their relationship develops is so natural, and it's helped greatly by a characterization where he has just enough of Sarah's husband in him, without it feeling like she only likes him because of that. He has enough individuality to make him stand on his own. But what makes him great is he represents something I think most of us wish we could experience in life. Through him, Sarah is able to get a new perspective on her life with and without her husband, as if having gone back in time to when they were younger. It's not necessarily a second chance, because that would only hold back her ability to move on, but a perfect epilogue to one story before another begins. And I mean, I know I gave a spoiler warning at the beginning but, SPOILER (kinda), the fact that they never even have sex (at least they don't mention it but who knows, maybe I just missed a hint) really helps the narrative from falling into cheap storytelling where THAT is how were supposed to know they're in love.

When it got to the last few pages, I was really scared that

something was missing. We're going at full speed with the story up until the last sentence. I still don't know if Sarah ever left the village, if Emil came with her, did they break if off? What? To this day, Daniel Cassidy has refused to acknowledge that, but again, I'll ask if I ever get the chance. Maybe he'll go easy on me.

This story was very satisfying, and a nice start to Daniel Cassidy's bibliography. I'm mixed on if I would recommend this to someone just starting out with his work, but hopefully people will go into this with the right expectations and give it the appreciation it deserves.

–Edit– It only gets better on the second read.

4

I wake up the next morning around 7 with a killer headache. I think I read up to chapter five last night, had another drink, and then might have given Aria a full plot breakdown through incoherent drunk ramblings.

In hindsight, I don't think she was a fan.

Good news is at least all the screwiness building up to the reading didn't ruin the experience.

Since I'm going back into work at Bookends today, I'll buy a new paperback copy of "Stargazing." I'm sure at this point someone saw my copy on the street and nicked it.

I'm also mixed on how I feel about going back this week. The closer we get to Thanksgiving, the less business we'll have. It'll be nice to be in my comfort place and not deal with mean customers, but it will also be more dull than usual. And to be fair, for every mean customer, there's always a nice one too who's eager to start up conversations and be friendly with you.

I arrive at the store just before nine for opening. Eliza won't be here for another hour or so, and I don't mind the time to myself. It helps me clear my head which I desperately need this morning.

Bookends

As if they'd been eagerly waiting for my arrival, the box of new *Stargazing.* books is sitting on the green couch of the back office. Before I can give myself a chance to forget about it, I grab a copy and put it in my bag, then set the bag aside on the desk. I'll charge myself for it later.

Any new books go onto their own special shelf on the front counter. One of those revolving metal racks that hold two shelves up and down that can each carry maybe two or three copies of a book. It doesn't mesh well with the aesthetic of the rest of the store, but new books already stick out like a sore thumb anyway. Especially when they're only ever Daniel Cassidy.

I place the books in empty spots on the shelf. Three copies of Cassidy's last book, *Stars Through the Trees*, are still sitting there waiting to be bought. Naturally, I loved the book, but after his previous works, I think people were more hesitant to continue supporting him. It definitely works in a new context as a spiritual prelude to "Stargazing," by slowly shifting his style from *Habits* and *Binds* back into more streamlined romance and his inclusion of cosmic themes.

About halfway through the task, there's a knock at the door.

"Not open yet," I call, without taking my focus off the rack.

There's a muffled, "I know, I just..."

The voice sounds awkward like getting into the store is like trying to ask a girl on a date for this guy.

"We'll be open in a few!"

Out of the corner of my eye, I see the person walk away from the door, but a moment later, he's in front of the window behind the counter and knocks.

At first I think it's Harry. Twice in one week, that'd be some-thing. But then I look up and a mix of shock and giddiness runs up my spine. I think today is going to be a "friendly customer day."

There in the doorway, with my copy of "Stargazing." in his hand, is the Daniel Cassidy doppelgänger.

Music starts playing in my head. No earbuds required this time. What song is it? It's light and sweet with a twinge of swing.

I see his mouth move but the music is all I hear.

Now he's pointing to the book, and his eyes look apologet-ic. Like he knows I blamed him for the accident. And that's all it was right? Just a silly accident? Who cares in the long run?

He gestures over to the door and mouths, "Okay?"

I don't know what he said building up to this moment, but I nod my head anyway and step to the side to unlock the door.

I open the door and there he stands, half a foot taller, and close to me, but in no way standing over me in the same jean jacket with that weird flower pin. It's a distance that says, "I don't want to intrude, but I *have* to see you." Or maybe I'm just projecting. Fuck, the likeness to Daniel is impeccable. The memory of last night flash-es in my mind, how I fantasized about him last night and now this man is here before me. It's awkward but I can almost convince my-self this is the real guy.

"I'm sorry for barging in but," he holds out the book for me. There's a large crease vertically on the cover where it bent when it fell on the ground. "I thought you'd want this back."

I don't know what to say. I look back and forth between his face and the book. Now that I hear his voice again, I'm so sure that it really is HIM.

"Do you uh… do you want it back?"

Yes! Say 'yes' Silvia, what are you doing?! You look like an idiot with your mouth hanging open like that!

"Y-… yeah, yes! Come in!" I step to the side like I'm inviting my home. Why? Silvia, get it together!

"No, it's okay, I don't wanna intrude if you're still closed."

I look at the open/closed sign hanging on the door and flip it to 'open.' "You're just on time," I say with a laugh and the most embarrassing smile on my face.

"Really, it's-"

I mean to reach for the book, but something takes hold of me and I accidentally grab his hand and nearly pull him in. "Please! It's amazing seeing, you know… ha ha… you!"

A hint of anxiety comes across his face. He knows I've placed him – I mean I bumped into him with his own book! – and he's probably worried he's going to have to deal with an annoying fan girl. Which, I mean…

But I still don't know what to say to him. I'm still holding his hand. He hasn't pulled away yet. Maybe he's just uncomfortable and doesn't want to be rude. Maybe he's scared! Oh shit, he thinks I'm a psycho! I quickly pull my hand away, taking the book with me, and hold it against my chest in both arms. Maybe it'll make me look innocent and harmless. I promise I'm not a psycho Daniel!

"Okay…" he starts. "Well, glad I could give it back." He glances awkwardly around the store. It's weird, from all his promos and interviews, he never came off this shy. It's definitely Daniel's voice, and he's still wearing the jacket I know all too well from his social media. Jeez, maybe I am a psycho.

His eyes then spot the rack of his books on the counter and I turn red with embarrassment.

"I guess you were all set though, huh?" His eyes return to mine, the first time they've become truly locked.

The faintest breath escapes me. My heart's beating at a hundred miles an hour, and my knees feel weak. Fuck, I think I even got a little wet when he looked into me.

God, if this was a movie I'd throw my arms around him and he'd dip me into a passionate kiss as the camera pans to a roaring fireplace. Take me, Daniel!

But it's not, and our eyes break contact. He looks glances at the door then says, "Okay, well… take-"

"I LOVED IT." I burst out and take a quick half-step closer to him. I'm nearly standing on my toes.

He jumps back a bit. Whether at my volume or, because I'm too close, I don't know. Maybe both.

I realize I came off too strong, and fall back onto my heels, dropping my head an inch too to stare at the floor.

"I got through five chapters last night." I almost say that I felt like he was writing about me, but NO! Jesus, Silvia, as if you weren't coming on too strong already!

His demeanor changes, but it doesn't look like appreciation. Just… interest, I guess. Or is it relief? It's hard to place.

"You are…" I glance around the room to make sure no one else is listening, even though I know we're alone. Then, in a whisper with a slight lean in, "Daniel Cassidy, right?"

He rolls his eyes the slightest bit and I know exactly what it means.

"No, no, no! I don't want an autograph or anything! I just… thank you, I guess."

"For what?" He's loosening up a bit. There's a small grin again.

I can't help but laugh again. He's actually here, still! Talking to *me*!

"Your writing, it um, helped me through some stuff."

This time his eyes roll, it's out of humor, and he leans back on the counter, but quickly fixes himself. It's like he thinks that was rude, like making himself comfy in someone else's house.

"Well, thank you then," he begins. "But I never really thought anyone would get like, that involved in them. That they would *help* anyone. They're just sappy stories."

He's just thrown my mind all affudle. That is a *lot* to unpack. So, let's break this down.

1) Holy hell, I just got an insider look into the mind of Daniel Cassidy that his publisher would KILL him for saying publicly. *Just* sappy stories! Aren't writers supposed to believe in the "deeper meanings" of their work? At least to sell it, right?

2) A little hurt. I tell him what the books mean to me and he (unintentionally, to be fair) invalidates how I feel. Not cool.

3) Could he really mean that or is he being humble? Obviously,

it's not all sappy romance. *Habits* is by no means a romance, and *Binds* is practically a straight-up, well… we all read it. I'm not ashamed.

4)   I love that he describes them as "sappy." Even if it's used in a bad way, that's the word I use. I still think it's a good thing.

"Maybe for most people, Mr. Cassidy."

His cheeks flush red when I address him as so. It's so cute! I never felt this kind of "golden retriever" energy from his press talks and social media.

"But I've read them all," I continue, "and there has to be some of your truth in there."

Daniel leans in. It's almost imperceptible, but it's definitely a lean, and I'm realizing how close we are. I never thought I'd get to meet him, let alone be alone in a room with him! But we're only inches apart now, and it feels like the universe is pulling us closer together. He smells like hazelnut coffee, with a bit of the cigar he smoked yesterday still lingering on his jacket. The smell of the cigar brings me back to summer nights when I was in high school. I'd sneak out to parties on Saratoga Lake with friends, and all the guys who thought they were so much more mature than we actually were would bring cigars. We were all idiots back then, but it was a great feeling and I'll always love that smell.

"How far did you say you got?"

I hug "Stargazing" closer to my chest and say through a silly, half-embarrassed-at-my-own-gushing smile, "Only five chapters."

An actual smile on his face! God, my heart's going to explode!

"I could have read it all last night, but I got to this weird part of loving it so much I had to tell someone about it so I gave my roommate this super annoying drunk ramble about it and then I eventually passed out," I say the whole thing with a smile on my face and at the last word I think that was an incredibly unattractive thing to say and become terrified of the impression I just made.

But he hasn't moved away. He's still smiling at me.

"So, the internal monologues? You didn't think they were too out of place? Or didn't take away from the story too much?"

I shake my head. "No, those were my favorite parts. Mr. Cassidy, I think you should know how much you're messing with the reader. I really have no idea if they just recently met or have known each other forever."

He steps closer still. I can practically feel the warmth coming off him. Is this my heartbeat I hear, or his?

"It can feel like that sometimes," he says. "Isn't that what people like about these books?" He lightly taps the copy of "Stargazing" I hold to my chest, but he may as well just be touching me. "The forbidden romances?"

My legs are about to give out. His lips are so close to mine and for a moment I almost give in, but...

A moment of clarity hits me.

Binds, chapter 17:

"Isn't that what you love about guys me?" Mason steps closer to Rose, who's now up against the wall and holds her neck in his hand. With his lips almost on hers, he says softly, "The forbidden romance?"

This asshole!

I step back quickly, creating distance between us, and hold up a hand to stop him from coming closer.

"What do you think you're doing?" I ask.

"I-... wh-... wait I thought…"

"I'm not that kind of person, Mr. Cassidy! I like your book, but that doesn't mean I'm just gonna sleep with you!"

Can you believe this guy?

"Wait a second, that's not-"

He tries to step closer, but I pull the door open.

"Thank you for the book back, but I think I need to finish opening."

He looks to the door, and back to me. Back to the door, back to me, completely bewildered. Good. You probably don't get told off like that too often, do you, Mr. Man?

"Please," I say sternly, gesturing to the street with a stern glare at him.

Without arguing, he says, "Okay, I'm sorry," and walks out.

I hate the way he says it, too. It's too, I don't know, somber? It's not the tone you usually get when you turn someone down for a hook-up. No, it was like he was genuinely apologetic for letting someone down. Which only makes it worse! It's emotional manipulation! Like, oh no I'm sorry for not hopping on your lap, you totally deserve to fuck me because I read your books? NO! I love Stephen King books too, but I'd never even kiss him! GOD! What is with these guys?!

I slam the door behind him and turn the open/closed sign

back to closed. But wait, no, It's well past 9. All right I'll wait for him to be out of sight so he doesn't get any ideas, then I'll change it back. Not like anyone's lined up to come in.

But now I'm fuming. After all that! Maybe I was setting myself up for this fantasy. Of course, he'd use his own writing to try to get with someone! But if it was from literally any of his others? I mean, he could have been more subtle. I was there, he basically had me! But then again, that's the problem too, isn't it? I was so close to giving in anyway. I was almost drooling over him!

Well, good riddance. Never meet your heroes, right?

I need to get my mind off of this. Any distraction is a good distraction right now. If I keep thinking about him, I'll just get irritated and might throw something.

I start going through any chore I can think of but it's a small store and it only takes me two hours to wipe down every glass surface to include every display cabinet, the counter, the door window, the front window, hell, even the tiny screen on the card reader. I vacuum every inch of the place, dust the bookshelves, and go through each and every one to make sure all the books are in the correct order. Alphabetical by author. I find a few dozen in the wrong spots, people never put them back where they belong, and that kills more time trying to put them right. I even count, recount, and recount again the money in the register just to be sure it's correct.

At about 11:45, Eliza comes in and I'm in a good state again. Until she says this:

"You'll never guess who I just saw outside. Daniel Cassidy!"

5

"Please, do not mention that name, Eliza."

"What's this? I thought you loved the guy."

I'm slumped over the counter with my head in my hands.

"Oh Eliza, he's just some creep. And is he really still out there?"

Eliza drops her handbag on the counter.

"No, I saw him in the window next door at that cigar place. He looked really down, but I knew it was him instantly. You should try to talk to him."

I can't help but throw my head back and laugh.

"I don't think so. Not a guy like that. Eliza, he was in here…" I recount to her the events you just witnessed. The whole time she seems so candid, like it's just another day in Saratoga that you meet celebrities. Well, maybe if this was summer, but still. And even more, she doesn't care that he was trying to hit on me like I was some groupie! Famous writers have groupies, right? Or is that just musicians?

"He was probably just nervous," Eliza argues.

"Oh no. No, he was a little too comfortable. He was practically breathing on me!"

Eliza laughs at my disgust. "Oh, I bet you hated that, ha ha."

I push myself off the counter and lean back against the cabinets against the front wall below the window. "Ha. Ha," I say as sarcastically as possible, then turn to look across the street through the window. Was he actually there? Has he been there this whole time?

"Maybe he wants to apologize," I hear Eliza say. Her voice is paternal, not just two girls gossiping anymore.

Without taking my eyes off of the creep writer, sitting just where Eliza said he would be, I say, "Yeah okay. If he wants to apologize, he can come back over and say it."

"I'm telling you, he's nervous," she says and walks to the back room.

I dismiss her comment, but follow and continue what I was thinking.

"Better yet, he can forget an apology. I don't wanna hear it."

"That's fine," she says, taking her laptop and glasses case out of her bag to put on the desk. "I'll go talk to him, then. I'm sure I can clear this whole thing up."

I can't believe this woman. I really can't believe her. After all this time working for her, she's taking some stranger's side? I stand there in the hallway with my hands on my hips.

"Really? Eliza, he'll probably flirt with you, too! That's the kinda guy he is, apparently."

"Oh, I should be so lucky," she laughs again. Like seriously?!

"EW! No! Please stop, Eliza."

"Listen, he wanted to give you your book back, right?" She's giving me a stern, but still friendly look.

"Mhmmm, so he could-"

She waves away my words before I can finish. "If he really is this pervert you think he is, I don't think he would have bothered with pretense. He would have left the book there on the street or kept it for himself. He came here to give you your book back. And from your story, it sounds like that was all he meant for. You wanted him in here. Did you even tell him you worked here when you bumped into him yesterday?"

"I… no. No I didn't."

Wait how the fuck did he know I was here? Did he wait on that corner all night until I came back?

Eliza approaches me and puts a hand on my shoulder.

"On your lunch break, I want you to go over there and sort things out with that boy. I'm sure everything was just a misunderstanding. He's not the kind of guy you think he is."

"Did he ask you to say that, Eliza?"

She smiles at me, "I can tell."

I can't fathom why she'd try this hard over that guy, but I'll compromise.

"I'll go when I get off today, if he's still there. I want to actually enjoy my lunch today."

Eliza is walking back onto the main floor.

"Then go now. You're on the clock, and that's an order.

Don't worry I'll be able to hold this place down for a few minutes."

That's a cheap move.

I see him through the window of the cigar shop when I leave Bookends. He's resting his head in his right hand, probably scrolling through his phone in the other.

Oh, my blood just boils at the thought of doing this. He doesn't deserve a second chance, so this better be quick.

Every step closer, my nerves get more and more intense. I can't even tell if I'm actually shaking or it's all in my head. I could lie to Eliza. Go to Starbucks instead for a few minutes then come back and say he was just as much a creep as I told her he was. But she's probably checking through the window to make sure I'm talking to him.

All right, suck it up Silvia. You can do this.

Daniel is sitting alone in the cigar shop. When you walk in you're greeted by the lounge area with great big arm chairs that look like they were made for 300 pound Mr. Monopoly type men. The place definitely goes more for a gentleman's club (not in the strippers and blow way) sort of vibe, with the humidor room further back. Past the lounge is a narrow hallway that leads to the humidified cigar room, where there are a number of tall, two person tables with chess boards. This is where Daniel is, with a perfect view of Bookends.

He stands as I approach and begins to say something, but I cut him off.

"I have questions for you," I tell him with as much authority as I can muster.

"Okay." His voice is so gentle.

I write it off as him trying to break my defenses. But no sir, Mr. Man. You're not pulling those tricks again.

"How did you know I work there?" I ask.

"Mind if we sit down?" He gestures towards the chair he was sitting in, inviting me to have a seat. What does he think this is, a date?

Instead of taking his obvious offer, I pull out my own chair and take a seat, and he follows.

"So, my question."

He exhales deeply and runs a hand through his hair.

"I saw you leaving yesterday. Before we bumped into each other."

"I could have been shopping there."

He laughs to himself. "No, I…" He looks at Bookends then back to me. "I've seen you in the window. I didn't mean to watch you or anything. I can only see from here when you're right up against that cabinet, there. But I can never see your face. You're always so focused on whatever's going on in there, you never turn my way."

I… wait how do I feel about this?

"Maybe once a day you turn this way, and I just…" He's at a loss for words and turning red again.

I'm holding back any show of emotion (a smile at the cheesiness) and he hides his face, running a hand through his hair again. I almost feel bad, but… this could just be another trick.

"I'm sorry for coming off the way I did. I didn't come over to try to… you know…"

Jeez, how much more red can he get. It's like even the idea

of sex is too much of a taboo for him.

"But I didn't come to just return your book either," he continues. "I just wanted to meet you. I tried to say hi yesterday, but you bumped into me-"

"Whoa, no, you bumped into me." I correct him.

He only laughs, "Ha ha, you had your headphones in. But it doesn't matter. Either way, let's just say I hoped to run into you. But once we did bump though, I got nervous, and you looked nervous, and then you were off!" He throws his hand out to emphasize his point. "And I just didn't know what to do, I was frozen for a sec, then I saw your book on the ground."

I have to think about this for a moment. Daniel Cassidy, has been here, right across the street from me for how long?

"How long have you been in town?"

"Too long," he laughs nervously.

All right fine, I'll go easy on him.

I let myself give him a friendly smile and ask, "How long though? Have you been watching me this whole time."

He's scared, "No! No of course not, I'm not like, stalking or nothin'."

"So, what are you doing here? If not just eyeing the pretty girls."

"Not the pretty ones. The beautiful ones."

What.

"One! Just one! But no, I mean, I'm sorry, I didn't mean it like that! Look, I got in town about a week ago."

"You came to Saratoga Springs for Thanksgiving. And

you've spent that time stalking me?"

"No, I said I'm not… it's research. You know?"

For some reason, I don't quite believe him.

"So, what's the next book about then? If you're really doing research."

In the heat of the interrogation, I didn't realize how close the two of us had gotten. The coffee smell is gone, and the smell of tobacco is there, but not as strong. He hasn't smoked this morning, just waited.

"I don't know yet," he says. "But it has to do with this town."

"But why here? Why Saratoga?" The pace of the conversation picks up. Like a real interrogation, and he's prepped.

"Family. I've learned some of this town's history from them, and it seemed like a good jumping off point."

"I thought you were from Iowa."

"Extended family."

"What family members?"

"Aunt."

"What side?"

"Dad's."

"See them often?"

"Not enough."

"Why this place?"

"Saratoga again? Trying to catch a slip?"

"Cigars."

"I like cigars."

"What about *Habits*?"

"You've got a lot of questions."

"You gonna answer?"

"No."

He falls back against his chair. The flush in his cheeks is gone, replaced with a look of glee on his face. He thinks he's got me again.

Maybe just a little bit.

"What do you mean, no?" I ask, still leaning in for the conversation.

"I get one question. It's only fair."

Fair? The audacity of this man.

"Fine. Fair."

He leans in again and asks, with a warm smoothness, "What's your name?"

There goes my heart again. I don't know what it is about him. Is it the earnestness in his voice? Or the welcoming, comfortable look in his eyes. Whatever it is, it's becoming harder and harder to see him as an entitled celebrity. So, what harm can a name do?

"Silvia," I say with my hand out to him. "Silvia Wright."

Takes my hand gently, and I swear he's about to kiss it. I'm not even sure how much I would complain if he did.

No, Silvia, stop. Calm down.

"Daniel," he says. "You don't have to keep up with the whole 'Mr. Cassidy' thing."

He's trying to break down the walls of professionalism. So, no, that would just be a win for him.

"I think I'll stay with 'Mr. Cassidy' for now."

"I'd prefer first names. 'Silvia' is too lovely a name to hide."

My legs shudder when he says my name. I definitely don't remember that line from one of his books!

We need to move on before he says anything else like that, or else I'll forget why I came in here or why I kicked him out of Bookends to begin with.

I clear the lump in my throat named "Lust" and say, "Back to my question. Why are you here? What about *Habits* and all the press about you 'cleaning up your act' and all that. You said you weren't even gonna vape again."

He shakes his head with a grin. "God, I hate that book. I tell ya, I got more crap for that book than I thought possible. It's just fiction, but everyone took it as a confession or like, 'deepest secret desires' and all that. The publicist said I should make all those promises so the books keep selling."

"Seems a little extreme to me."

"You read the book. Some of it was a little too disturbing." He leans in then and says, "Believe me, I never did any of that."

I want to question him then about *Binds*, but I can't. That'd be too hypocritical.

He continues, "What about you? That book almost scare you away?"

Obviously, it didn't. I'm still here, aren't I? But I can't make it easy for him. Gotta be diplomatic, Silvia.

"It was a little scary," I tell him. "I never believed any of it actually happened. Especially the part about Detroit and the-"

"Yeahyeahyeah, please, we don't have to talk about that part," he laughs it off but he's clearly uncomfortable with the topic. But it's not like I didn't expect some kind of reaction.

I continue, "Anyway, it still comes from somewhere, right? And everyone struggled that year. I know it can be easy to get lost in your head like that. A lot of," I take a deep breath, thinking about the family drama that came up during the lockdowns, "a lot of frustration and anxiety. Had to let it out somehow."

"That's nicer than most said."

"In context with your previous books, and the timing of everything, it seemed like a natural progression. Even if it did get a tad disturbing."

"So, let me guess. You like the sappy stuff better?"

I laugh, "got me there. Ha ha, usually. But I take it you don't feel the same?" I try to teasingly imitate him and say, "TheY'Re jUst sAPpY stOriEs."

"Okay, okay I get it, I'm sorry."

Wow, what a smile he's got when he blushes like that.

"I was nervous," he says. "It slipped out. I didn't know how much you liked them. But if it were up to me, they'd be more grounded. Like *When Harry Met Sally*. Hold off on the sappiness, let it build up until it overflows and explodes in the ending."

Did he really just reference my favorite movie? My smile is way too big now, and eyes are wide again. *This* is the Daniel Cassidy I'd hoped to meet.

"Why don't you do that then?" I ask him.

"The publisher," he answers, the disappointment obvious.

"They want sap. I think the only time we got it right was with *Lisbon*."

Interesting…

"I gotta ask. That title, it isn't a reference to the place, is it?"

"What makes you say that?"

His face says he knows exactly what's coming next and I just know my guess is correct.

"There's this song I like…"

He picks up the sentence, "… by Wolf Alice. The album was part of the inspiration."

There is no. Fucking. WAY!

"Do you promise you're not stalking me?" I try to make it sound as obviously a joke as possible, but he goes tense with embarrassment anyway.

"No! No, really…not for more than a week anyway."

I can't tell if that was an intentional joke or he's just trying to get out of the awkward place I put him in. So, I try to save him from further embarrassment and giggle.

"Cute Daniel. Not too creepy, I'll let you off with a warning."

"How about a date instead?"

Interlude
Runaway Lover

Released: July 31st, 2018

Synopsis: What are you to do when the One That Got Away returns just before you're supposed to say "I do?" Liz Cambry just answered that question, and was swept off her feet for her fairytale happy ending. But now her history of rash, wannabe romantic choices is finally catching up to her.

-Page count: 218
-Read: January 20th – 21th, 2021
        August 3rd – 3rd, 2022
-Rating (Goodreads average): 4.1 /5 Stars
-Rating (Mine): 4/5 Stars

Review: I'll try my best to avoid spoilers on this one. It's crazy how Daniel Cassidy's shortest book can cram in so much character!

The way it's told in a non-linear format, with every chapter bouncing from one defining moment in Liz's life to another, represents really well the scattered mind of someone desperate to fix themselves and not knowing where to start. And in the end, it doesn't really matter where you start sometimes, it's just there, an all consuming chaos that just exists inside you. It's a little depressing but what so far the trend I've found in Daniel Cassidy's original trilogy of books is that we follow people with tremendous baggage overcoming themselves. This one takes a darker turn than *Summer Snow* did, as in that one, the main character Sarah is thrown into a bad situation, whereas in this, Liz is just not a great person. But I don't think it would necessarily turn the reader off, following a protagonist like that. They're not a "you love to hate," kinda girl, you just don't realize they're a bad person until it kind of just clicks and you accept it. Does that make sense? What I mean is, the opening wedding scene is played out in this ultra-fantastical way where, of course you're gonna root for her to bail and be with her "one true love." By the time you realize, 'oh wow, that guy really didn't deserve to be ditched like that,' and 'maybe she didn't really think this through,' you've already moved on, and it's too late to go back and scream, 'stop! What are you doing, are you nuts?!'

This really is a mark on Daniel Cassidy for his ability to drag the audience along, letting us fall into our own expectations on life only to hold a mirror to us and ask, 'were you really okay with that?' But it doesn't even seem like he's cheating us because, although I haven't read the book a second time, I did reread the first chapter for the sake of this review, while it is ultra-fantastical, the full story is still there. The reader kinda just blocks out the fact that she's being incredibly short sighted because we just want in on that fantasy.

Bookends

After doing my research, I haven't found a ton of bad reviews for this, but most of the ones that do exist criticize this book for being misogynistic, as it's written by a guy, criticizing a woman's need for self-fulfillment. To that I say, fuck off. Every person in the world has flaws they have to come to terms with, that's not exclusive to a single gender. And he doesn't criticize in an underserved way.

The flaw it does have though, because all books do, is the consistency. It feels like this book may have been the teeniest bit rushed, and not because of the length. There are just a few bits here and there that contradict each other. I can excuse if a book isn't airtight against plot holes, but the time these came up just really took me out of it.

I don't think this needs to be read in any particular order for Daniel Cassidy books. It's a great little snack of a book that you could read in a day.

6

Holy hell! I can't believe this is happening! Our date is set for Saturday, and I absolutely have to finish before I see him again. And though I'm loving it, and all things in life should be amazing, these next few days are going to be unbearable.

After meeting with Daniel, the day slows to a crawl. A total of four customers come in all day, and only one buys. Two of them are browsers, and the last one grabbed a million and a half things off the shelves before realizing there would be a sale later in the week and dropped everything in a corner. So that was fun to re-shelf. I try to tell Eliza he should get a lifetime ban from the store, but again, she thinks I'm being dramatic.

At any time when no one is in the store, I read as much of the book as I can. But now that I've met him, it's so much harder to get through. I hear it now in his shy tone, especially in the monologues. In this new context, it feels like they are no longer for deeper insight into Dillon and Louise's relationship, but a confession of things he wished he had time to tell her. I also can't get more than three sentences read without getting distracted, thinking about seeing him again. It only makes it harder knowing how badly he wants it too! You should have seen the way he lit up when I said yes to the date. Like I said, it's that "golden retriever" energy.

By the end of the day, I've only gotten through chapter six, and about half of chapter seven.

The store closes at 4, and by 4:15 I'm home.

Aria is there already. She's cooking up stir-fry.

The whole way home, I could barely contain my excitement, and Aria gets a full-on assault when I walk in.

At first she doesn't believe me. In her words, "I think you've finally cracked. But that's okay! That's okay because my therapist is great. I can set you up with her." And it doesn't help that I don't even have a picture with him to prove it. But eventually she starts to come around, and then she's disappointed in me for initially kicking him out.

"Aria!" I give her a friendly shove. "I'm not a slut like that!"

"Oh, come on, I would! You're really gonna tell me you didn't want it?"

In the right moment, with him? Who am I kidding? But not like *that*!

"He's a celebrity-"

Aria interrupts. "To you. Not to most, he's just a writer. But go on."

I give her a look and gesture to say 'calm down.' So, what if writers aren't at movie star level. But arguably they can have just as much impact on people through their work.

"He's a celebrity," I continue. "I could have gone my whole life without meeting him and been happy." Pause. "Buuuuuuuuut…

now that I *have* met him, I don't want to waste time on some fling."

Aria pulls the stir fry pan off the stove and asks, "So, how long is the big-time celebrity staying around? Any plans on having him over? I'd just recommend cleaning up and hiding your toys. Ooo, or better yet, leave them out. Maybe he'll like that."

I take my full plate to the other side of the counter and sit down. Why can't she get off that topic? But I won't humor her. At this point it's just annoying. Still though, her first question catches me off guard.

"What do you mean?" I ask.

"Well, he's not staying here forever. He's from where, Ohio?"

"Iowa."

"Same place." She goes to the fridge and pulls out two High Noons (they take up about half the fridge. It's not a brag, just a confession). One for each of us. As she does, she says, "He said he's here for research, right? He's gotta go back sometime."

I've been so caught up in the excitement of all this, that fact never really sunk in. But I don't want to believe it. At least, I can't, no, won't believe he'll leave so soon!

Okay, but what if he does? And what if things go really well while he's here? Long distance isn't impossible these days, so there's that.

But what if he didn't mention it for that reason? What if he knew he screwed up once already by being too forward and now it's just a different angle? Oh, the bastard!

No, no, that's crazy! He was too sincere. It was in his eyes.

Call me crazy but his eyes don't lie.

"Silvy! You good?"

"Yeah, just got lost in thought. I'll see him on Saturday, and I'll ask. If he doesn't plan on sticking around, or say…" I lower my voice as if I'm telling her a dirty secret, "wants something long distance…"

We both laugh. Me with giddiness, her with second-hand embarrassment.

"… then hopefully it'll still be a nice evening out and we'll go our separate ways. At least I'll have gotten to meet him."

But I know, and Aria can probably guess, that those aren't my intentions.

I can recognize my own faults. And a big one is, if you haven't noticed already, I tend to get ahead of myself with things I'm passionate about. Here I am, having only known the guy for a few hours and I'm already talking about a long-distance relationship! I'd be lying if I said I didn't briefly picture what our wedding would be like. That, mixed with my fear of confrontation(even though it worked out, I'm still annoyed at Eliza for making me go over. Out of principle) is how we ended up with Harry. We moved in together just two weeks after we started dating. Just in time for quarantine. I was still in the honeymoon phase, so all the issues we had I either chalked up to anxiety and stress from the situation, or ignored completely out of complacency, and want of happiness at any cost. 'Everyone has their issues, these are completely normal things,' I'd tell myself. Things improved for a time when quarantine ended, but the longer things went on, thanks to Dan's (wow, I'm actually calling him that!

Or should I stick to Daniel? Which one sounds better?) writing, I saw the cracks for what they were, but it took me over a year to jump ship. God, that was a painful year. But I still don't know what hurt more, the lack of effort and romance he brought to the relationship, or giving up on him. I know, I know, that's the wrong mentality, but at least it's a real emotion. One of the only emotions that I'd felt that year.

We carry on dinner with other topics of discussion. I've said my peace, and it'd probably be healthy to let other things occupy my mind.

Aria updates me on Richard. It seems like they *are* a thing now, but not to be a shitty friend, I doubt it'll last past Thursday. Officially anyway.

After dinner we watched a movie from her laptop on the coffee table. Aria has just about every streaming service, but I don't get it. By principle, I think everything should be owned physically(i.e. All the books in my room), but also, there are only about a dozen movies I've seen and cared for. I can't even remember the last time I went to a movie theater. There'd probably be more I'd watch, but there have been none based off of Daniel's books. I think there was discussion of adapting *Binds* now that the "Fifty Shades" movies are done but the studios wanted to keep that market entertained, but the project probably slowly faded away.

The thing about movies for me is they always feel too shallow. With a book you're allowed so much more time to develop the characters, and you get better looks into their heads and backstories. If a movie can pull off that level of depth, that's great. Very impressive. But it just doesn't happen often enough for me to get invested. The few that I have loved are:

- *When Harry Met Sally* (All time greatest, I can watch it on repeat)
- *Wall-e*
- *The Princess Bride*
- *Misery* (That's the only horror I can do, and oooooo it's good. Daniel, I promise I'd never do that to you)
- *Sabrina*
- *Some Like It Hot*
- *The Apartment*
- *The Elephant Man*

Yeah, that's probably about it. Other movies I can respect for what they are, like *Lord of the Rings*, but they're just not my cup of tea. I'm sorry to all the guys reading this for that last comment.

Aria skims through for what feels like hours, asking me "how about this one?" "What about this? This looks cool!" But most of them are horror movies and Aria, come on, not the mood. I don't give a solid yes or no to any of them though, which she's not unused to. Eventually she'll pick something regardless of what I think and we'll both be on our phones the whole time, but she'll still be annoyed that I'm not paying attention.

She finally settles on an 80's horror movie called *Alien*. Wow, creative title, I'm sure I'll be blown away.

That's another thing! Horror in movies are so cheap!

OoOooOOoOOOoo, spooky monsters, AAAHHHH!! LOUD MU-SIC! That's not real horror, that's just quick, easy shock! Now in books if you can scare someone, that's impressive. The only visuals are ink on paper, but in good writing it will still transport you to that horrific scene. I remember reading *Misery* for the first time and literally sweating during the shunting scene! Oh my God, have you read that? It's crazy! At least the movie did it justice, even if it didn't go all the way. Stephen King, I know you've heard it before, but you are absolutely incredible. But no Daniel Cassidy.

Speaking of, is it too soon to text him? I don't remember how to do this. I haven't had a first date since 2019! Jesus, has it really been that long? What would I even say? Do we just talk about how excited we both are for this weekend? And I don't want to get too into deep conversation. I've always felt like that should be saved for the date, you know? You have to be face-to-face when you get down to the nitty gritty of who a person is. That may sound ironic now after my whole spiel about books vs. movies in developing characters. But it's true.

"Aria, what should I-"

"Shhh!" she scolds me, pretending she's invested in the movie but not even looking up from her phone. And it's not like anything's going on yet. It's just tracking through the ship with no dialogue. And not in the good world-building way like *Wall-E*.

I whisper to her, "What do I say to Daniel?"

She ignores me.

Whatever.

I start to text 'hey!' but then think, *wait, is he supposed to text first? Should I just wait for him?* Yeah, that sounds right. He should come to me.

I turn my phone over and wait.

Wait…

Waiting…

Still waiting…

JESUS WHERE IS THIS GUY?!

Maybe the waiting would be easier if this movie was better! The characters are awful. "Oh look! Something that clearly looks like an egg in this clearly alien spaceship! Lemme just stick my head in it!" Wooooooowww. Smart, dude.

Screw it, I'll text him. I'll keep it simple. Just remind him I'm still here.

-Hey!

Is that a good start? Or should I say something else? Also, holy hell I just texted Daniel Cassidy! Daniel, I mean. I can call him that now.

-Just wanted to say, you're welcome
again at the store! That was only
a temporary ban I gave you earlier
haha

That's good. It's light and friendly, and maybe something to get the ball rolling? Hopefully? But now we wait.

At least the movie has picked up a little bit. We've got some infighting with these characters and this Ripley girl is cool. Nice outfit and hair. If Aria wants to do something for Halloween again next year, Ripley would be an easy costume. And it's a cool name too. I'll add it to the list of potential baby names.

My mind begins to wander, waiting for Daniel to text back. I should just watch the movie. I might even like it if I actually gave it a chance. Although with Aria buried in her phone, I'm sure I could change it and she wouldn't even have noticed. I should have said we should watch *When Harry Met Sally*. I feel like I'll see it in a whole new light now after what Daniel said.

Just thank (thank God!) my phone vibrates. A text from… are you kidding me?

Harry.

> *-Hey*
> *-Your dad texted about thanksgiving*

What the hell? Why would-

UUUGGGHHHH. My parents never really accepted the breakup, especially with the way I wanted to handle it. Staying friends and all that. In their eyes, we're just having a break for now, but once we figure out our own individual lives, we'll get together. For them, breaking up after four years was a silly thing to do. We'd made it that far, and for them, I overreacted in a "rough patch." Yeah, a four year long "rough patch."

-Oh? What'd he say?

-Invited me
-Don't worry
-not coming
-don't wanna make it awkward

Oh, my Lord Harry, you only need one text to say that.

-oh, sorry about that. Weird. No i told him you weren't coming. He must've forgot.

I turn my phone over and focus on the movie again. In comparison to having a conversation with Harry(today of all days), this movie feels like the best thing I could do with my time.

But he texts back. And I won't be rude and ignore him.

-Its k.
-just wanted to let you know
-Hope its good one though!
-You still doing the tree after dinne?
-*dinner?

-probably. Dad never lets me leave
until we do. But i think it should be
left til the 1st.

I put my phone down and just in time because WHAT THE FUCK?! A little penis looking thing just popped out of John Hurt's chest! Okay, no, that scene was scary. Fantastic build-up, awesome effects and the cast really sold it. Especially my girls Ripley and Lambert(? I think that's her name).

-Well then I guess I'll have to come
back.

What?? What the hell is he thinking? Shit, I give him an inch and he just runs with it. I know he's not *trying* to ruin my week but PLEEEAAASEEE!

-excuse me? I really don't think
thatd be a good idea.

-what? But i thought you said I
could come back?

-No, i know i didn't. Please don't
come over harry

-Harry?

Wait, now I'm confused. A second text comes.

> -*Nooo come on*
> -*christmas trees go up november 1st*
> -*gotta get in the spirit early*

Shit, that wasn't Harry saying he was gonna come back!

-Oh my god Daniel! I'm sorry! Some-
one else was texting me! No please,
come back!

> -*k good, i was gonna say, haha. If*
> *you kicked me out twice in one day i'd*
> *really be heartbroken. I'd been think-*
> *ing about that date all day haha*

Ohmygodohmygodohmygod! He's been thinking about it "all day!" I think I'm going to die of happiness! I can't contain my happiness and start shaking on the couch.

"Silvy, calm down. I'm watching the movie." Eyes still on her phone.

Me calm down? Aria, you need to calm up! This is so exciting he's been thinking about *me*!

"Aria, I don't think you understand! Look!" I show her my phone.

She takes a moment to read the text on the screen then says, "huh. That's pretty cool."

"Pretty cool? Aria!" Even with my annoyance I can't help but have the biggest smile on my face. I'm sitting on my knees almost on top of her with excitement. "He's been thinking about me! All day! Me!" I fall back onto the couch feeling like a princess having been swept away by my prince, with all the giddiness in the world bubbling up in my heart!

I couldn't care less anymore about Ripley and whatever is going on in that silly movie! Right now, nothing could knock me off of my cloud.

> *-if you want help with decorating the store though, let me know!*

Harry.

I'll leave that on read for now.

7

Wednesday goes by slowly but inoffensively. The day is spent at home, alone. Aria is unfortunately working all throughout the week, which sucks because her family moved down to Westchester earlier this year. To help her feel better, I've invited her to join my family for Thanksgiving.

Harry is kept at arm's length, and Daniel is kept close. But he doesn't text too much. I can only assume he's busy doing research for his next book. I wonder what it'll be about! Me maybe? Holy hell, that'd be something.

He said when I saw him that his Aunt mentioned the history of Saratoga Springs and he's using that as a jumping off point. Oh! Maybe it's a period piece! That would be a first for him, and very exciting to read. But then, does that mean he's not working on the sequel to "Stargazing?" It was originally announced as a series. He must be taking breaks in between each book. Either that, or he already has one or two of the sequels completed and is just sitting on them until the publisher is ready to sell. Anything is possible.

By Thursday, I'm on chapter 12 of the book. For reference, it's 14, and 289 pages. I keep wanting to check Goodreads to see what people are saying about it, but I'm terrified something will be spoiled, or someone else's bias will seep into my subconscious.

I could finish it today, except Thanksgiving.

The way my family looks at Thanksgiving is it's only a prologue to Christmas. We have the big dinner and everything, with a big chunk of extended family from my mom's side to include, but not limited to, Aunt Rita & Uncle Tom, with their two kids Jared(14) & Brandon(12), Aunt Lorainne and her boyfriend Dale, with her kids Lily(20), Rose(19), Iris(18), Lavender(17), and Matthew(16), and Grandparents Nona and Pop(I know, we weren't too creative with that one). Every other year, my dad's side swaps where they're all going to be, between him and his brother, Uncle Gerry. This year, it's Uncle Gerry. But while it's my mom's side that always comes, it's my dad's traditions that we go through.

I show up around 11. They live just north of Broadway where all the old Victorian houses are. I've only just beaten out my older brother getting there.

"What's up nerd?" It's his only term of endearment, and not at all trying to be mean. It's more like a fake-mean because we all know out of the four of us(yes, I know, God help my mother), he's the biggest nerd. Comic-cons through and through. Thankfully his wife Bailey is on the same page. She, unfortunately, won't make it today. Like Aria, she has a demanding job that doesn't care about holidays or spending time with family. But I don't think I'm legally allowed to talk about what she does.

"Hey, Lucas," I say as I step out of my car.

He's sitting on the front porch with my parent's dog, a little beagle named Sally, in his lap. "Ready to help out?"

"It's blasphemy to decorate this early. But I don't want to be left out."

He stands up to hug me and Sally jumps off his lap trot alongside him.

"How you been buddy?" He asks.

I haven't yet told any of my family members about Daniel. If I was selfish, I would have asked him to come to dinner with my family just to show him off. I can't do that, but I still think it's worthy of an announcement. I just don't want to be annoying and seem like I'm begging for everyone's attention. As Aria said, he's a book celebrity. Most of my family probably won't even know who he is, as much as I hate to admit it. For now, I'll act cool. Cool as a cucumber. Nothing crazy going on in this girl's life. I'm not acting weird.

"Oh, not baaaaad…" My stupid smile shows I *am* in fact acting weird. But luckily I'm talking to Lucas.

"That's good," he says plainly.

Inside, my dad is in the kitchen cooking, and my mom is bringing boxes of Christmas decor up from the basement. The moment the door opens, Sally shoots through and runs back to the kitchen. I love the sound of her tiny paws smacking against the hard floor. It was the thing I missed the most when I first moved out of this house and in with Harry.

"Hey Dad!" I call to him.

From the kitchen I hear him call back, "Silvy?" Then his head pokes through the hall. "Thought you'd be here later!" He then returns to the kitchen. He doesn't mean it in a negative way, I don't think.

Lucas and I walk to the kitchen together and my dad and I go through the pleasantries. Nice to see you, how you been, I'm fine, food smells great. But then he adds to it and turns it into unpleasantries.

"Where's Harry?" He asks.

I don't have to see it, but I can feel Lucas roll his eyes behind me. He does the smart thing and leaves the room. Probably to help Mom with the boxes.

"Dad," I try to speak with as much patience as possible, "He's not coming, and you know that. Why did you even invite him?"

He doesn't even look at me to answer. He just keeps working around the kitchen, hopping from the appetizer plate to the charcuterie, to the turkey. For him, it's just another thing. "Silvy, it's a rough patch. Breaks happen, that's fine. You were together for years, he's practically family. And you said so yourself you're still friends." For the last part at least he looks at me, but for some reason that makes it feel worse. As if he's saying, 'See, you did this to yourself.'

"Well, he's not family anymore. And we're *only* friends. I've made that very clear to him."

He gives me a look of, 'Okay, sure kid.' "And how's that working? Does he feel like you're *only* friends?"

"I don't think it matters." I can feel my heat rising at the questioning. Why can't he just have my side? "He can think whatever he wants but that's on him."

"Who are we talking about?" My mom passes by through the hall, carrying a box marked "Village."

Before I can answer, my dad says, "Harry. He's not coming this year."

As if he's coming next, dad?

"He's not?" The genuine disappointment in my mom's voice is appalling.

"Oh my GOD!" Nope, done already. I'll see you in a few. Let me cool my head first. I quickly grab a drink from the fridge, a Corona, first thing I see, then speed walk back through the hallway into the living room. Sally follows after me. At least you won't bring up Harry, will you Sally girl?

The TV is on in the living room playing the Macy's Thanksgiving Day Parade, so I make myself comfy cozy on the couch.

Lucas comes, sliding the Christmas tree box. My parents have one of the fake ones that comes in five different sections, about twelve feet tall in total, with fake frost and everything on the needles.

"I kinda had a bet going on with myself for how long it'd take them to bring up Harry."

"Yeah well, one of these days they'll get it," I tell him, eyes locked to the TV. Right now I know he's one of the few that gets it, but I don't want this to turn into a heart-to-heart.

"Maybe when you're married. Or you could just come out as gay. Either one." He laughs.

I laugh too, a bit. "Yeah, no. That'll just be a phase for them."

He walks over and drops down on the couch next to me.

Sally immediately bails on cuddling up with me and hops over to his lap again.

"Already put in your work for the day?" I look at him and gesture over to the boxed-up tree.

"Eh. It can wait."

We sit in silence for a moment, watching the parade. That's all you need sometimes. I feel like one problem shared by books and movies – maybe plays too, I don't know – is every moment has to be filled by something. Very rarely can you get a solid five minutes of nothing and it's still engaging. Like after the heroes get into a big fight and all the henchmen are dead, I'd like ONE scene of the hero just sitting there. Catching their breath or rehydrating. No words. Just sitting there. For five minutes. And now I feel better. See? All it takes.

When my mom comes into the living room with more boxes, she's accompanied by my two younger brothers, Josh and Tyler. The rest of the siblings. Yes, I'm the only girl, and yes, it was a struggle growing up. Still love them though!

Just behind them stand their girlfriends, Izzy (Josh's of about a year now. Lovely girl, but sometimes a little *too* opinionated, and not the best filter), and Tyler's new girl whom I haven't yet been introduced to.

I know, I'm throwing a lot of people at you, I forgive you if you can't keep up. I can't either sometimes.

"Lucas, you done helping already?" My mom asks him.

Lucas sighs and gets up. Sally reluctantly walks back to my side of the couch. I don't know what it is with the dog. She's always been Lucas' biggest fan.

I look back at Josh and Tyler, raise my glass to them, and give them a "Hey bros."

Josh and Tyler are two years apart, 22 and 20, respectively. They could almost pass for identical twins, except Tyler has my mom's green eyes and is half an inch taller.

The Wright family's all here, now we just wait for the extended family, who should be here within the next hour or so, which means my mom is ready to put us all to work.

Box after box after box after box comes up from the basement. It seems like a third of them are marked "village," with small ceramic houses, shops, and people all bundled up and wearing ice skates, to be placed strategically all around the living room. That's any flat surface with at least an inch of free space, whether it's the coffee table, piano, windowsill, bookshelf, the top of a book even, or the soundbar under the TV. Hell, if my dad could balance a figure on top of the TV, he'd do it. And even though he tells us to "go crazy and put stuff wherever," he always comes in intermittently to correct the placement.

During the decorating, Tyler introduces me to his girlfriend Camille. Right off the bat, I get a good feeling about her. She has the most beautiful smile and an attitude that screams, "I just want to be your best friend." She'll be good for him.

At noon, the Thanksgiving Day parade wraps up, and after a quick commercial break, they air *Miracle on 34th Street*. The original one. My dad is always sure to have a Thanksgiving movie, or at least a Christmas movie that begins with Thanksgiving, playing non-stop after the parade ends. This one I can enjoy. It's just so pure and innocent, I think it's actually illegal in most parts of the world *not* to like it.

By the time my Aunt Lorraine gets here with her whole family, the inside of the house looks like a winter wonderland, minus the tree. That goes up after everyone leaves and it's just us again. It feels like Camille did most of the work, maybe trying to make a good impression on the Wright family.

Aunt Rita and Uncle Tom arrive about twenty minutes later with their kids, and Nona & Pop shortly after that. I don't know how those two are still mobile. They're almost in their 90's, but walking around like they're 70. I still can't believe they're allowed to drive.

Everyone is mingling and eating from the charcuterie board (shark-coochie board as Lucas and I joke), making small talk and updating each other on their lives, or gossip they've heard around town. But here I am, hanging out with Lucas and playing with Sally, just DYING to tell everyone my news! I mean, they're all here so I could do it now, but this is a big deal! I'll be patient until dinner.

Miracle on 34th Street ends and *A Charlie Brown Thanksgiving* takes its place on the TV. This is getting a little ridiculous.

Finally, my dad calls us all to the sunroom in the back of the house. It's just big enough to hold all 21 of us. The table we use is really about four tables, all slightly different heights(by an inch at most) and sizes, covered by two tablecloths. Lucas sits to my left, and Camille to my right. Good company.

Once everyone is seated, my dad leads Grace, and we dig in.

Now's my chance to share the news. Should I stand?

Before I can figure out how to say it, my Aunt Lorraine asks me, "So, Silvia, are you still working at that bookstore?"

Perfect! You're making this easy for me, Aunt Lorraine.

Now it won't feel like I'm just begging for attention. All the other kids are still having their own conversations, but I'm sure they'll tune in.

"Yes!" I tell her excitedly. "Things are actually going really well right now. Just this week I-"

My Uncle Tom cuts in, "Where are you at? Barnes and Nobles?"

I turn to him and correct, "No, Bookends. On Phila Street. Just off Broadway. But yes, it's going great. I just met, actually-"

"That place is still open?" Uncle Tom asks.

I begin, "Ye-"

My mom cuts me off, "They're probably closing soon. They had a good run though."

"Mom!"

She looks at me, half nervous. "What? That's what you said?"

"When? I never said they were closing!"

She gives me a 'oh come on' look. "Last time we talked you said no one comes in anymore."

"Okay that doesn't mean we're closing, it's just a... I don't know, a rough patch." As soon as the phrase comes out, I know exactly what I've invited.

My dad chimes in, "Does that means you're not certain it's over?"

I can't do anything but ignore him.

"The bookstore is doing fine," I tell my Uncle Tom plainly.

As if not listening to the last few pieces of the conversation, my Aunt Lorraine chimes in again. "Well then what will you do after the bookstore?"

"I… what? I'm not doing anything."

"But you'll need new work, right? What's your degree in, again? I'm sure work should be easy to find," says Aunt Lorraine. I feel condescension in her voice, but I really can't tell if it's in my head or not.

"Marketing," my mom interjects again.

Josh's turn to chime in. "You think she'd be better at advertising that store."

The comment gets a few small laughs, but all I'm thinking is, 'What the fuck, Josh?'

"No, come on," my dad says through a smile. "She does a great job with our social media. More than the rest of you do for the family business." He points his fork at my brothers.

"I'm too busy," says Josh.

"I don't have a marketing degree," says Tyler.

As if it were queued, everyone looks to Lucas for an answer.

Please help me out Lucas.

He gives me a blank look, like he was only half paying attention to the conversation, then turns back to the bloodthirsty mob. "I think Silvy had something to say."

What the fuck? In a good way Lucas.

For a moment there is silence, and all eyes are on me again.

I should stand, shouldn't I? No, that's dumb, I'll just say it. "I met someone the other day." Then to tie it into the conversation at hand, I say, "at the bookstore."

The reaction is non-existent by most of the family except for my parents, who look shocked(hopefully in a good way, hard to tell), Lucas, who's smiling at the news, and Camille, who's excited and even claps a little. She's a treasure!

"That's nice," Nona says quietly as she reaches for the cranberry sauce.

"And he's famous," I add for the clout.

Now people are more engaged. Skeptical, but engaged.

"What's his name?" My Mom asks.

Here comes the big reveal. I'm trying so hard to hold back a smile, but my face is going red with excitement and Camille is the only one matching my energy.

"Daniel Cassidy!"

No reaction.

Camille tries to look excited still, but it's clear she doesn't know who I'm talking about.

With a little less enthusiasm, I add, "the writer. He did…" Shit, what book can I mention that they would know but isn't dirty? "*Summer Snow*? *Runaway Lover*?"

Nothing.

A little quieter, *Lisbon*?"

"Well," my dad chimes in, "They can't all be best sellers, can they? But either way, that's good to hear. Happy for you, Silvia." He turns to Aunt Lorraine, "She does still help us out with the office here and there. We've offered her a full-time thing-"

"He wrote those books *Habits* and *Binds*."

SHOCK. All. Around. The table.

Okay, most of the table. (Un)fortunately, pretty much everyone over 18 at the table knows who I'm talking about now. Except my grandparents. Thank GOD they don't know. Lucas is half smiling, and Camille looks like she just heard the best dirty secret and she's all in. For the unfortunate part, my parents are a little conservative when it comes to that type of media.

"That pervert?" My dad asks.

"He's not a pervert, dad. He's really sweet."

"Silvia, have you even read those books?" My mom asks.

"Have you?" I ask in a quick response.

"I know enough about them, it's disgusting."

Lucas now, in an admirable, but futile show of support, "*Habits* maybe. I heard the other one was good."

For a moment eyes are back on him and I'm able to breathe.

"I heard." He clarifies.

I'm cut off again before I can speak but this time I'm not complaining. Camille says, "I think that's so cool! How'd you meet him? He wrote that *Vanilla* one right? I liked that one."

I love this girl.

I recount the story of our meeting to the table, leaving out some of the more intense parts though. "He said something I can't remember that gave me a bad vibe, and I kicked him out. But after talking to Eliza, I realized I overreacted and met up with him…"

By the end of the story, I think I have everyone more or less on my side. Everyone except my dad. He seems very put off by the whole thing.

Interest in Daniel Cassidy fades very quickly after my story. Camille asks a few more questions like "what are we going to do on our date," and if I'm planning something long-distance. Why am I the only one that didn't think about this?

After we eat, my dad brings the boys into the back for a drink and a Thanksgiving Day cigar. Camille and I help my mom with the dishes. The cousins and aunts are either in the dining room finishing off the dessert charcuterie plate, or watching whatever Christmas movie is on TV. Where Izzy got off to, I have no idea.

The smell of the cigars wafts into the room. It's a pleasant smell, but the moment it hits my nose, I crave the hazelnut I smelled on Daniel.

"Camille, can you go find Izzy?" My mom asks.

"Yeah! No problem," she's off, and I'm alone with my mom.

"Your dad wanted me to talk to you."

"About?" I ask as I scrub one of the dinner plates.

"Harry."

"Jesus, Mom." I almost drop the plate in the sink.

"Look, you say you're not getting back together with him, that'd be fine. But it's obvious you're not doing anything to let him know that."

"I'm seeing someone else now. As if breaking up with Harry wasn't enough." For some stupid reason, I really thought the news of Daniel would make everyone forget about Harry. I pick up another plate and scrub harder, scrubbing out my frustration.

"Does Harry know about this new guy?" Faux sympathy slides through her teeth. She wants me to think she's asking for my own good, but I don't feel her heart in it. It's once again all about Harry because *I'm* the one who treated him unfairly apparently.

"No, and it's none of his business to know! It hasn't BEEN his business for months!" The plate slips from my soapy hands and chips in the sink. I begin to shake with anxiety. Tears well up inside me, and I feel like I'm about to explode. Bits of Silvy gore spread all over the room, dripping off the walls and ceiling. My mom would clean it up while saying, "Poor Harry, he'll be so sad about this." And on the counter, she'd find my heart with the faintest beat, and give it to him as a gift. "She wanted you to have this."

But I can't explode. I can't even say anything else, I can only cry! God, I hate myself sometimes. All I wanted was to come over and share my happiness with my family but all anyone cares about is my ex! Instead of trying to defend myself in vain, I rush out of the kitchen and run up to my old room.

My mom doesn't even try to stop me.

I lay in my bed for I don't know how long. It's been years, but my parents have left my old bed sheets on, and a few of my old stuffed animals are there. I cuddle with Georgie, this terribly ragged stuffed green dragon, my favorite as a kid. 'That's not a name for a dragon,' Lucas would tease. He thought he had a say because he gave it to me as a Christmas present when I was two.

Footsteps sound through the hall, walking in my direction. There's a knock at the door and a soft, "Helloooo? Izzy?"

I shouldn't say anything. Just pretend I'm not there.

"Hey! Silvy, you okay?"

Camille, you're lucky it's you, so I'll be honest. Muffled by the pillow my face is buried in, I say, "No. I'm dead."

"Oh. That's not good." She walks in and sits at the foot of the bed. "What will we tell Daniel?"

"Tell 'im I died ob harrbrey. I loss uh will."

"I'm sorry, what?"

Aria is much more used to dealing with my self-loathing than Camille. She can't translate as well.

I begrudgingly rise off my stomach and rotate to sit next to her. "Nothing. I'm fine."

But she can see I'm not, in fact, fine. My face is tear-stained like I just got ditched before prom. Which I can sadly relate to, and that makes me feel worse.

"Good," she says softly. The genuine care in the way she says it does so much to warm my heart. "Because I don't know how to get a hold of Daniel Cassidy."

I laugh. "You can call him Daniel. He said it's okay."

"If I meet him, I'll try to remember. But what are the odds of that? I'd have to be a real lucky girl."

"Oh my god," I start crying a little more, but happy tears this time. "Why couldn't you meet Tyler sooner?" I don't care if it's weird, but I need a hug.

* * *

We come down a minute later, once I've had time to compose myself.

Aunt Lorraine and her family are getting ready to leave. I

say my goodbyes and 'hope to see you again soon's.' Their departure signals Aunt Rita and Uncle Tom, who say they should head out, but stay for another 15 minutes.

Looking around, I realize I missed Nona and Pop leave, and I feel a bit of guilt for not saying goodbye. But they live around here, so I see them often enough.

Now that it's just immediate family again, Dad's ready to put up the tree.

This is a timed event. We begin once the movie *Planes, Trains, and Automobiles*, starts playing. We watch the movie while we work but we absolutely HAVE to be done before Steve Martin gets on the final train at the end of the movie. My dad requires complete silence and attention from everyone in the room to be on the screen, so that we can all appreciate the emotional beats. He's seen this movie every year since it came out and never gets tired of it. It's insane.

Everything is finished, and the movie ends around 9ish. We say our goodbyes, and I do my best to keep it brief so my parents can't get me cornered again. All I want is for Saturday to come. At least I can be thankful for two things. 1) I made a new friend today, and she's amazing. 2) Harry didn't show up today. I didn't expect him to, but you never know.

8

Harry just showed up.

It's not right at opening, thank God, but he does make an appearance during the Black Friday sale.

I came early today to create a nice design on the chalkboard we put at the corner of Phila and Broadway that reads:

Support Small Business!
Half off everything!

I figure if we put "everything" it'll attract both people that know who we are and people that are out shopping for good deals on any type of gifts/unsure what they're looking for. I also put a second chalkboard right outside our door so people don't mistake us for Witch's Brew next door.

Nyx is putting out her own sign as I walk by. A strong scent of basil emanates from her shop.

I give her a wave and call, "Good luck today, Nyx!"

"I'm covered. Smudged the place. I can do yours if you want. Just a small fortune, but worth it."

Holy hell, I can only imagine the heart attack it would give Eliza if we let a witch cast spells in here.

"I think we'll be all set. Maybe next year Nyx," I say and enter Bookends.

From the minute we open customers start coming in. The first one of the day happens to be walking by as I flip the open/closed sign, and Bookends is exactly where he needed to be. He's looking for a first edition of *Eyes of the Dragon*, one of Stephen King's more obscure works, for his wife. I know I've seen it somewhere in the back, and as I'm looking around, a couple(maybe in high school) enters. I apologize to the man for not being able to look anymore, "but the owner should be in soon and we'll be able to help."

It's one of Eliza's few rules for employees (only me), that if there are more than two "groups" of customers in the store at a time I have to be behind the counter where I can see everything.

"That's all right. I'm sure I can find it online," he says.

He begins to walk away but I step in front of him. Hopefully, it wasn't too aggressively.

"No, it's no issue! Really! I know we have it, I just gotta watch the counter. Please, it'll only be like 10 minutes, I swear!"

Begrudgingly he concedes, and I return to the counter.

*-Eliza! Might be busy today. Hope
you'll be here soon!*

She probably won't text back, but at least she'll see it and act.

The high school couple is pawing through the young adult section saying things like, "Remember this one?" and "I used to love this book," as if they hadn't seen them in decades.

Mr. *Eyes of the Dragon* is trying to keep himself busy, browsing through the sealed case of high-priced books. Every once in a while he gives me an impatient glance, even if he doesn't mean to. I don't blame him either. It'd only take me a minute or two to find it, but if Eliza walked in now she wouldn't be happy.

To save myself his glances, I turn and look out the window to see if Daniel is in his spot. A hint of betrayal pierces me when I see he's not there, as if he were a soldier who's abandoned his post.

An excited gasp comes from the high school girl. "Oh my god, look!"

I shift my focus to her and see her pull *A Court of Thorns and Roses* off the shelf.

"I can't believe it's here," she says with a laugh, half to herself. Her eyes are glued to the book and she flips through, unbelieving she's found it.

I don't hear the rest of what she says to her boyfriend because she drops her volume down to a whisper as if she's in a library, but I can guess what she's saying. ACOTAR(as the fans call it) is a popular book and not hard to find. She, like I was when Eliza put it up, is surprised it's in with the other young adult books because it's definitely not for kids. Lots of dirty stuff. I haven't read it yet, but it's on my list. Pretty much anything fantasy-related, Eliza puts in the

YA section. And since Eliza still considers people my age (26, by the way) to be "young adults," that's where the dirty fantasy books go. I don't agree with it, but it's not my store.

Sabrina, I hear her boyfriend call her, keeps the book in her arm and they continue to browse. I love it. The book has found a new home.

Just a few minutes later, Eliza walks in and greets me.

"Morning! Did you see my text?" I ask her.

"Yes." She looks around the store and is happy to see so many customers right around opening. "Sorry it took a bit. Couldn't find parking. Broadway is absolutely PACKED today."

That's wonderful, and I'd love to make small talk with her, but Mr. "Eyes of the Dragon" is full-on staring us down now.

"Eliza, I know you just got in, but can you watch the counter for a sec? Someone needs help."

"Yes, yes, go on," she says with a smile and we swap out.

I lead the man to the back room and I scour through the stacks to where I'm sure I last saw it. Thankfully the man's patience is rewarded after only a minute or so. The price sticker only says it's $15. Surprising. I thought this book was rarer.

In the short time it took to find the book and return to the floor, about seven more people have entered. It's times like this I wish Eliza had more employees on hand. Granted, some of them are only coming in to browse and might not buy anything, but this small store gets crammed fast. At least everyone seems polite. No one's stepping on toes or getting in someone else's way.

It all looks well and good, a nice middle finger to all the

condescension the store received over dinner last night, but Eliza sees me enter the room and gives me a warning glance.

Here comes Harry. He's pretending to check out the local history section, but the moment I'm in his peripheral, he acts all surprised as if he had no idea I worked here.

"Hey there!" he says excitedly with a little wave.

Way less enthusiastically, I give a wave back but don't say anything. I just purse my lips and keep my eyes forward towards the counter to swap out with Eliza, who in turn goes to the back room.

And what do you know? He follows.

I do my best to ignore him as I check out the man I've been helping, but Harry waits patiently behind him like he's next in line.

The book only costs $8.02, which I think is a pretty good deal. But as soon as it's in the bag, the man takes off. No "have a nice day" or anything. Some people.

Now it's Harry's turn.

"Good morning!" He says with the same excitement.

"Hey, Harry. Funny seeing you again so soon." How uninterested can I sound without coming off as rude? Does he even deserve the attitude I'm giving him? To be fair, he's never in here with malicious intent. He's only ever trying to be friendly. But the combination of what my parents keep saying, Daniel entering the picture, and seeing him twice in one week because he just doesn't get it, I can't help but be extremely bothered by his presence. Right now, even though I know he isn't, it feels like he's trying to bother me.

"Oh, you know, just here to-"

"Support the local business. Yep, we feel supported." Shit,

okay that was a little too harsh.

His excited little smile falls to a struggling grin. "Yeah…" he lets out slowly.

I drop my head a bit in guilt. "Sorry, Harry. I-"

"It's all right," he says sympathetically like he feels bad that I feel bad. "You doing okay?"

"Yeah, no I'm fine." I rub my temple, trying to pretend I'm just tired, but I know he sees through it. "Good morning, Harry. How was your Thanksgiving?" Small talk. Good. Maybe he'll feel how awkward it is and willingly leave me alone so I don't have to feel guilty about it.

"Good," he says. "It was good. Small. Most of the family was at my grandparents', but my brother and I stayed at the apartment."

As he talks, the high school couple walks up behind him.

Harry sees them and steps aside. "Go ahead, we're just talking," he says.

Sabrina places the books on the counter. *ACOTAR*, *The Martian Chronicles* by Ray Bradbury, *Are You There God? It's Me, Margaret* by Judy Blume, and *Pretty Girls* by Karin Slaughter. Her boyfriend already has his wallet out to pay. What a gentleman.

I begin ringing her up, but Harry keeps talking. Distracting me.

"What about you? Decorations all put up?"

I have to be polite. I can't show any rudeness in front of customers. Gotta keep up that neighborly atmosphere of the store where everyone gets along. But the more I engage, the less he'll take the hint. He might actually believe I'm actually just tired and don't mind him being here. Ugh.

"Yep. Mom's side came around. And Tyler has a new girl-friend. She was wonderful. Oh, Shit!" I realize I rang up *Are You There God?* Twice. "Sorry, just a sec," I say to Sabrina.

As I correct the charge, Harry jokes, "Wonder how long that'll last."

Blasphemy against my new best friend? Not cool.

"Hopefully for good this time. I think I'd rather keep her around than Harry."

Shit.

I realize what I've said and look him in the eye. He's trying not to show it, but it's clear he's hurt.

Oh my God, I can't believe I just said that. I quickly rush through the transaction without saying another word to him. He won't push it either. Not in front of customers.

Once Sabrina and her boyfriend are gone, Harry leans in and asks in a low voice where the pain is most obvious, "Can we talk? Silvy?"

Anxiety starts to rise again. He hasn't asked to "talk" since we broke up. He hasn't even outright mentioned getting back togeth-er in any capacity because he doesn't have to. Up until now, it seems like he's assumed we were one day just going to be dating again. Like we didn't even realize we were doing it.

"N-now's not a good time, Harry." I feel like I'm shaking again, like my whole body has been set to vibrate. You wouldn't be able to perceive it, but my bones are rattling around in there.

I look around the room to see if anybody is ready to check out. The numbers have thinned, only four people wandering, and none of them look good to go.

"When is?" Harry asks.

"I don't know. Just not right now." I feel like I rushed out those words. Time is moving slowly around me, but on the inside, it's moving at hyper-speed.

Someone, please save me.

"What about on your lunch?"

Any time but then. Or better yet, never. No time ever. Let's not do this. Let's just stop existing in each other's lives.

"I… later, Harry."

"When's later?" He keeps getting a little closer, and a little quieter, very careful not to make a scene.

"I…" I don't know. The words are caught in my throat. What do I say? How do I not make it harder for him? He's been on this for months, and okay fine! I strung him along a bit, but it was only to be nice! I can't be the bad guy for that!

But here we are. He's the one that's well-composed. I'm the one struggling through this. I'm the one that's red in the face. I'm… but what if he's just really good at hiding it? He's still been here most weeks since the breakup. He's still trying to make it work!

"I'm seeing someone, Harry."

He winces, just the slightest bit, but it's enough to see that a piece of him just died a little.

There's a moment of silence between us, and for the life of me, I have no idea what he's gonna say next. Did he finally snap? Is

109

the cool composure gone now? Or at least on its way out?

Please, someone, anyone, come to the register. Save me.

No one. Instead of saving me, another person leaves the store.

"I'm sorry, Harry."

I think another terrible silence is about to begin, but Harry takes a deep breath, pulls out, and says bluntly, "Good. That's good. I'm happy for you."

"Good?"

"Yeah. That's great, Silvia. I hope he's… I… good. I hope he's good to you."

When he says my name like that, it- no. No, I'm not doing this to myself. It's just going to make me feel worse.

"How long has uhhh… when did this…" I can't tell if he's trying to be diplomatic, or genuinely can't come to terms with the news. Or he's trying to be sincere and keep up being just friends in the face of defeat.

"Tuesday," I say quickly.

Another customer walks in. I shoot my head around hoping it's Daniel to save the day. See, I do have a boyfriend. Just because he goes to a different school doesn't mean he's not real. I'm totally not lying.

"Tuesday." He confirms.

"Yes." Some of the tension begins to leave me.

"Cool."

"Yeah…"

"What's his name?"

What?

I ask, "What?"

"What's his name?" Harry asks again.

A customer comes up to the counter. An old lady (she must be 100) with a tiny dog in her purse. She has a Zdzisław Beksiński coffee table book. Great choice ma'am. Really one for comedic timing, aren't ya?

Harry backs off a few inches to give the woman space.

I say a quick prayer in my head, thanking God for this moment of levity.

But impatience gets the best of Harry. He asks, "He does have a name, right?"

This son of a bitch really thinks I'm lying, doesn't he?

Before I answer, the old lady points to the rack on the counter of new books. "That's the one that just came out right?"

"Yes," I say. "Just this Tuesday."

Her face lights up. "I'll take one of those too."

Her smile makes me smile. "Here you go, ma'am."

"Thank you, darling," she says as she takes the book. "I love this young man. *Binds* was wonderful."

JESUS. Didn't need that picture.

I look back at Harry. He's still waiting for an answer, so I nod towards the book in the lady's hand.

He only gives me a blank stare.

Holy hell, this guy can be clueless.

I ring the woman up. She pays in cash, and I take my time counting her change. She doesn't seem to mind. Her eyes are glued to the cover art, then she flips it over and runs her hand over the picture of Daniel on the back cover. Keep your hands off my man, woman.

"Here you are, ma'am." I hand her the change. "Bag?"

"No, I'm all right," the old woman says and puts the coffee table book in her purse. The dog doesn't seem to mind. She leaves, still studying the Daniel Cassidy book, and another customer walks in.

With her gone, Harry steps closer again.

"Silvia, if you just want me gone, why don't you tell me honestly?"

"That's not it, Harry." Why did I say it like that? But it's too late, the thought's planted already that I don't want him gone. "It's Daniel Cassidy." I reach over to the rack and grab another copy of *Stargazing* to hand to him.

"What's this?" He looks at Daniel's picture on the back, and his face contorts in a weird way like he's trying to place the face. It shouldn't be hard though. He's literally holding Daniel's book in his hand, it's not like a random face in the crowd of someone you might have known in high school.

A book, Harry. For the last few months you've been buying all my favorites but you *never* grabbed a Daniel Cassidy book?

"I bumped into him. The writer's in town and we're going out tomorrow."

Harry laughs. He actually laughs. "Are you kidding me Silvy?"

Okay, yes, I totally see how he thinks I'm messing with him. I wouldn't believe me either. But it annoys me anyway that he thinks

I'm lying.

"I'm serious. He's here and he asked me out." I stand a little taller when I say it, taking pride in the fact that of all the girls in Saratoga, hell, all the girls he's met on any book tour or anywhere he's stayed for research, he asked ME out.

"You know, I've tried to just be a friend. You know? I'm at arms length, I don't try to be overbearing, but I don't know why you have this… this… animus towards me!"

"Animus? What the fuck does that mean?" my voice rises a bit, and I'm sure heads turned but I'm locked on Harry in slowly growing anger, and a little bit of confusion.

"I read it in one of your books," he says, a little embarrassed. "Hostility… I think it means. You're being hostile to me and I don't know why!"

A customer walks up behind Harry. "Everything okay?" the familiar voice asks.

"FINE." Harry almost shouts in response, but his eyes stay on me. "Silvy, I don't know what else I can do to keep you in my life. You don't want a relationship? Okay. I can be friends. But when you feel like you have to make up a new boyfriend just to push me away-"

The customer cuts in again, but his question is directed towards me, "You've got a man now?"

I'm no longer mad at Harry. I mean, I am, but my joy overshadows it and I can no longer hold back my smile. I might even die of laughter when Harry sees what's going on. But even if it were my time, I'd refuse to go because I've developed such a love for that hazelnut scent.

"Listen, guy, back the F-" He turns around and swallows his words when he sees the customer's face.

Daniel Cassidy. Perfect timing, like in one of his books. The music starts up in my head again, that light and sweet with a twinge of swing, but this time it's more triumphant like he's about to carry me off in his arms.

We both ignore Harry, who's now fully embarrassed and speechless. Maybe a little starstruck?

"So, this boyfriend of yours," Daniel begins, "you planning on seeing him anytime soon?"

My legs shake in the best way. Did I just bite my lip? Fuck...

"I was supposed to tomorrow. But if he's free today..." I lean in a bit over the counter, resting my chest on my arms. That's not too forward, right? From the right angle, meeting him last time could count as a first date, and it's not like I'm showing off my breasts. They're just there. In case he looks. Fuck, I really can't control myself in front of him, can I? I'm saying "fuck" a lot. Calm down, Silvia.

"He might be, but it doesn't look like you are right now." He steps closer.

"I am after five."

If this was my store I'd close up right now. Just kick everyone out except for Daniel.

He rests his arms on the counter and leans in towards me. Not too close though. He's not making a move to kiss me(unfortunately), just closing the distance a bit.

"I think he'll be free by then. Might have to move some stuff around but I can make it work."

"Excuse me!" Harry literally cuts in, waving a hand between us.

I'll be honest, for however long this moment lasted, I completely forgot he was here.

Harry continues, "You're serious, Silvia?" He looks at Daniel, "this is the real guy?"

Daniel stands straight and addresses Harry politely, with a handout, "Hi." It's not said pompously, like 'Yeah I just stole your girl, what are you gonna do?' It's just polite.

Harry debates for a moment what to do, then shakes Daniel's hand anyway. "You're... Daniel?"

"And you are?"

"Harry. Silvia's... friend."

I look around the room, people are glancing at us, barely trying at all to pretend they aren't. Wow, if only that old lady had stayed a minute longer she probably would have died of a heart attack. "*Binds* was wonderful." Holy... hell.

Harry looks at me, then to Daniel, then back to me, realizing his mistake. His face begins to show hints of blushing, but he's somehow able to hold it back.

"Well... I uh... cool..."

"I really didn't mean to interrupt," Daniel says. "I just needed help finding something."

"That's fine. I'll just... I'll head out. I'm sorry Silvia."

Harry starts to rush for the door and my customer service instinct and need to not completely obliterate his heart kicks in, "Come back around soon!" Fuck, I hate myself.

It's now just me, Daniel, and three other customers who have gone back to minding their own business. With every second passing since Harry's leave, I feel myself gaining a sense of serenity. I can go back to imagining it's just the two of us. The other people in the store have been here for a minute and none of them are carrying any books. Just more browsers.

"So, what can I help you find?" I ask him. Is my voice a little dolled up so he thinks it's cuter? Maybe. Did I lower my glasses down my nose a little bit when he looked away? Possibly. Don't judge.

"Is it just books you've got here? Or like…" He trails off, pretending to study the room.

"Just books. Oh, and magazines. We've got a few over there. Why? Trying to find one of your old interviews?" I tease, and thankfully he laughs.

"Ha ha, no. Actually, I was looking for this really cute girl. Auburn hair, blue eyes with bits of green, and the cutest damn nose I've ever seen."

He's keeping this bit up then? I'll allow it. It's cute how committed he is to it. Like he's never flirted with a girl before and is running with the first thing that came to mind. But it works.

"Freckles?"

"Just a few," he says through that handsome smile.

"Hmmm…" I tap my index finger on my lips like I'm deep in thought. Should I bite my finger? Would that be hot? No, too much Silvia, too much. "Five o'clock?"

"Five o'clock," he confirms.

116

Interlude: Lisbon

Released: Nov 13th, 2018

Synopsis: Georgie and Roe. When you've known someone your whole life, it's easier to overlook their flaws. When you're in love with someone, you want to overlook them. When the two are combined, is it even possible to know when it's time to break free?

Follow Roe's journey of heartbreak and hope as she's torn between a comfortable yet toxic, surface-level love, and the fear of being alone in the world, unable to find love again.

-Page count: 531

-Read: March 2nd - 10th, 2021

March 10th - 16th, 2021

Nov. 13th - 21st, 2021

May 8th - 15th, 2022

July 27th - August 4th, 2023

-Rating (Goodreads average): 4.3 /5 Stars

-Rating(Mine): 5/5 Stars

Bookends

Review: What a strange, tragic, optimistic, and overall beautiful book. This book seems to take pleasure in sitting somewhere between solid narrative and an abstract concept. Really, if it weren't for the synopsis on the back, I'd still be trying to figure out what the hell I just read. The book goes from chapter to chapter without clear direction, yet they still somehow work, flowing from one to the next. It's like a music album that's dipping its toes into 'concept.' There's one album in particular it reminds me of, which is Wolf Alice's *My Love is Cool*, which makes sense because of all the references. Georgie from *You're a Germ*, the hallway scene, the themes in general of this toxic surface-level relationship, I mean come on, *Lisbon* is even one of the songs on the album!

But does this idea work when converted into a book? According to the critics, surprisingly it does. IDEK anymore how many awards this book was nominated for. But what do the critics mean? Absolutely nothing. It's all about the reader. And this reader absolutely. LOVED. IT.

It was definitely a hard read to start with. The first half as a whole is pretty depressing. And when you get to the halfway point, it feels *okay, this has to be the end, there's no way there's more because there's no way out of this situation*. It really guts you in the most brutal way. It's one of the few books that really made me cry, not at the climax. Believe me, that was a long night, getting through that part.

The second half is a beast all on its own. And thank God, because I don't think I could have taken another 200 or so pages of depression. So, if you're reading the book and thinking about giving up because it's too heavy, then please trust me. You HAVE to keep going. Spoiler I guess, but it's not just a great personal comeback, it's a grade-A triumph! And yes, even though it's a personal, emotional victory, we still get a bonus with a newly fulfilled romance.

Please, if you don't own this book, drop everything you're doing and buy it RIGHT NOW! I will be reading this many, many more times after this.

9

I wonder what he has in mind for our date. I daydream about it while I wait for the clock to reach five. We'll go somewhere private and he'll write me a beautiful poem. I'll never share it with anyone, just something between us. Or is he the kind of guy to keep work at work? Should I even talk to him about his books? Would he think I don't want to get to know the real him? I do! I really do. I want to know the little ticks and imperfections no one else knows about. He usually keeps his private life off of social media except for the basics. You know, if a certain event in his life gave him inspiration for one of his books and the influence his family has had. But really, until he started writing, so much of it is a blank. That's what I want to know.

It's thankfully been a great day for our little shop. Right before noon, we had a massive rush of customers. It was a little scary, I won't lie, because a ton of them were coming in with cups of coffee and hot chocolate, and with how small this place is and everyone bumping into each other to get around... oh my Lord... I almost had multiple heart attacks thinking about books being spilled on. If it's like a drop on a page here or there while I'm reading. That's fine.

Adds character to the book. After noon, it cooled down a little bit but still had a nice flow, and by 4:30 it was completely empty. I think God is looking out for me because I expected people to be browsing up until we have to boot them out to close.

4:40. I know I've got time, but I hope to see Daniel waiting outside.

4:45. Patience, Silvia. There's no clock in the room, but I hear ticking in my head, cruelly reminding me how slowly time passes.

I let time pass and after what feels like an hour I check my phone. 4:47. Goddamn it.

To pass the time, I ask Eliza if I could close out the register.

"There could be more people coming!" She shouts expectantly from the back.

I walk to the back office where she's pricing books and tell her, "Ellie, no one's been here for twenty minutes."

She turns around and looks at me like I just told her I want to quit. "Have you got somewhere to be?"

I never told her that Daniel came in. I was worried that if he came in again and she knew, she would have asked him to stay for a book signing. That, or whatever she could think of on the spot to bring more people in. Would it have been good for the store? Yeah, but it wouldn't be fair to him. And if I told her that he asked to change plans over text she would have dismissed it right there. "You can't make a date over text. He should have come in and asked you," she'd say.

"Tonight I do. I just want a little time to get ready."

"Date with Mr. Cassidy?"

You got me, Ms. Eliza May.

"Mhmmm. He said he'd be here at five."

Eliza looks at the time on her computer, and then back to me. "It's a little late to ask for time now, don't you think? What happened to Saturday?"

"He must have gotten impatient," I laugh.

"Seem's that's going around." She sighs. "All right, close out the drawer."

Yes!

4:50. I rush through the task. Total at the end of the day is $4,390.76. See mom? We're doing just fine here.

I look outside again. Still no sign of Daniel. That's fine, it's fine, everything's fine. He's got 10 minutes. And if he's here a few minutes late? That's fiiiiine. He's a busy guy. Out there doing his research all day. Or... I guess just being a human being and doing his Black Friday shopping. I wouldn't have minded doing that with him. Seeing who he gets presents for is a good way to know who's important to him.

4:55. I rescind what I said about it being fine. I should probably bring in the Black Friday Sale sign, shouldn't I? Don't want people coming in now.

5:00. It's almost dark. Where the hell is this guy?

Whatever. It's time to leave. I walk to the back to grab my bag and coat, give Eliza a hug goodbye, then leave.

And who's there just outside the door waiting for me?

"Hey, you," he says awkwardly but cutely when I open the

door.

"Hi!" That might have been a little loud.

The cold air hits my legs and makes me shiver. The black turtleneck was a good idea, but the skirt? Maybe not so much.

"It's freezing out here. How long have you been waiting?" I ask. "I didn't see you."

"I just got here. Christmas shopping had me tied up till the last minute and I had to rush over here."

"Oh, you didn't have to rush!" I laugh out the lie. Yes, you did. I didn't like the wait.

"No, I'm glad I did. I definitely wouldn't have been able to wait any longer."

God, that smile. My heart leaps and there's no way to respond to him. I can only stare.

"Do you wanna go?" He asks. "It's a little cold for a skirt isn't it?"

My immediate reaction is the wrong one. "You don't like it?"

"No! No, you look lovely! You're beautiful! It's just really cold is all."

"Oh, okay yeah, ha ha." Get it together Silvia. He's just trying to be nice. Don't take everything as a negative.

"So. Do you want to get going?"

Finally! Someone said it.

"Yes! What'd you have in mind?" I ask. "Dinner to start?" Is that boring? It's a first date, shouldn't it be more... I don't know... more? Dinner's something you do every night. But it's five, and I haven't eaten since breakfast so that's where my mind goes.

"Dinner's a good start," he says. "Mind if we get out of 'toga though?" He steps to the right, in the direction of the parking garage down Phila Street, and I walk with him.

"That'd be great. Where are you thinking?" I walk almost arm and arm with him, hoping he'll wrap his around me. If he says anything about it, I'll just say I'm cold.

"How about Lake George? I can drive if you're comfortable with that."

Yes. Yes, I am. I shouldn't be with someone I just met, but yes. And as he asks, do you know what he does? He lets out his arm just a bit. It's not wrapped around me, but he totally wants me to hold his arm.

I gently place a hand on his bicep, and when he doesn't say anything I put my other hand on him and pull myself closer to rest my head on his shoulder.

"I'd like that, Daniel."

Daniel's car is parked in the same garage as mine, but there's nothing weird about that. It's just the closest place. For some reason, it's not as sleek as I'd expected from him. I expected a Camaro or Mustang. But nope, just an older Impala.

He opens the door for me like a gentleman. There's a framed photograph on the passenger seat. At first glance, it looks like it was from the Civil War. He grabs the photograph so I can sit down, then runs to the other side to get in.

"What's that?" I ask him as he starts the car.

When it turns on, music starts playing at a low volume. The

band Pale Waves. 'Television Romance.' This guy has great taste. I'm so glad it's not something like Dave Matthews who everyone in this town is for some reason obsessed with.

"It's uhhh… a gift for a friend of mine. He's a historian." Daniel pulls the car out of its parking spot and we're headed to dinner.

"Is he helping you?"

Daniel looks at me inquisitively.

"With the book. Your research," I add.

"OOH! Right," he laughs. "Yeah, no, he's a big history guy. We help each other out with work."

"Is he a writer too?"

"Not as much anymore." Daniel drives through downtown Saratoga, avoiding Broadway. Smart move, it's probably so congested up there. "He used to write a lot of historical books"

"Fiction or non? Would I know him?"

"A bit of both. Reggie Phefferberger. Read anything of his?"

I think hard, but the name doesn't ring any bells. I don't even remember seeing any books with that name come into the store.

"I'm sorry, no."

He shrugs it off. "Don't worry, I don't blame you. But we don't have to bring Reggie in on this date. Let's keep it just us."

I know he doesn't mean it like this, and it's just me ruining a good moment, but when he says 'just us' the terrifying thought of Harry showing up to ruin the night pops into my head. It's stupid, I know.

I can't let myself ruin the night though. It's just us.

Daniel's right arm is on the armrest. His hand only lightly on the stick shift. Should I go for it? I've already held his arm, this is a reasonable next step.

The song playing on the radio changes. The Girl From the North Country Fair, Bob Dylan & Johnny Cash. Daniel almost skips it but I stop him, "Wait, I love this song." My hand is just over his on the dashboard. For a moment we look into each other, and my fingers close over his.

The car comes to a stop at the light just before we turn onto the highway. The world wants us to have this moment.

I let our hands drop onto the center console, but then he slowly pushes over and lays his hand on my thigh. My muscles clench. He doesn't place his hand too high, or try to get between my legs. It's not a sexual touch, only gentle… sweet.

He starts, "Are you-"

"It's fine," I say, looking from his hand, back to his face.

Okay, you can go a little bit higher, Daniel.

The light turns green and we turn onto the highway. While the rest of the song plays, neither of us says anything. It's an un-spoken understanding that we're both just taking in the moment. I hope/pretend he doesn't do stuff like this often. Whatever he's thinking for tonight, I want to be the only girl he's ever thought of doing it with.

I hold his hand a bit tighter, and he squeezes my thigh. We both laugh a little.

Here and there through the song, he tries to sing along under his breath. It's only short bursts like he doesn't know all the words. I don't mind.

The songs bounce around that ride from classics like Sam Cooke to bands like Paramore and Wolf Alice. *Your Loves Whore*, a Wolf Alice song comes on and we both sing along at the top of our lungs.

After the song ends he tells me about seeing them in concert last year. Oh my God, that pissed me off, haha. I tell him, "I was dying to go to their concert here last year! They played in Albany."

He looks at me like I've offended him, "Why didn't you?!"

"I'm sorry! Ha ha, my ex and I had tickets but he got really sick like the night before. And I felt bad going without him."

"Silvy… what?!"

"Oh! EEUUHHH!" I pretend to vomit. "Please, no 'Silvy.'" I say it politely, and I'm still laughing a little so he doesn't think I'm too offended.

"What's wrong with 'Silvy?'"

"My ex called me that. Well, everyone does, but *he* did specifically. And I don't really want any reminders of him when I'm with you."

"All right, Sil, my bad."

Sil? I think I could roll with that.

He pulls off the Northway, onto exit 21. The village is already decorated with snowflake-shaped lights and wreaths on all of the streetlamps. In the park by Dunham's Bay, inflatable snowmen and reindeer are becoming friends. It looks so beautiful I wish it would snow again to complete the picture.

Daniel finds parking on the main street, right next to the park. As we hoped, the village is pretty dead. Lake George gets all the tourists in the summer. Canadians come south, city people come North, and everyone meets right here. But in winter it's almost entirely deserted.

When we get out of the car, Daniel checks something on his phone, then says, "We gotta eat quick. What are you feeling?"

"Trying to get out of our date already?" I ask half joking, half concerned. Was it something I said in the car? Did I not talk enough and make it awkward? Should I have let him put his hand higher on my thigh?

"No! Course not," he laughs at me. "The place we're going to closes in an hour or so."

I walk around the car to his side and huddle close to him. The wind blows hard and freezes my face and legs. "And where are we going?"

"Hold on," he says and grabs something out of the back seat. "You're freezing. I don't have spare pants, but here." He hands me a beanie. Daniel Cassidy wears beanies. Okay.

I put it on and give my thanks through a shiver. Beanies have never really been my style, but I think that's going to change now. I'm keeping this beanie. Even if it's only one date.

Daniel then holds out his arm for me to hold, but quickly changes his mind and – thank GOD! – wraps it around me. "Pizza good to start?"

Again, not what I expected from a date with Daniel Cassidy,

but what exactly *did* I expect? A five-star restaurant at the top of the Chrysler building after a ride in a private jet? And once he says it, I see the sign for Capri, which to be fair, is the best pizza place for about 50 miles.

I tell him it's fine with me, and he escorts me across the street, running from the cold.

He orders two slices of chicken/bacon/ranch, and I get buffalo chicken with a garlic knot. He doesn't hesitate to pay. I feel like that shouldn't be a thing that makes me like him more, but some people think that guys paying for everything on a first date is too outdated and unfair. Screw that, I'm happy to be treated like a princess. I'll thank him later. With a kiss at MOST, Let's make that clear...

Calm down.

We sit down at a booth in the front corner hidden behind the kitchen. There are two other groups there. I'm glad it's quiet here, but a part of me hopes someone else in the room will recognize Daniel. I don't want him getting swamped with attention, I only want to show off(just a little bit) that I'm here with him. You can't blame me. Everyone who loves someone wants to show off their lover.

"You feeling okay?" Daniel asks me.

"Huh? Oh, yeah of course! Why?"

"You keep looking around like you're looking out for some-one."

"Do I? I'm sorry." I drop my head in embarrassment. Why be embarrassed? I have no idea; my mind just tells me I'm being weird.

"Can I ask you something personal?" He doesn't smile

when he asks. By the way he asks, I know it's a question he thinks might be *too* personal, but he feels it's important anyway.

"Sure, I think I'm a pretty open book." Okay, Daniel. How personal do you want to get, because I have a few questions myself.

"Who was that guy earlier today? I thought he was an ex, but you said you'd see him later so... I don't know, I just..." he lowers his voice a bit and looks away, maybe embarrassed to make eye contact. "I don't want to be strung along I guess. Like you're just here because, you know, the books."

The question takes a moment to sink in, and when it does I can't help but laugh. One 'ha,' but really. Fucking. LOUD.

Now the other diners turn and look at us. Daniel turns to look at the wall, avoiding them.

"Oh my Lord, no!" I reassure him, "No, Daniel, I came out tonight because my Mom keeps asking when I'm gonna give her grandkids and you were the first guy I saw. So, are we gonna do this or what?"

He looks at me, sees my smile, and (thankfully) laughs. "Okay, I can work with that. But not until the third date. I'm not some whore, haha."

Keep this up and it'll have to be the second date.

"Deal," I say with my hand out.

He shakes it with a firm grip. "Deal," he says, then starts eating.

After a moment, I begin to understand he's waiting for me to answer his initial question. I hate to bring Harry up now, but it's clear that seeing him in the bookstore threw Daniel off a bit and if we ever want transparency in this relationship then it has to start now.

"Harry's my ex," I start. "We dated for about four years and broke up last September. I've tried to be friendly with him, you know, let him down easy, but-"

"But he's not going anywhere."

I pause, feeling like that was more of an accusation than an assumption. "Yeah. I thought it'd be easier on him if we let it die slowly. But he comes into the store every week and it's so obvious how bad he wants to get back together."

"So, why don't you just tell him it's over?" He takes another bite of his pizza.

"It's not that simple." Is he really asking me this?

"Why not? If it's over, it's over."

I can't believe this line of questioning, and I give Daniel a look that shows how I feel.

He takes the hint. "Sorry, just wanted to know who he was."

"Okay, I've got a question for you now."

"As you wish."

"What is that?" I point to the red pin on his jacket.

Daniel looks down and nearly blurts out, like he's been dying for me to ask, "It's a poppy."

"Huh... so what are you secretly an opium dealer?"

"What?"

"What?"

"No, it's a veteran thing."

I'm totally lost. When I think poppies, I think *Wizard of Oz* and Opium. Which, to be fair, *Wizard of Oz* and hard drugs go hand in hand sometimes.

Daniel continues, "Poppies are a symbol for fallen soldiers. It started in World War I. You know the poem 'In Flanders Fields?'"

I shake my head. Army stuff isn't my thing.

"In World War I," he starts, "soldiers in Europe were buried where they fell. There wasn't time or manpower to give them official burials. And in Flanders Field where many died, poppies grew over them. Now because of the poem by John McCrae, poppies became a symbol of the fallen."

"So, why do you wear it? Did you know someone who… I mean-"

"My dad," he says. There's an ounce of pain in his voice but he composes himself well. "Iraq."

Oh my God…

"Oh my God, Daniel… I had no idea…"

I try to think about what I know of him. We know he was born and raised in Iowa and had a healthy relationship with his parents. But again, so much of his past prior to the writing is a blank. There's never been a mention before of a death in the family.

"It's okay," he consoles me as if I'm the one that needs comfort. Or is that the wrong way to think, assuming that he needs support? "He's remembered. He was a lot older than me and joined the army when I was real young. So, I didn't know him for a long time, but I think even in memory he was a great role model."

I put my hand over his. I think I can understand why he doesn't wear the pin all the time. He doesn't live off of sympathy. He wears it for himself so he never forgets.

Daniel turns his hand over under mine and wraps his fingers around me. A light smile touches his face.

You're a very handsome man, Mr. Cassidy.

We let a minute pass while we eat. When I finish he takes our trash to the bin and then asks, "Ready to go?"

I grab my bag from the booth, stand and put my hand on his arm, and say, "You still haven't told me where we're going."

"Just down the road. Don't worry, it'll be fun."

We walk down the main street of Lake George Village together, only about a block until he stops under a big, flashing neon sign. And he asks me, "How good's your Skee ball?"

Oh Daniel, you poor, poor man. Get wrecked. In the summer between my freshman and sophomore year of high school, I took my first job. Working at the bowling alley/arcade in Saratoga. Given that no one cares about bowling anymore, the place was typically empty. Saying that now, I realize I may just have an obsession with underperforming businesses. Anyway, with all the downtime, I learned all the tricks of the trade for arcade games, and may or may not have perfected my Skee ball game. But I won't tell Daniel that. I'll let him have his fun.

"Oh Lord, haha… I can't remember the last time I played. I'll be terrible," I tell him.

He puts his hand on my lower back and walks me in. "Well, how about this. I appreciate that you're not here just because of the books. But I know that you didn't get to all of your questions in that interrogation the other day. Right?"

I roll my eyes. He's right, but again, giving him the satisfaction would make it too easy for him.

"I may have had a few more," I say.

"Thought so," he laughs and pulls out his wallet to buy an arcade card. I kind of miss the days of using quarters in arcades. Or the little gold coins. Hitting the jackpot as a kid and receiving an endless flow of gold coins made you feel like you just won the lottery. Now it's all digital and dull.

Daniel continues, "But I also want to know you better. This can't all be about me. *SO*, we play a round, and the winner gets to ask anything. And you have to answer truthfully, no matter how embarrassing. Fair?"

I already know how this is going to turn out. On one hand, I could absolutely annihilate him and end up getting a better one-on-one than any journalist could ever dream (except maybe Gabriella from *Binds*, but I don't even want to compete with her). On the other hand, he could keep winning, play it safe with the first two questions, (what'd you study in college? What's your favorite book of mine?) then the third would be 'When was the last time you touched yourself to my writing?' But I'm confident in my skills.

"You're on, Mr. Cassidy." I take the arcade card from his hand. "Oh, I'm sorry," I say flirtatiously, "Daniel."

I swipe two lanes and the game begins.

I let him roll first, just to gauge where he's at.

He fumbles it and gets the bare minimum, 100 points.

Okay, easy game. I roll, landing in the 300-hole. Your mo-

500. Daniel rolls a smooth five hundred.

"Lucky shot," he says with a shit-eating grin. It's a cute one, but he's still rubbing it in.

All right, Daniel Cassidy, I won't go easy.

I roll my next ball. 400.

He rolls. 500.

"I think I already know my first question," he laughs.

"First? How many rounds are we playing?"

Daniel only shrugs.

Each roll becomes more and more aggressive. Life and death hang in the balance of this game, and the points start racking up. A 500 is sunk. A 400. 500 again. Someone sinks the 1000-point hole. The lanes fade together. I'm not even paying attention to how I'm shooting because somehow it's turned into a race as well. I throw two balls in rapid succession, and when it comes to the last ball of the round, it's Daniel's turn. The score is 3900 to 3700, with me in the lead. Daniel could easily win this round.

He takes his time, like his life depends on this win, pulls back his arm, breathes deeply in a hilariously over-dramatic way, shoots the ball, and…

3900 to 3800.

"OOhhh nooo, too bad," I tease. "Good game though."

His eyes roll from the scorecard to me. "Good game. So, what would you like to know? For you, I'm an open book."

Okay, let's think. I can ask him absolutely anything I've ever wanted. With so many options in front of me, my mind temporarily goes blank. I could ask him what the plan is for the whole "Stargazing" series. It would be a perfect time right now to ask him about a long-distance thing and not get any roundabout answers. But the first thing that comes out is a question I've always had about his first book, *Summer Snow*.

"What happened with Sarah and Emil?"

He laughs a confused laugh. "Ha, what?"

"In *Summer Snow*," I say. "It ends so abruptly, we've all just wanted to know, you know… what happens to them? Does she stay around?"

Daniel laughs through my whole question and then asks, "That's it? Ha ha, I… I mean I guess it all works out for the best."

"Oh, come on, that's not an answer!" I punch his shoulder playfully. "I won, you gotta tell me!"

"All right, fine! Fine. If that's really the question burning on your mind. Uhh… okay…" He falls deep into thought and I swipe the cards again.

"While you think, I'll give you a second chance to get a question of your own."

The second round begins and he lets loose his reserve. 500 after 500 after 100 after 500 point hole. So much for being a gentleman. But I won't complain. I want to tell him anything he wants to know about me.

Before we throw our last balls, he comes up with an answer to my question. "Sarah found happiness. That's what happened."

"That's not what I asked!" I exclaim. "I asked what happened to her *and* Emil."

"Did you want them to be together at the end? Do you think that would have added anything more to the story?"

"Well...I mean..."

"The book was about her moving on, wasn't it?"

It's almost like he's asking me out of his own curiosity, rather than looking for confirmation. I suppose he's getting at it being my own interpretation.

"Well yeah, but it was still a romance between them."

"Then if you think it needed that to be a happy ending, then they ended up together." He rolls his last ball and gets the first 1000-point hole between the both of us for that round. 4600 to 3800. There's no way I'm coming back from this.

"That's such a cop-out!" I almost scream at him in playful annoyance.

"I'm sorry! Ha ha, but that's how it is. She found her peace, the story ends. If you want more then you've got your own imagination."

"Holy hell, that's not a good enough answer but fine." I roll my ball and land a 400. "Your turn. What would you like to know?"

"I'm actually gonna save it for later."

I'd like to argue but... the way he says it. So assured, so cool, so... yes, Daniel, anything you say.

We move on from Skee ball and work around the arcade. It's cheesy, and far from the high-end kind of date I expected (five-star at the Chrysler building), but it's the most fun I've had on a date in years. The games are all rip-offs, but we play them with our whole hearts, avoiding the ones that are only there to give you tickets, and playing the ones that are actual games. Children and families are running around, waiting impatiently for the high payout games, leaving us with the fun ones. Their screaming and shouting with excitement, combined with the music and sound effects from the games, it's enough to give anyone a headache, but for me it's all blocked out by this moment we're living in. I can picture it as a movie scene. One long, almost slow-motion(but not quite) shot of us walking through the room, where the whole background is blurred out and all sounds are at a low muffle except for the song that plays for the audience. We'll throw in a few clips of us playing games, winning tickets, or just laughing together. It's one of those scenes where no dialogue will do our emotions justice.

After Skee ball, Daniel goes easy on me(or at least he thinks he does) for all of the competitive games. But any second when we're not playing against each other, he can't take his eyes off me.

"It's all the lights in here," he says. "The way they fall on your hair, and light up your eyes…" He's looking at me through the glass of the claw machine. We're trying to win an off-brand squish-mallow, a little frog guy who's absolutely adorable. I'm on the claw working side to side, and he's supposed to be telling me how far back to go, but he's too distracted.

"What about my eyes?" I ask.

Daniel abandons his job. He walks around to my side and puts a hand on my cheek. "I've never seen eyes as beautiful as yours."

Kiss me, Daniel. Please, kiss me now.

I close my eyes.

He leans in, but there's a brief hesitation, and he pulls back.

I open my eyes. He's not looking at me anymore but past me. "What's wrong?"

"I think we should get out of here."

I turn to see what he's looking at, and right behind me is a little girl no older than 8, with her nose pressed up against the claw machine. She's staring at the frog fake-mallow with obsessive intent. Okay, yes, it would have been weird to passionately kiss with her right there. Am I still disappointed though? Also, yes. But if he wants to get out of here because there are too many eyes, I don't think I'll complain about what happens next.

He takes my hand and we start to leave, but then stops, turns around, and releases the claw. It drops down onto the frog. A perfect grip. The frog drops into the prize bin and the girl starts jumping up and down with excitement. It'd be cruel not to just let her have it, and Daniel isn't a cruel person.

"Here you go," he hands the girl the frog and she happily runs away. He then puts his arm around my waist and as we walk out he says, "Don't worry, next time we come I promise I'll get you the best prize."

Good. Yes. There was a stuffed Toad from the Mario games (you know, the one with the mushroom head and the little blue vest) on the shelf and he's the cutest little guy, I really wanted to win that.

"Who says I didn't already win it?" I say. FLIRTATIOUS-LY.

Kiss me, Daniel!

We cross the street to the lake side of town, then up and around the docks until we get to the pier at Shepard Park. I'm freezing again but Daniel keeps me close.

At the end of the pier is a bench. We sit down together and

listen to the sounds of the lake. It's peaceful. The lights from the houses on the other side of the lake reflect on the water, bobbing up and down playfully with those of the stars above.

I lay my head on Daniel's shoulder, and he holds me tighter.

"I really like you, Sil." It feels out of nowhere, and there was almost a stutter in his voice. "I uhh... I don't want you thinking I just wanted a fun night with a, um, a fan girl."

I turn my head so my chin rests on his shoulder now, and ask, "What do you mean?"

He breathes deeply. "I'm sure you know I won't be in town forever, and..." he rushes out the next part so I don't have a chance to cut him off, "and I don't want to assume anything," back to his nervous, calculated voice, "I don't want this to be for just tonight."

I can't believe he's saying this...

"I'd like to come around here again sometime. I saw you eyeing some of the prizes," he laughs. "And I don't know if you've heard it before or not, but your karaoke in the car was fantastic. If Wolf Alice comes around again for a concert, I... I'd like to be the one to take you. And more than anything..."

He puts his free hand back on my cheek.

"... I'd like to kiss you."

I close my eyes and lean in.

I expect a slow dramatic kiss, but he rushes to my lips, unable to hold himself back any longer.

It's one date, one kiss, but I am unbelievably... unarguably... inconceivably... head over heels, in love with this man.

10

The night could not have been more perfect. Daniel and I sat together on that pier for a little while longer until it became too cold, and then he drove us back to Saratoga. We didn't talk the whole ride. I only laid my head on his shoulder, and his hand held my thigh. When we got back to my car, I half expected him to ask if we could carry on the night at one of our places, but he didn't even hint at it. He only asked if we were still on for our date tomorrow night and when I said, "Of course!" he kissed me and said he'd see me then!

Is that weird? I mean, it's polite of him to not try anything, or push his luck but… let's be real. Aria may have been a little bit right about Daniel and I. In the context of how well the date went, maybeeee I would have been okay with him coming over. I don't have to let him go all the way, but we could have still messed around. I just get annoyed at myself because what I expect out of a man's behavior and my own wants sometimes aren't the most in line. Remember that old movie *Hitch*? I know, I said I don't care for movies, but that doesn't mean I haven't seen any. Well, that came out when I was a kid, and it really shaped my idea of what dating was going to be like. They have this whole thing about how it's on the third date when you share your first kiss and find out if you're really in love or not.

Obviously, we didn't wait three dates, but I grew up thinking those were the rules. Subconsciously, I still believe sex shouldn't come until at least the third date. But what I believe and how I act aren't always the same. So far with Daniel though, it doesn't seem like we'll be rushing into it. Am I complaining? Maybe a little. But I can appreciate it too. It only took one date with Harry for his hands to be under my shirt. In hindsight I could have been more strategic about it, made him wait. But really all it did was give me this expectation of "that's how it is now."

Driving home alone wasn't the most romantic end to the night, but I appreciate him for it. I really feel like he wanted me for me. And all things considered with celebrities, it was absolutely perfect.

Interlude:
Treasures of the
Deep Desert

Released: May 7th, 2019

Synopsis: In 1913, Dr. Scarlet Banks is on an expedition in Saudi Arabia, searching for the mythical lost Madinat Alhikma, the City of Wisdom, fabled to hold all the darkest and most sacred truths of ancient history. After years of searching, the first clue to the location of the city is found, and along with it, a mysterious group intent on killing anyone who gets close to the city.

With her life's work almost in her grasp, Dr. Banks must reluctantly team up with a shady guide through the desert, the only man willing to cross paths with the mysterious killers. Death is on their tail, and around every corner, but what could prove to be most dangerous, is the attraction that grows between them.

-Page count: 310

-Read: April 20th - 23rd, 2020

Bookends

August 1st - 7th, 2022

-Rating (Goodreads average): 2.9/5 Stars

-Rating(Mine): 4/5 Stars

Review: What a 180 from V+C! Not to complain or anything, I mean, it was great! It was just so different.

I'll be honest, this is only my second Daniel Cassidy book, and from what I know, this is the only one that leans into any kind of adventure storytelling. Something about it just works though. The action is cheesy, and a little cliche, but in a fun way that says "homage" much more than "lazy." I feel like this is all really backhanded compliment stuff, but I did like it! It was cute. Had a real *King Solomon's Mine* vibe.

The romance in this book does a hard shift from sensual to sappy. Or, I guess since this came out before V+C, that one had the shift. Ugh, I should just read these in order of release. Anyway, I liked it. It was over the top, but in a good way. It's all very melodramatic, maybe leaning into guilty pleasure.

It's not really enough to get me reading more action/adventure books, but if Daniel Cassidy writes more like this, I'd probably give it another shot.

11

I feel like I'm walking on clouds. This whole morning I'm riding a high, a fun buzz before the dizziness is too much. But I am dizzy. Just a silly girl dizzied up with love, like Buttercup when she realized who Westley really was, or Annie Wilkes when she found Paul. Okay, maybe not the craziness of Annie, but that level of happiness.

The snow is falling again on Phila Street as I walk to work, and it feels like Christmas snow came early. I'm basking in the feel of the cold, soft snowflakes in my hair, imagining myself as a snowy princess, bouncing with every step I take. I want to stop in every shop I pass and tell them the good news! I want to rush to the nearest boutique and buy the prettiest sundress, then parade through town uncaring of the cold breeze running by my legs! I want all eyes on me, and everyone not jealous, but excited for how excited I am for life this day!

I'm so happy I can almost forgive Eliza's totally reasonable expectation for me to come to work on a day like this. Especially after I told her two weeks ago I could work today. But how was I supposed to know where life would take me?

As I approach Bookends, I see the Black Friday Sale sign has been left out overnight. I could have sworn I brought them in before closing. At least, I thought I got the one at the entrance. Oh well, simple fix.

I grab the sign, then reach for my key to unlock the store but the lights are already on inside, and the door's unlocked. Did Eliza forget to lock up before she left? Shit, she's getting too forgetful nowadays. And Saratoga isn't as safe as it used to be. I hope no one came in last night.

The moment I step in, I hear something in the back room. I lean the sign against the counter and call out, "Ellie? That you?"

I hear no response, so I close the door behind me and slowly walk towards the back.

I ask again, "Eliza? Are you back there?" This is why I need to carry pepper spray on me. Today is not the day for someone to fuck with me or my store. But I don't have pepper spray, so I grab the heaviest book on the shelf within arm's length.

With each step closer I take to the back hall, my nerves start to rise. I hear a noise again like breathing, but it's so brief that I just can't tell. Slowly I poke my head around the corner and any nerves I had wash away.

"Ellie, what are you doing?"

She's sitting with her head in her hand over her computer and jerks around quickly when she hears me.

"Oh! Silvia! You scared me. What are you doing here this

early?"

I lay the book down on the nearest shelf and walk into the office. "Ellie, it's almost 9. Why are *you* here this early?"

She closes the computer and stands up, walking past me to the main floor and I follow. "Oh… busy," she says. "You know. Hoping to get some late Black Friday shoppers today. Oh! Why'd you bring this in?" She picks up the sign and puts it back outside.

"We're not still doing the sale, are we?" I ask.

Eliza is moving around in a weird, tense way. I'm noticing now she isn't even making eye contact. In fact, it seems like she's actively trying to avoid it.

She says, "I think we can do one more day, don't you?"

"I guess… I mean, if you say so."

Her demeanor is so shifty. Eliza steps around the floor for the next hour or so in quick, abrasive movements, and continues to refuse to make eye contact with me. From my spot behind the counter, I study her as she organizes the shelves and brings the higher-value books into the back office. That first part alone is a cue that something is off. Organizing the shelves is my job. But when I offer to go through them, she laughs awkwardly, like she's trying too hard to be friendly, and reassures me that she has it handled. She doesn't though. I take mental notes of the books she's moved around or put back on the shelf after customers decided last minute they didn't want them. When she makes a stop in the back office, I walk around the floor and see that very little of what she put away is in the right spot. She never even locked the high-value cabinet back up after opening it.

Something is clearly wrong today and I can't let her carry on like this. Thankfully, no one except the two of us are in the store today, so I'm not worried about leaving my post.

"You got a minute?" I ask politely.

Eliza is rummaging through the stacks of books up against the wall, skittering through them with her eyes only centimeters away from the spines. She's so focused that she doesn't hear me.

I ask again, "Ellie? Are you feeling all right?"

"Hm? What was that sweetie?" She cocks her head up but still doesn't make eye contact. "Someone need help?"

"No, just me." I step closer to her. "What's going on, Ellie? Come on, talk to me." I put my hand on her shoulder to show my care, but it's like she's on vibrate mode.

"I-" Her voice becomes shaky, "I have... just c-checking prices." She grabs something seemingly random off the shelf, a first edition hardcover of *Bonfire of the Vanities*, and brings it to the desk.

I see she has eBay open. Eliza always has some things up on the site, but it's usually the rarest of the rare, or books she has way too many to sell in the store. No in-between. But now I see, next to the computer is a stack of high-value books from the case.

"Eliza," I say in a stern, but friendly way, to really grab her attention. "What's going on?

She gently closes the laptop, not all the way, but just enough that it looks like she's embarrassed that I caught her on a dirty website.

"Silvy..." She takes a deep breath. "I don't think this old store is... I don't think I can keep up with this anymore."

I take a seat on the couch, the end closest to Eliza. Okay, so it's stress, I get that. The holidays are coming up and it's just the two of us trying to meet the needs of a busy town. "You had me worried there for a sec," I laugh. "Ellie, if you need some time off don't worry about it! I think I'm capable of covering down on you for a few days."

She tries to eke out a smile, but it feels half-hearted. "I know… I know you could. But it's not like that."

"Oh, sure it is!" I reach out and put a hand on her arm. She just needs some warmth and friendship. And that's what we are in this moment. Friends. Not an employer and employee. "Look, I know it's only gonna get busier the closer we get to Christmas. I think I can handle the stress for a bit."

"Silvy, really, it-"

"I mean it. There-"

She cuts me off harshly. "Silvia. Please, listen a moment."

I'm taken aback, but okay. Maybe my peppy mood isn't right for this moment. Read the room, Silvia.

Eliza continues, starting with another deep sigh. "This isn't about stress or the holidays. I've been running this place for fifty years. Business had never been fantastic, but we always got by. When Carl died, the store pushed on, and I owe so much of that to you. Now though… (she sighs), I guess time is up for Bookends. We're not making ends meet anymore. I just can't afford to stay open, or I'll be digging into my personal savings to keep it afloat. I'm sorry Silvia. I just can't keep going."

I can't believe what I'm hearing! Sure, business isn't great but we still manage!

"But Ellie, what about the sale?"

"What about it?" She asks gently.

"We killed it yesterday! We made almost $4500!"

"Silvy, it was Black Friday. That won't happen every day."

"Yeah, okay, but it shows people still have interest in this place. And it'll be a busy month. I promise you, Ellie, we can make it just fine. Maybe we just have to do better marketing for it. I don't know, maybe I can make you an Instagram page, or a TikTok."

"Silvy, it's all right. Really. I'm old anyway. It's time to move on."

I stand up. Whether it's because I want a way out of this insane conversation, or if it's real, I swear I hear footsteps on the main floor.

"This is ridiculous, Ellie. You have nothing to be worried about with the store."

She tries to speak, but the more she talks, the more she's going to get herself down, so I push on.

"It's just the stress getting to you. It happens. You'll see. December will come and go, and Bookends will be alive as ever. I'll do what I can to promote it more," I say this as I walk back to the front, not letting her get a word in. I feel bad about it, a little rude even. But again, how can I let her wallow in her own self-doubt? That would be the real sign that I'm not a true friend.

I make my way back to the floor and find busy work. I can occupy my time by reorganizing the shelves, and while I do so, I can brainstorm ideas of how to bring Bookends back into the public eye.

First of all, social media is a must. Eliza has always been cautious of it, feeling like an online presence would take away from the intimate nature of the store. Well right now, Mrs. Eliza May, I think that's what you need if you're so worried about it closing down. We also need better advertising around Saratoga. There are plenty of small mom-and-pop shops I'm sure we could partner with. Hell, we could work with some of the coffee shops in a plan where we give the customer a coupon for a free coffee, or discount at one of those places. Then people will stop here first, get something to read, then go and relax at one of the cafes. Or better yet, if Eliza is all about the intimacy of the store, we could convert the second section of the floor into a lounge. Come on by, grab a book, and make friends in the reading corner. What if we hosted a book club? The ideas are reeling in my head, I should really write them down! Oh! Maybe Daniel could help too! Is that too much to ask this soon?

I text him anyway.

-Hey! Good Morning!

That's a safe place to start. Now how long will it take for him to text back? Jeez, I feel like I'm back in high school texting my crush. I remember Lucas would always tell me I should never text first, and ALWAYS wait at least two minutes before responding so I don't seem desperate.

Well, I already broke the first rule. And I'm sure at this point he's past playing silly games. But I may not be.

Back to the task at hand while I wait.

Bookends

Wow, Eliza, you really weren't in the right mind this morning. A hardcover of a Robert Louis Stevenson book is stuck between two of the "Fifty Shades" paperbacks. There's a manga(wow I didn't even know we had any of these), with reference books about the history of Saratoga. Everything is all sorts of messed up, and even after a half hour, I'm still finding errors. At this point, I concede that this wasn't all Eliza. Just a lot of bad customers.

Pro-tip. If you are a customer in someone else's place of business, and you change your mind about something after you grab it, please put it back where you found it. Otherwise, you're an asshole.

My phone vibrates, and I check it.

It's Daniel!

-Good morbing!

-*morning!

-still on for tonight?

Holy hell… a different text for each sentence.

Fuck. Me.

12

By the time we get to closing around five, I think I may have proved Eliza wrong about business. We haven't done nearly as well as yesterday, only pulling in about $1500, but it's still a fine amount. It's okay though. Most people did all their shopping yesterday, and we're still doing a sale(for some reason), so I'll count this as an off day. But like, a *good* off day.

Customers have been fine, mostly quiet, but what's gotten me through the day has been anticipation of seeing Daniel again. I really shouldn't be nervous, I mean, last night went so well, but I still feel giddy thinking about seeing him again. I still don't know what the plan is for tonight though. We texted sporadically throughout the day, he wasn't the best at keeping up, but we never came to anything solid. Only that he'd be by again around closing to see me.

I really wouldn't mind if we just spent some time here. Bookends is probably the only place we'd find any real privacy. Even if we went back to my apartment, chances are Aria will be around, and I don't want to be so forward as to assume we could go to his. He's probably staying with family while he's here anyway and we *definitely* aren't at that level yet. Thankfully, Eliza took off a few hours ago to do more online listings at home because she "couldn't focus here."

I told her patiently, "Ellie, you don't have to sell these online. People love checking them out here."

"I don't need them to 'check them out,'" she rebuked. "I need these books to sell."

If you ask me, she just needs to be a little more patient. Books like these only become more valuable with age and she's cashing in her chips too early. But she doesn't seem to care. Holiday stress.

I wanted to close the store at 4:30 just to be sure no one came in as I try to leave, or see Daniel and swamp him with attention, but regardless, I'll have to hang around until he shows up. It'll be a risk staying open, but we've been empty for the last hour and a half so I'm confident-

In walks an old man.

He's a cute little thing, with a very nice sports coat, hobbling in on a cane and wearing thick glasses. His lips are so tightly pursed but with a wide smile on his face. The man must be over a hundred years old, guessing by the depth of wrinkles on his sagging face, and the way his entire body shakes when he takes his tiny steps. It takes me a moment to realize it, but I'm glad Eliza isn't here to see the man because he's the spitting image of her late husband Carl. Today of all days in her state would probably ruin her.

But it's not Carl, nor a ghost of him. Just an old man who gives me a nod and mouths 'hello' before hobbling slowly towards the non-fiction aisle. It feels like it took him five minutes just to make it ten feet. He may not have come in last minute, but I can assume he won't make it out on time.

I have to hurry this man up before Daniel gets here.

"Is there anything I can help you find?" I ask the man, as I stand to the side of the counter.

He perks his head up quickly, and looks at me through the massive lenses, still smiling. His mouth opens and shuts with a nod, and he points to something on the shelf, but no words come out.

I step a little closer, "Sir? Are you all set?"

He nods again, opens and shuts his mouth in a quick gasp-like sound, and returns to browsing through the shelf. Must be mute or something. That can come with old age, right? Harder to talk?

Well, unless he finds a way to ask for assistance, I don't know what I can do for him. I just hope he understands that we'll be closing soon. I try to tell him so. "Sir, we'll be closing the store in twenty minutes!" and gives me a thumbs up, then hobbles around to the high-value cabinet.

I send Daniel a quick text, not wanting to annoy him but just wanting to see his name on my phone screen again and double(triple) check to make sure he's still coming.

-Closing up soon. One guy still hanging around though. Shouldn't take long to close!

His response is almost immediate.

-I'll be around in a bit

-hope the day went all right!

Daniel, you're great, but please. That could have been one text.

-Great! Can't wait to see you!

Shit, is that too much?

The old man begins tapping on the glass of the high-value cabinet and smiling at me again.

I walk over, looking eager to assist him and ask, "Is there something you'd like to check out?" I see the book he's pointing towards, *Don Quixote*. It's a rare hardcover edition that we have priced at $350.

He stops pointing, then does a signal with his hands like he's flipping through the pages.

"Would you like to check it out?"

He nods and again tries to speak but nothing comes out.

"Okay, just a moment. Let me get the key." I return to the counter and grab the key that hangs in the space below the register, then open the cabinet for him.

The book feels like it's about to turn to dust in my hands. Some of the pages are torn at the spine and beginning to poke out through the edges. The front cover is so worn that it's almost impossible to read the title. But the old man doesn't seem to care. He beams when I hand off the book to him, and thankfully handles it with the utmost care. As slow as he was walking, he flips through the pages, and I'm nervous for a moment that his shaky hands will rip the pages right out, but he seems to have gained steadiness the moment the old leather touched his skin. He even looks younger and handles the book like a newborn child.

Why can't we have more customers like this guy? And it sucks that he can't talk because unlike the people that come in and only talk to yell at retail workers, I believe *he* would be full of engaging conversation.

I watch him as he flips through the pages. It really makes me happy seeing how excited he is, yet handling the book with such care.

"Just let me know if you need anything else, all right?" I ask gently with a hand on his shoulder.

He nods and holds the book close to his chest then continues shuffling around, shaking as much as ever but not letting the book slip from his hand.

A few minutes go by. It's almost 4:50 and I tell the man that we'll be closing soon.

He looks at me and smiles as if to say, 'that's nice dear.' He now has a small pile of books in his left arm with *Don Quixote* on top.

I hope he's planning to check out soon. Something tells me he's the kind of person that only pays in cash and exact change, and at the rate he moves, we'll be here all night.

My phone vibrates. A text from Daniel.

> *-Walking up now*
> *-traffic wasn't great*
> *-parking hard to find*

Bookends

-sorry!

-you free yet?

-not yet. One guy still left. About to
make him cash out if he doesn't hur-
ry up.

Before the text even delivers, I see him walk through the door. My heart beams and I feel the warm and fuzzies all over. I don't think I'm the only one that feels this way either.

Daniel's smile shines on me in a way that could have melted all the snow in Saratoga.

There's a lump in my throat again. It feels like we're back at that first (second really, but first official) meeting when he returned "Stargazing."

Thankfully, Daniel isn't as awkward as I feel. He's walking past the counter and before I know it right by me, pulls me in close and we kiss.

"Well, hello there!" I say as our lips break away.

"Hey Sil. Not too forward, right?"

"Not at all." I lean in to give him another kiss, then tell him, "But calm down just a bit. Still one more." I thumb back to the old man.

His back is toward us, and I'm guessing his hearing is only slightly better than his speech.

"Want me to hurry him up?" Daniel laughs as he asks.

"Oh yeah, be my bouncer again and just," I kick the air, just in case the man *can* hear us. We both laugh quietly, then I say, "No but really, he's fine. He's a nice guy. Reminds me a lot of the owner's husband."

Almost on cue, the man turns and walks towards the counter. Daniel steps back away from the counter.

"All set?" I ask the customer.

He lays the stack of books gently on the counter and reaches for his wallet.

I ring up his order, totaling $568.34, a third of what we'd made throughout the rest of the day, and just as I expected, he pays in cash. The man counts every bill methodically, slowly laying them down next to each other by bill size. Thankfully he has three hundred dollar bills. The rest though... smaller.

I give Daniel a mostly fake-annoyed look, which he reciprocates. Then proving my point further, the man reaches back into his pocket and counts out change. Yaaaaay.

The old man catches my look over at Daniel and takes a look for himself. On seeing Daniel's face the old man laughs, then... what? Is this sign language?

"I'm sorry, sir. I don't know sign."

I see it in his face that he's trying to find a different way to communicate, but Daniel speaks up.

"Yes," Daniel says and signs back as he speaks. "Just started."

The old man laughs at Daniel, then looks at me and points excitedly at Daniel, which turns to a thumbs up directed at me. He then signs back to Daniel something that turns him beat red, and they laugh together.

I'm dying to know what they're saying, but I also really want this man to finish paying.

"Thank you," Daniel says. "Glad she," he pauses for a moment then, "you both enjoyed the book."

Oh, I have to know which one they're talking about. It's obvious the man recognized Daniel.

Attempting to signal them along, I pick up the cash from the counter and count it again to make sure it's the right amount.

"Just the thirty-eight cents, sir." I remind him.

The man jumps back to counting the change, pays, and shuffles out the door, waving the whole way out.

I trail behind and flip the closed sign the moment he crosses the threshold. It's 5:08.

"Holy... HELL! I thought he'd never leave." I say as the door closes.

"He wasn't that bad," Daniel says. "Nice guy."

I walk up to Daniel, "Why, because he liked your book? Which one was it?"

"You don't want to know," He laughs, and leans against the counter.

I mirror him playfully and say, "I think I can guess then. *Binds?*"

"His wife was a fan. I didn't need the rest of the details."

The mental image is disgusting and I have to laugh it out of my head.

"Jeez, I'm surprised either of them could even handle that!"

160

"Yeah, I'd prefer not to think about it. Or that book at all, most of the time."

Most of the time? Is that where his head's at now? Was that a flirt? I take a half step closer to him.

"What was your inspiration for that one anyway? I think we're all dying to know where your head was at with it?"

The way he looks into me when he speaks, fuck... I immediately get a mental image of the two of us as characters from a scene in the book. Which scene? I won't tell. I have to reserve at least some modesty.

"I don't think you're ready to hear where it came from," he teases.

We draw closer together.

I say playfully, with my hand running up his arm, "You won't even tell your biggest fan?"

"Don't you know the biggest rule of writing?"

I already know what he's going to say, and it's cheesy as hell, but the way he says it, a slow, warm, almost whisper in my ear, my legs shake and I feel myself getting wet.

"Show... don't tell."

Fuck...

His lips are on mine again, and a hand on my cheek. I don't even realize what's going on at first, it's just happening. But now that it is, I don't want it to stop. He places his other hand on my hips and pulls me closer. Are we seriously about to do it right here?

The kisses are passionate and hard, like he's been waiting ages, not hours to see me again. Slowly, he moves from my lips to my neck, and oh GOD! how I love how he feels. It sends a shiver up my spine, and he almost pulls away, maybe thinking he's gone too far but I don't let him go. Not until a moment of clarity hits me and I realize we're still right by the storefront window.

"Daniel, wait!" I push him off of me gently, not letting him go too far. "Not here, like this." I tip my head over to the window.

"Oh, right," he agrees with a laugh. "Wasn't even thinking. Just since last night, all I've been thinking about has been seeing you again. Got a little carried away."

I tease, "I've been on your mind but only get a handful of texts?"

"Well, I didn't want you to think I was some kind of stalker," he smiles. "Unless you're into those tropes."

I know this isn't helping the mood, but I'm almost glad we're just talking now. When he's here in front of me, or when he's kissing me, or hell, even when he looks at me, I want him. I want him so bad. I want him to tear my clothes off and fuck me however he wants me. But any moment where I have a moment to think clearly, I'm glad we're not doing that. Is it that I haven't had *anything* for the last few months? Last night solidified the idea that he's not just here for sex and I really want to hold on to that. Yes, I want us to take our time, and yes, I want to ride his face, but it feels like having one will ruin the idea of the other. I just hate how conflicted I am over this!

Goddamn it. Okay Silvia, slow. See if you can hold off until at least the third date.

"Nope, none of the toxic ones. Enemies to lovers, stalkers, professor & student, not a fan. I like the straight-forward romances.

No surprises. But how about we take this somewhere else? I haven't given you the tour yet have I?"

I'm worried he'll be disappointed that I'm now outright murdering the mood, but his face betrays no hint of it. In fact, he still looks like he's just happy to be there.

"That'd be nice," he says warmly. "I feel like I've been here a million times but never really saw it."

I take his hand and say, "Well then, let's begin."

From the moment I start, I lose all sense of control. I give him the full rundown of the store, not just which shelf is which, or how it's organized, but almost every other book it seems I'm taking off the shelf to give him (*him*, Daniel Cassidy the *author*) a history lesson on, or my own personal review. We spend nearly twenty minutes going through the history and non-fiction books that are mostly about Saratoga, and how I understand but am so annoyed with everyone's obsession with horses in this town.

I bring him next to the high-value cabinet. Of the nearly three dozen items in there, I have a background or story associated with almost all of them. Most are first edition or collectable hardcovers, or infamous misprints to include an "extra-wand" copy of *Harry Potter and the Philosopher's Stone*. As a special treat to him, but mostly because I love holding these delicate pieces of history, I unlock the cabinet and let him flip through the pages. He's particularly interested in a copy of Stephen King's *Thinner*, and I mention I've been dying to find a copy of "Rage" for the longest time. Thankfully, he knows exactly what I'm talking about and oh my god could he get any hotter?

By far the longest part of the tour is the children's shelf because naturally, we've got the classics. Daniel's eyes immediately go to a first edition "Miraculous Journey of Edward Tulane" (with the colored photos, because we run a classy establishment here at Bookends), and now it's his turn to lecture me on how much the book meant to him as a kid.

He tells me, "My aunt used to read this every time she came over." He laughs and says, "We cried so hard every time Edward was lost, and my aunt would say, 'Okay, that's enough for tonight,' but I'd never let her stop reading. We stayed up until two in the morning one time reading it."

I'm in love with the way he glows when he talks about the book. I was the same with that one growing up, but I stay silent for a moment as he studies the pictures, letting him treasure this moment of nostalgia. After a minute or so, I say, "I loved that one, too. That and *Tale of Despereaux*. We would listen to that book on tape on car rides all the time on family trips."

He looks up at me from the book smiling, but doesn't say anything. It's almost a confused smile.

"You have read it, haven't you?" I ask him.

He purses his lips through his smile and shakes his head slowly.

"What's that one about?" He asks.

"Holy HELL, Daniel!" I laugh. "How have you *not* heard of Despereaux? It's the same author, Kate DiCamillo! The one about the little mouse with big ears? And soup! It's so beautiful!"

"Dumbo mouse and soup is a 'beautiful' book? Ha ha, I

guess I'll have to give it a shot! Got a copy here?"

YES! Yes, I do Daniel!

"I think I could find one," I tease, then scan the rows for a copy. "Maybe if you ever do a children's book you could learn something from her. Or take inspiration."

I find a copy of the soupy mouse book and trade with him for "Edward Tulane."

Daniel takes the book and says, "I'm not sure if children's books are in my wheelhouse. Especially if it's by the guy that wrote *Habits*."

Fair point, Daniel.

"Well, maybe people will have forgotten by then. Gotta break out of the mold sometime right?"

"I'm not sure if that's the right phrase, but, sure."

I roll my eyes playfully at him. "Sorry, I'm not the writer, knowing every fancy idiom or whatever."

We laugh together, and he closes the distance between us.

"Trust me, I'm not all that great with words either."

"I beg to differ."

"Really, sometimes it'd like…"

He's at a loss for words. Maybe just to make a point and make me feel better. Probably that.

I finish his sentence, "That the editor does all the work?"

The distance he closed opens up again. Was that rude of me to say? Did I assume too much?

"Daniel, wait I didn't mean it like that."

"No, I know. It's just… yeah. I guess. Like by the end of

165

it, it's not even my own words anymore. Kinda hard to take credit at that point sometimes."

Am I the only one that feels like this took a weird turn? I didn't realize that would hit a chord with him, but I think I can understand where he's coming from. You work so hard on something you have so much passion for, only for someone else to take it, scribble all over it, and point out every minute flaw and failure.

Trying to sound sympathetic, I put a hand on his arm and ask, "So what's *yours*?"

"What do you mean?" A light returns to his eyes.

"If you had to pick out one thing from all of your books that is 100 percent you, what would it be."

Now he's completely glowing again like he's been waiting all his life to be asked this question and he finally gets to answer.

"How far into 'Stargazing' are you?" He asks.

Shit! I'm still on chapter 12 and so close to finishing but haven't touched it for days! I've been so caught up in spending time with Daniel I completely forgot to actually finish the thing!

"I'm almost finished," I tell him. "Just been distracted lately."

"Distracted in a good way?" He asks.

I don't think either of us realized it at first, but we're slowly backing towards the office hallway.

"In the best way."

We cross the threshold and I'm nearly up against the wall of the tight hallway.

"What's distracting you?"

"Well, there's this guy… he keeps popping up around here. Makes it very hard to focus on anything."

"Uh huh," he says with a disarming smile that makes me melt. "And what are you gonna do about this guy? Seems like he's really into you if he keeps coming around."

"Hmmm… I think I've got plans for him," I say as I run my hands over his shoulders and pull him in close.

"What kind of plans?" His voice is gentle, and he's leaning in for a kiss.

Forgive me, reader, but I sidestep and take his hand to lead him down the hall. "I'm going to finish the tour," I tell him. "This is where I come to escape."

"So, this is the secret clubhouse?"

I laugh, "Yes, and it's super exclusive. Only the coolest kids can come in."

"Oh, my apologies, I didn't mean to barge in," he says sarcastically, and takes a few steps back out of the office, then knocks on the wall as if there's a door between us. "Permission to enter the super-secret exclusive Bookends clubhouse?"

I play along, "What's the password?"

He looks around the rooms, trying to think of something, then throws out a guess, "Wolf Alice?"

"Hmmmmm…" I tease.

He gives me a 'come on!' look.

"I guess that's close enough, you can come in."

He mime's opening a door and walks through.

"Oh, thank you very much. It's freezing out there! So am I

a member of the club now?"

"Not quite yet."

"No? What do I have to do to be a member?" He steps in.

"You still have to pay your dues."

"What's the price?" His hands are on my hips.

No more time for games, I think you've been patient enough. I *definitely* have.

I fall back onto the couch, pulling him down with me, and in no time, he's kissing my neck, and his hands are under my shirt, massaging my breasts. Fuck... I haven't felt this in too long. Even the first feel of his fingers over my nipples makes me want to come. I wrap my legs around his waist and pull him in closer, and can feel him getting hard.

His hand traces down from my stomach, out of my shirt and over my crotch.

I moan in ecstasy, and reactively grab his hand, holding it there. His face is still buried in my neck, and neck kisses are my weakness!

I'm getting closer and closer, I'm almost there and I hear a bang! Or pop? What the fuck was that?

Daniel seems to hear it too and he shoots up, looking towards the hall.

"What is it?" I ask.

But Daniel doesn't have to answer.

From the front of the store I hear Eliza! (What the fuck is she doing here?!) call, "Silvy? Are you still here?"

"Shit!" Daniel and I whisper simultaneously.

I call back to Eliza, trying to compose my voice. "Y- Yes! I'm in the back, just a sec!"

Thank God we weren't fucking yet!

"What are you still doing here?" Eliza's footsteps draw closer to the office.

Daniel and I scramble to our feet, and away from the couch, just in time for Eliza to walk into the hallway.

"Ellie! Hi!" I say WAY too loud, she almost jumps. "What are you doing?"

"It's my store, aren't I allowed to be here? Better yet, what are you *two* doing here?" she asks, eyeing Daniel, but not in a mean way.

I put my hand on Daniel's arm and introduce him, "Ellie, this is Daniel Cassidy. I was just showing him around the place before we go out. Daniel, this is my boss, Eliza May."

"It's nice to meet you," Daniel says, and walks over to Eliza to shake her hand. "This is a really beautiful place."

"Thank you, Mr. Cassidy, it's wonderful to meet you too," Eliza says politely. Then to me she says, "I left my computer here. Just came to pick it up. You won't be here much longer will you, Silvy?" She looks back and forth between Daniel and I while she asks.

"No!" I say with too much nervousness in my voice. It's obvious she knows what we were up to, or at least planning to be up to. "No, we're headed out right now."

I take Daniel's hand and escort him through the store.

"Have a great evening you too!" Eliza calls, then follows it up with something that I'm not really paying attention to.

I'm too embarrassed to say anything except "yeah, sounds good!" to whatever she said, and am nearly sprinting to the door, but Daniel finds it appropriate to say his goodbyes.

"Thank you! We will, take care!"

Why does he have to be so polite? Whatever, now we just have to figure out a back-up plan for tonight.

Outside, he tells me he doesn't have a plan because what we *were* going to do tonight ended up being last night's plan.

He offers, "why don't you come back to my place? I'll make dinner and we can just have a private night."

Private? Just me, him, and his extended family he's staying with? No thanks. We'd have better luck with privacy at my apartment just as long as Aria's not around. And even if she is, I'll hopefully be able to kick her out.

"How about mine instead? I'll still let you cook."

"If that's what you'd like to do," he says and holds out his arm for me to hold onto as we walk to our cars.

13

Please don't let Aria be there! Please don't let Aria be there! Please don't let Aria be there!

I called her once and texted her about twenty times just on the drive back to the apartment but she hasn't answered once.

-I'm bringing Daniel over! Please please please please please go out tonight! Things are getting serious!

-Aria! WHere are you?!

-Text me back! Please leave the apartment!

Just a few of the texts.

When I pull into the parking garage, Daniel's car right behind me, there's no sign of Aria's car. Unfortunately, this doesn't mean a whole heck of a lot. The garage is almost filled and she could have parked outside. All there's left to do is pray.

Dead God… PLEASE HELP ME OUT!! Amen

As we walk up to the apartment, I'm so painfully obviously nervous. Daniel holds my hand and asks, "Are you feeling all right?"

"Why?" I ask way too quickly.

"Your hand's shaking. And you look…"

He's going to say I look sick. I just know it. Smart move not letting it out.

"I'm fine. Just worried my roommate's around. She's… she's uh… she's not the most discrete."

Daniel laughs it off. "I'm sure we'll be fine. Even if she is here, what's the worst that'll happen?"

The worst is if we have one more interruption I might just snap. I don't say this to him, can't let him think I'm a psycho this early.

The moment we reach the door, a realization hits me.

"Shit! We never grabbed dinner."

"Oh, right," Daniel says, seemingly unbothered. "You uh, want me to run back out quick and grab something?"

On one hand, this isn't a bad idea. It'd give me time to make sure Aria isn't around and that she doesn't *come* around, or if she is here, that I can get her out. On the other, we've had too many distractions as is and I just want to get him alone.

I sigh, "No, no it's fine. We've got stuff inside to make. I'm just sorry it won't be a romantic dinner."

He gives me that disarming smile again and I'm reminded that I shouldn't feel so bad when I'm in company such as his. "Sil, if I'm with you, any dinner can be romantic."

EEEeeeeeee! This man... uggghhhh, yes, I love him. But compose yourself, Silvia.

"What do you say we go in?" He asks after a moment of silence I hadn't registered.

I nod excitedly with this stupid smile on my face.

As I reach for my key, the door opens and who is there but the one person I don't want to see. Predictable? Maybe. But fuck it. I'll look at it this way; if enough bad or annoying shit happens, eventually I'll have built up enough karma that the good stuff will happen. Just throw me the cliches early so we can get it out of the way!

"Are you two gonna come in or what?" Aria asks. "We can hear you in the hall ya know."

"We?" I ask her, and peek into the apartment. Sitting at the counter is some guy I've never met. "Ari, who is this?" I ask her quietly.

Aria moves aside to let us in and introduces us to her company. "Silvy this is Rich, one of the guys I work with. And you're Daniel, right?"

Daniel shifts his focus to her, and polite as ever raises his hand to shake and say 'hi,' but Aria for some reason decides they're past formalities and hugs him! What the fuck is that about Aria?

"It's great to meet you," she says in an overly charming voice. "I've read almost all of your books."

"Oh yeah? What'd you like?" He asks.

I don't think Aria hears it, but there's a hint of sarcasm in his voice. The question is a challenge for her, not an invitation for conversation.

She doesn't take the bait though. "The Vanilla one was fun. I-"

Before she can finish, Daniel cuts her off with "I'm glad you liked it. And Rich, right? Nice to meet you."

Richard doesn't stand up to greet Daniel, but at least reaches out to shake his hand.

"What's up," Richard says as monotone as possible. Like come on, this is Daniel Cassidy! Then to add insult to injury, he adds, "You a writer or something?"

Daniel gives a brief chuckle, not letting the insult to his fame hurt him, and says, "yeah, something like that I guess."

While they exchange greetings, Aria whispers to me, "You really weren't fucking around? That's him?"

"It is. Why didn't you text me back?"

Through a smile I can't quite place, she tells me, "Phone died. Sorry!"

"Well, can you leave? Daniel and I wanted to be-"

"I'm sorry!" she says for everyone to hear. "We were just about to start cooking?" Aria walks over to the cabinet next to the refrigerator, and I'm left baffled.

I rush over to Aria.

"Seriously! This is important to me!"

"Silvy, I was here. Rich and I wanted a night alone too."

"Why can't you go to his place then?"

She stops pretending to look for something to make for dinner and addresses me directly. "His roommates are around."

174

"What is he in, college? How many roommates does he have?"

"Three. They all rent a house together, so it's hard to get privacy at his place."

Daniel had been trying to talk up Rich, but he turns to us and says, "Sil, it's okay, we can all eat together right? We can always go out after."

"Yeah, *Sil*, let's all get to know each other."

I swear I could smack that shit-eating grin right off of her fucking face.

No, Silvia, don't say that. She just can't read the room and you know this. She's never been able to, and now that Daniel's here she doesn't want to. Aria is harmless but goddamn it is she oblivious sometimes.

Begrudgingly, I agree. "All right, fine. Who's cooking then?" I look from one person to the next, hoping someone will speak up.

Aria is only looking at Daniel. Daniel is looking awkward, unsure what to do. Rich is staying out of it, but glances briefly here and there at Daniel, probably still trying to place him. I give them all a look like, 'well come on!'

Daniel, thankfully, is the one to save us. "I guess, I mean I already said I'd cook. What've we got to work with?" He walks over to the open cabinet standing between us, then asks me, "Do you have any cheese?"

I check the fridge for him even though I already know the answer. Aria and I are cheese goblins so yes, we have plenty.

"All right cool," Daniel says, grabbing a can of tomato soup and bread out of the cabinet. "My skills pretty much end at cooking, but there are a few things I make well."

While Daniel cooks, I try my best to give Aria subtle hints to please back the hell off of Daniel. I get it, it's Daniel Cassidy, but seriously, we're trying to have a date here! She's got her own man to pay attention to, even though he doesn't seem to be interested in much going on around him. Even when Daniel asks Richard what kind of grilled cheese he wants, Richard barely looks up from his phone. I almost feel bad for him. He might not be with Aria tonight for the most wholesome reasons, but I don't think he expected to play fourth wheel while his date fawned over a celebrity. If there's no getting Aria off of Daniel until dinner's over, I might as well try to make Richard feel welcome.

"Sorry we got in the way of your plans tonight," I say to him. I know it wasn't our fault Aria didn't look at my texts. She never told me they would be around so it's not like I had any reason to believe they would be here, but I don't know what's on his mind and I want to be polite.

"It's nothing. Not like we had plans. She just hit me up." He doesn't look at me when he speaks, just glances up quickly at Aria and Daniel.

"Oh…" I say, honestly not surprised at all. Quick hook-up maybe? "Well, you're lucky anyway. Aria's a really great girl."

He says nothing but finally gives me a disbelieving look.

I laugh, trying to keep everything in a good place. No matter how out of hand Aria acts right now, I wouldn't let anyone(except for myself) talk bad about her. "I'm serious!" I say with a smile,

"Trust me, I've known her in and out forever."

"Hm. Why's she hitting on Ian then?"

"Daniel," I correct. Holy hell this guy really doesn't pay attention. "She's just friendly. And I don't know if you know about him," – holy shit, did that sound really bitchy? – "but Daniel's a famous writer. Can't blame her for wanting to meet him."

Another flat "hm" from Richard.

All right fuck that. I tried, didn't I?

Thankfully, Daniel announces dinner just in time to save me from this painful attempt at conversation.

There are only two stools at the counter, and I do not have the motivation to ask Richard if Daniel and I can sit. Aria offers me the other seat, and I almost take it before realizing that leaves her standing with Daniel and that feels like a power move. Like she's standing over me with MY man. Am I looking too deep into this? Doesn't matter. We're eating fast and getting this over with. I really don't think I could spend another minute in this company. Unfortunately, I know Aria isn't going to let us off easy.

"So, Daniel," she starts once she's taken her seat. "Are you working on the next book yet? Is it dedicated to anyone special?" She eyes me when she asks.

See Richard? She's just trying to be supportive. She's doing it terribly, but it's an attempt.

Daniel gives me a look that makes me blush. He says, "I uh… I've got an idea. Not sure where to go yet. But yeah, I think it'd be for someone special."

The overload of warm and fuzzies he gives me by saying

that makes me choke on the tomato soup I'm sipping down and accidentally spit it out in Richard's direction.

"OH MY GOD I'm so sorry!"

Richard wipes away the drops of soup on his face, and it's probably the first time all night he's shown the slightest bit of emotion. It's not annoyance or anger, weird, but hard to place.

Aria acts like nothing happened and continues, "What's it about then? Another one of the spicy books? Maybe a sequel to that one uh, *Bondage? Bonds?* No, *Binds!* That one, maybe a sequel to that?"

Holy hell Aria, how do you not know his most famous book! Especially if you've apparently 'read them all?'

Daniel laughs awkwardly, "Ah haaa, I don't think that one needs a sequel. Or anything like that."

"Maybe something similar then? You've gotta be *reeling* with ideas you wanna, I don't know, experiment with."

Daniel gives me an unsure look, like he's asking my permission to answer this not-table-appropriate question.

Instead, I answer for him. "I think the tamer stuff is better." Not completely true, but, if it helps Daniel out of this. "The one that just came out has nothing spicier than some passionate kissing and it's already one of my favorites."

She bounces back quickly, "Well not all of us want slow-burn romance with no payoff."

"Who says there's no payoff? *The Princess Bride* didn't have any sex but it's still one of the best romantic books ever."

"One of the best isn't the best. But why don't we ask the author?" She turns to him and beams, flashing a smile to try to get him on her side.

He takes a moment, looking back and forth between us, totally ignoring Richard who couldn't care less.

"Sex is a bonus, I think." His answer catches both of us off guard. Aria probably because she's shocked he wouldn't take her side with all her cozying up to him, and me because those are some strong words for someone who frequently, graphically, talks about sex in a lot of his books. He continues, "I don't know, if we're talking romance, it's rarely necessary to build up the romance. It feels cheap, kinda, using sex to show that two people are in love. Like you said, Sil, the Princess Bride didn't have any sex and we never doubt the love the characters have for each other. Or in *It Happened One Night*, you've seen that right?" He looks around the room for approval but we're all giving him blank stares. Even Richard looks up. "There's sex in the movie, but at first only teased for comedy. When they do have sex, it's after the big payoff where they profess their love, and is the literal last minute of the movie, and only to pay off a joke set up earlier." He laughs to himself, "It's a really great movie, one of the best."

"Good luck with this one," Aria thumbs me. "Strict no-movie policy."

"That's not true," I say. "I like a few, most just seem pretty shallow."

Daniel looks at me, surprised. "Shallow? Movies are like, the best way to tell a story!"

Aria and I both look at Daniel again.

I ask him, "What do you mean? You have so much more

freedom with books. You can go as in depth as you want and really develop your characters so much deeper than a movie can."

He rebuttals, "I've read plenty of long books that have nothing to say, and I've seen ninety-minute movies that leave a huge impact on me. It's not about the medium you use to tell a story, it's how well it's done. And if we're talking about length and "freedom" being factors, then film is MUCH more impressive. There are so many more limitations with movies, it takes so much more talent to craft a well-rounded story. Haven't you ever read a poem that stuck with you? That's only like a page, but you can't forget it."

He has us all stunned.

I never expected someone like him to knock his own profession. And Aria, well I really don't know what she's thinking. In all likelihood, she's probably still stuck on Daniel's take on sex.

To add further surprise to the conversation, Richard chimes in.

"Deep."

"Thank you, Richard," Daniel says politely.

"No prob, Ian."

"It's Daniel," all three of us say in unison, then after a moment laugh at each other.

Richard is back to being silent and nods his head.

"Well, Daniel," Aria begins, "Thank you for dinner." She gets out of her chair and puts a hand on Richard. "I think we'll retire for the night. It was great meeting you, Mr. Cassidy."

Aria and Richard walk into her room and I say to her before she's completely disappeared, "Daniel's fine!"

She makes a sound I can't quite make out and the door closes behind them.

"Nice friend you've got," Daniel says in a tone I can't make out.

I sigh in mild distress, feeling like having Aria around, and her constant pestering made him too uncomfortable. "I'm sorry about her, Daniel. She really is wonderful, just, you know, doesn't always read the room.

"Oh, no, she's fine," Daniel smiles. "She's nice, just got excited. I mean, clearly she's happy for you. That's the mark of a good friend, right?"

I shrug, wishing that if that's what a good friend looks like in serious moments, I wouldn't mind too much an 'okay friend.'

"How about I clean up quick, and we call it a night?" He asks.

I look at the counter and see that Aria and Richard have left out their dishes for us to take care of. Thank you, Aria. I really can't with you sometimes. I breathe deep and rub the bridge of my nose.

"No, thank you, Daniel, but I got it." I reach over the counter and grab the dishes. I'm not going to wash them tonight. They can sit in the sink and *maybe* Aria will deal with them in the morning if she's the first one up. Chances are low, very low, but worth a shot.

After taking care of the mess, Daniel and I go into my room. I feel like a kid, wanting to show off how cool my bedroom is with my overflow of books, but I'm hoping that him, of all people, will appreciate it. The first thing I notice though, is that my Daniel Cassidy books are out of place. A majority of them are sitting on my nightstand. Aria must have gone through them. If she was trying to do her homework before meeting him, she could have looked him up on Goodreads or something. This makes me think she put them there so that he'd notice and, I don't know, think my obsession is cute? Again, I see where you're coming from Aria, and if I'm right, I appreciate the misguided attempt at your support. But he already knows I'm obsessed; I don't think strategic book placement is going to change anything.

Daniel doesn't notice Aria's plot, but looks around the room and says, "So... you like books, huh?"

I sit on the end of my bed, hoping he'll take a seat next to me, but he continues to skim through the books.

"I may have a minor obsession," I joke back to him.

"Have you read all of them?" He pulls out a copy of *It Happened One Summer* by Tessa Bailey and holds it up towards me.

"Most. That one I have."

He laughs, "Okay so you've read this but never heard of the movie this book takes its title from?"

I stand to defend myself, and playfully take the book from him, pretending to be more offended than I really am. "It was fun! I'm sorry I haven't seen every movie ever made."

"Yeah, but it's such a classic! Okay, what about this one?" He pulls out a book sitting just below Chuck Palahniuk's *Invisible Monsters*, a Joseph Conrad hardcover collection. "Or anything from this? *Heart of Darkness*?"

"Okay, yes, kinda. I started it. But-"

He cuts me off and pulls a book off the top of the shelf.

Twilight. He gives me a coy look, and he doesn't even have to ask what I know he's thinking.

"Okay, EVERYONE read that in middle school!"

"Middle school?" He laughs, "This is on the top of the shelf, when was the last time you read it?"

"That's- that's not fair. I-"

He gives me that look again.

I pause for a moment and my lips purse in petty annoyance. I tell him quietly, "April."

"What was that?" God, if it wasn't Daniel Cassidy, I'd smack that beautiful smile off his face in a heartbeat. But it is Daniel Cassidy. And that smile does stuff to me I cannot talk about in polite company.

"April!"

"So you have time to read, and re-read *Twilight*, and these cheesy, by the numbers romance books, but you haven't finished *Heart of Darkness* yet?"

I grab *Twilight* from him and hold it up against my chest with *It Happened One Summer* like I'm defending them from the mean man that just doesn't get it.

"It was hard! I'll get around to finishing it eventually. And who are you to knock romance books?"

"Come on, Sil. One, I'm only teasing." He takes the books from me and puts them back on the top of the stack. "You already know how I feel about romance books. I just have a high standard," he teases again, and we start moving closer to the bed. He sits down first, and (God, please let this be the right move), straddle his lap.

Daniel continues, trying hard to look unphased, "But you're right. Who am I to say anything?"

"Exactly," I say with my hands on his chest. "Just gonna come in my room and make fun of what I like?" I lean in slightly.

"Would you like an apology?" He just won't drop this teasing attitude, will he?

"'Sorry' won't cut it.'

"All right, how can I make it okay?"

Did he seriously just make a Wolf Alice reference? Fuck it, I'm not even mad. That was cute.

"I bet I can think of something."

No more waiting, no more teasing. Our lips meet, and a new atmosphere of burning passion envelops the room. We fall back together on the bed and kiss. I feel his hand on my cheek and run my hand through his soft hair.

It was one thing seeing him in town. I thought I was in a dream when he came into the store, and every time after that brought me deeper and deeper into the dream. Now, I'll refuse to wake up. What completes this idea of a dream is, what are the odds he would have really been into me too?

And he seems *really* into me right now. With each kiss, he moans louder and louder... almost, no, yeah, hold on it's too distracting. I want to get into the mood, but this isn't like when we were back at the bookstore.

I stop kissing him, back away a bit and ask him, "Are you okay?"

Confused, he says, "Yeah. What's up? I thought you were

into it."

As he talks, I keep hearing the moaning, and we realize it wasn't either of us. It's coming from Aria's room.

We laugh awkwardly, and Daniel says, "I kinda forgot they were right next door."

"I *did* forget. Wish I still could. It's really just a mood killer knowing she's right there."

From Aria's room, we hear a scream, whether pleasurable or painful is hard to tell, and then some aggressive dialogue is exchanged that we can't make up.

"What do you think they're getting into?" Daniel asks.

"I have no idea. I try to block out when Aria talks about sex."

More strange exchanges make their way through the wall, and it sounds like one of them wants to be spit on, but it's hard to tell exactly what it was, and who said what.

We laugh again, and Daniel stands up and goes to the door.

"What are you doing, you perv?" I ask and jump up to listen with him. To be honest, I promise I'm not a pervert, but there is a bit of curiosity as to what exactly they're doing. It's way too much to be just casual sex.

The sounds of aggressive lovemaking are getting louder and would be impossible to ignore if we tried. I'm surprised the neighbors aren't banging on our door already.

"Is this something you always have to put up with?" Daniel asks.

I sigh and tell him, "She's usually better about it. She has plenty of guys over, but most of the time is decent enough to keep it quiet."

An aggressive voice shouts through the walls, "Fucking take it, slut!"

Daniel and I laugh, and he asks something that I didn't realize I needed an answer to. "Which one was that? Ha ha!"

Wait seriously, I couldn't even tell.

Then much more clearly, we hear Richard's cries of pleasure, and (no shame) I become very uncomfortable. "Yes mommy! Please give me more!"

Daniel and I stare at each other in disbelief, and he's the first to laugh.

"Well, good for him," Daniel says through his laugh. "At least he's comfortable enough with himself."

"What are you?!" Aria screams through the walls.

I don't think I can repeat what he said at that moment if I don't plan on going to church anytime soon to ask forgiveness.

They continue shouting their... I don't know... terms of endearment(?) at each other, but "I can't take anymore. Just too much," I say and lead Daniel by the hand back to the bed. I sit down, but he hesitates a moment.

"I didn't think I had to ask, but there's nothing like that I need to worry about with you is there?"

It takes me a moment to realize what he meant and I blurt out, "OH! God no. I'm not- no- no toys, ha ha. The kinkiest I get is my vibrator." FUCK ME WHY DID I SAY THAT?! My face goes the deepest shade of blood red and I want to DIE!

But Daniel just laughs at me as if it's nothing. "Well good. I don't know if I'm ready for whatever that is." He climbs on the bed next to me and runs his fingers up my back. "I think the pace we're going's just fine."

I turn and lay down on my side to look into his eyes. "Just fine? Or...?" I know I shouldn't be too unsure of myself like this, but I think back to our fun in Bookend's office. What if he thinks I'm too easy? What if he thinks I'm too reserved? Does he think I want to keep getting interrupted? Am I not putting out enough for him?

In a sweet, understanding voice he says, "We can take our time if that's what you want."

Relief washes over me. I exhale all of the pressure I've felt building up in me since we first met. I didn't think I'd be so content *not* having sex with Daniel Cassidy.

"We just met this week," he says. "And I'm leaving tomorrow for I don't know how long. I'm not gonna be the guy that comes around just to take advantage of you then leave." He puts a hand on my cheek. "Sil, I just really like spending this time with you. Getting to know you. And I hope that you'll still be around when I come back."

Daniel Cassidy could have any girl he wanted. He could download Tinder and in 15 minutes have a girl fawning over the famous writer that he is. A few times since meeting him, I've almost completely thrown myself at him, but that's not what he wants. My eyes start to water, but I won't let myself cry right here. And it doesn't help that I didn't realize when he said he 'wouldn't be in town forever,' that meant he would only be here for the rest of the weekend.

"I will be." It's not like I have anywhere else to be.

He kisses me again, and I add, "But you'll stay tonight, right?"

The question catches him slightly off guard, but he's not against it. "If you'd like."

We're able to block out the noises Aria and Richard make, and find comfort in each other's arms as we lie in bed. All I can hear is his heartbeat as I lay my head on his chest. He holds me tight and kisses my head, and we soon fade away into the best sleep I've ever had.

Interlude
Titles Are Hard to Come Up With

Released: Sept. 10th, 2019

Synopsis: The portrait of a painter's dead wife begins to speak to him. A group of high school kids spend the last night of summer on the beach and let out their deepest secrets about each other. A loner makes a last stitch effort to win his ex back over karaoke. Two lifelong friends wait to enter heaven together. And more...

-Page count: 201

-Read: June 5th - Sept. 11th, 2020

-Rating (Goodreads average): 3.1/5

-Rating(Mine): 4.5/5

Review: The reviews on this one are WAY too harsh. Is there an overarching theme to these stories? No. But individually, they're all really great. I also didn't read it all in one go. I read one short, read a book, read another short, you know. Broke it up. That could be why the lack of theme didn't bother me.

What I got out of it was, Daniel Cassidy wrote four romance books in rapid succession, and between them, or during them, other ideas came up. But he's a romance writer, and that's what the market demands of him right? His mind can't be focused solely on romance forever. The collection is very scattershot of different ideas, very few having anything to do with romance. And I guess that's where an overarching theme can be found. It is Anti-Romance. Anti-Daniel Cassidy, by Daniel Cassidy. And it works.

My personal favorite was Karaoke Night, the one about the boy that tries to win back his ex by singing Karaoke at the café(bar? I don't know, it wasn't really super clear) where she works. It's awkward but feels real for an awkward kid trying his hardest to show this girl he's in love with what a real-life fantasy ending can look like. Does it have a happy ending? I don't know. It's left ambiguous, but I'm leaning more on the side of no.

On record, Daniel Cassidy said he wasn't planning anymore collections like this, but I'm hoping things change. I'd like to see what he does with a novel that's not entirely focused on romance. And then I'd like him to go immediately back to romance because I don't want to wait too long for more of the good stuff.

14

When I wake up, I half expect to see Daniel dressing and trying to sneak out. I'd have to act unoffended that he's leaving so soon, because what did I expect from a one-night stand? It takes me a moment to realize the reality of the situation. I haven't shared my bed with anyone in so long, nothing seems right. I can barely even remember what happened last night for a minute or so. It slowly comes to me that, no, it wasn't a one-night stand. And Daniel isn't getting dressed. He's still in bed asleep next to me.

I turn over to look at him and run my fingers through his soft hair. He stirs but doesn't wake. I don't think he ever said when he had to leave, but I won't waste a moment. Slowly, I pull his arm over me, and nestle up against him.

Daniel radiates a comfortable warmth, like I'm being wrapped up in a blanket by the tree on Christmas Eve. Once awake, I can never fall asleep, but right now I'm content with lying in bed all day as long as Daniel is here to hold me.

After some time of silence, save for the beat of his heart, I hear a mumble, half yawn,, "Goob morning beautiful." It seems he can't say 'good morning' right in text or in person.

"Goob morbning to you too handsome," I say, hoping he thinks it's cute.

He tightens his arms around me and kisses my forehead. Is this a little much for a first night spent together? Maybe. But it feels natural, like it's been months already and I don't mind it one bit.

I ask him softly, "Are you hungry? I can make you breakfast. Or coffee if you want."

He doesn't say anything, just nuzzles me, and I assume he's falling back asleep.

I tap on his chest with my one free hand. "Excuse me. Mr. Cassidyyyy," I whisper. "It's time to get up." Just because I *could* comfortably stay in bed all day, doesn't mean I *want* to.

"I'm awake," he just barely squeezes out, but his eyes stay shut.

I don't want to bring it up, but this may be the only way to get him out of bed. "Gotta get up. Don't you have to travel today?"

He scrunches his face in annoyance and slowly picks himself up. "If you really want me to leave so badly…"

"Oh stop," I laugh. "I don't want you going anywhere!"

"Then I guess I'll stay right where I am," Daniel says and drops back down on top of me.

"No! Daniel!" I'm laughing so hard I can't breathe and trying to push him off, but he's planting himself there, pinning me between him and the mattress. "Get off!"

"Nope. We're staying here today. HHHHOOOOONNNN-KKKK SHHHOOOOOOOO…"

"Daniel, you are NOT doing this! Ha ha! Get up!"

"Can't hear you," he says. "I'm asleep. HHHOOOONN-KK SHHoooooo memememe…"

"I swear I'm gonna kill you!" I push as hard as I can.

"No, you won't."

"Oh, are you awake now?" I say with a pretend-stern look and stop trying to push him.

"Nope. I'm asleep." He opens his mouth to do another over-the-top-fake snore and I quickly cover it with my hand.

"Seems like you're awake. Now get up or I'll kill you!"

Through my hand he mumbles, "Nb boo bown. Ooo fambus."

"What was that?" I ask, removing my hand.

"Too famous. You'd be all over the news. I'm sure it'd be good for your store, generating popularity with a 'true crime,' but something tells me you wouldn't like the spotlight."

"What? Me? Not wanting the spotlight for a murder? Shocking. I guess I'd just have to be very careful."

He backs off, and I sit up in bed.

Daniel then continues, "Plus, you'd have to live with the guilt of killing off Daniel Cassidy forever. No more of his books to read. Oh no," he teases.

"How about this; I'll let you live, but you can't have breakfast with me."

He pretends to check his watch and says, "Aw, if only that was a threat, ha ha. But I've got a train soon. Can't really stay too long anyway."

"A train? Who takes trains anymore?"

"First stop on the press tour is the city. I'll be there for the week, then travel down along the coast to Florida, then across to California. Gonna be a lot of time on the road."

Shit, I can't imagine spending that much time in a car. Or on the road in general. Of course, I've always played with the idea of doing a road trip with friends, especially after reading *Stars Through the Trees*, but every time I actually get close to any form of plan it just becomes too much work.

"Well… fine. You *should* stay for breakfast then. One more decent one before you go." I'm sure he'll be eating fine on the road.

He teases again, "You're not very good at standing your ground, are you?"

"Oh, I'm still annoyed. You're just lucky I'm a decent person."

Daniel jumps off the bed, and feigns reverence, "oh, thank you for your kindness. I'm truly in your debt."

I laugh and throw a pillow at him. "Shut up! Do you want to eat or not?"

* * *

When we leave the bedroom, Aria's door is open, and I can see that she is still lying in bed. Richard is nowhere to be seen. There are also a few objects lying on the bed with her, I assume she meant not for anyone to see. Probably should have closed the door on your way out, Richard.

I sneak over to her room to close the door so we don't wake

her up, but the moment my hand touches the knob, she turns over and looks at me.

"Heyyyy buddy.." I whisper. "Good morning!"

"Is Daniel still here?" She asks.

Weird, but, okay?

"Yeah, we were just about to eat? Did you want to join us?" As soon as I ask, I regret it. But no turning back now. "I was thinking of making pancakes."

"Can I have chocolate chips in mine?"

I wasn't offering to make her any, just stating we were having them, but whatever. It's just how Aria is.

"I don't know if we have any, sorry!"

Daniel's voice sounds from the kitchen. "Looks like you have a small bag left."

Thank you, Daniel. More work.

Aria says, "perfect. I'll be up in a bit."

I roll my eyes and start to walk away, but Aria chirps up again. "And coffee please?"

We'll make her breakfast, but I leave without acknowledging it.

Daniel takes control over the kitchen like last night, doing the cooking while I clean the dishes. I should have known Aria wouldn't touch them. Even if she did wake up before us, she probably would have been too "busy" to clean up. I know I'm complaining, but I don't entirely mind. I mean, its time spent with Daniel, and I know that as soon as breakfast is over he'll be leaving so I might as well stall as long as I can. With Aria and cleaning, it's just the principle of the thing.

Aria comes in just as the first pancake finishes cooking and is more than happy to start eating.

"Did you make any coffee?" She asks in her sweetest voice.

Again, I don't verbally acknowledge, but yes, the coffee was brewed and I hand her a cup.

"UUGGHH THANK you, Silvy." She takes a sip. "You're a gem."

Daniel gives me a look like, 'This is what you deal with?' and I respond with a look to say, 'Unfortunately.'

Not noticing our exchange, Aria asks us (with her focus clearly on Daniel), "So! Did you too have a fun night? Silvy isn't *too* much of an obsessive fangirl is she, Daniel?"

I turn red with embarrassment and annoyance, but Daniel seems unphased.

"Ha ha, she's an appropriate level of fangirl. The ones that are too much are the ones that linger on the celebrity part of it," he says with a coy smile, the subtext clearly going over Aria's head.

"And how do you deal with girls like that?" I ask, playing along with his jest.

He turns to me and says, "I'll humor them. Tell them what they want to hear and if they don't leave me alone I give them a fake phone number and tell them to hit me up sometime."

Aria interjects. "Okay but like, what if you get a creepy stalker fan that just doesn't take the hint?"

Daniel and I look at her, wondering if she's messing with us.

His tone shifts from playful and teasing to respectful, yet, matter-of-fact. "I guess, odds are I'd never see them again with how much I travel, unless I really wanted to." He glances quickly at me, but I'm stuck on the reminder of him traveling, and I no longer want to have this conversation.

"So! Aria! When did Richard leave? I don't think I heard him this morning," I say hastily in an effort to steer the conversation.

Daniel returns his attention to the pancakes.

"Fuck if I know." Aria probably doesn't even care that he left. She takes a sip of her coffee and says, "Might've been last night. I was out pretty early, I think."

"Are you two dating now, or what?"

She laughs, "HA! No!"

Almost apologetically, I say, "It just seems like it's been a while for you too. May as well be right?"

"Silvy, it's been a week."

I have to hold my tongue, but I want to remind her that a week for her is almost a full-on commitment with a guy.

Aria continues. "He's fun, but really, not something I can see as long term. Besides, I want to keep myself open for if something better comes."

I'm turned away from her at the moment, but something about the way she says that make me feel... ehhhhhh... weird and uncomfortable inside. Maybe it's just me, and my ideals of what love and romance are, but a person like that who's never content with what's in front of them, especially when it comes to love, talking about it like it's something that can easily be disposed of just grosses me out. These things are sacred, and she's speaking heresy.

197

Daniel is, again, the one to speak up. "Keep looking for something better and you might not see what you've got."

"Okay mister writer," Aria says with a small clap. "Look at you with the… the, I don't know what you call it. The fancy sayings."

Daniel and I laugh at her, and he flips a pancake onto the stack that's built up during the conversation.

He says, "Thanks, I think that was a compliment. But you know…" he places some pancakes on a separate plate and hands it to Aria. "I think Sil and I are gonna eat out on the balcony."

Aria moves the slightest bit in her seat, but Daniel stops her.

"Alone," he says. "If you don't mind."

Aria falls back into place in her seat and says with a coy smile, "Didn't get enough privacy last night? Fine, fine, I get it. Rather sit in the cold than sit with me."

I roll my eyes at her.

Daniel grabs the plate and our drinks, and I grab a sweater out of the bedroom, then we step outside.

The air is sweet and clear this morning, and not too cold. We're lucky today. It's feeling more like early fall than we usually get this late in November. There are a few flakes of snow on the railing and on our seats, the last remnant of the flurries we've had the last few days. With no traffic passing by below, it's all together a fine morning, with fine company.

We sit quietly for a few minutes, enjoying the atmosphere, and Daniel's incredible pancakes, but I can't help but wonder if he's thinking about leaving. Not like, I think he wants to leave right now, but if he's thinking at all about what it means for us when he does have to go. I should just let things come naturally, but I need to know what happens next and I ask him, "So when's your flight?"

He lets out a deep sigh. Okay, it was just me dwelling on it then. Now I feel bad.

"Noon. Leaving from Troy. And taking the train."

"Right, the train…"

There's a moment of silence between us, and I feel the need to tell him – even after all we said last night – that it's okay if this week was all I'll ever see of him. It's a lie, obviously. I just don't want to get my hopes up any more. Last night is already beginning to feel like a dream. A beautiful dream, but still a dream.

I begin to speak again, and he cuts me off.

"I *am* coming back, Sil."

Keep it together Silvia. Don't start tearing up again.

I ask him, "When? I'm sure you'll be home in Iowa for a while."

Almost before I can finish my sentence, he says, "As soon as the book tour is over. I'm coming right back here."

I breathe deep, trying to keep my emotions from getting the best of me, and look out to the road. One look into his eyes and I'll be stuck between belief and disbelief of what he's saying and go mad, not wanting to believe him because what he says is too good to be true. His words are sweet, but really, how can I believe him?

Daniel can see my conflict clear as day. He leans in and says gently, "I don't want to leave you with any doubt. How can I prove this?"

Finally, I do look at him, and I think for a moment. What's

the one thing Daniel can do that no one else in my life can? It's not hard to figure out what it is.

"Write to me," I tell him.

He laughs in a manner of relief. "Write to you?"

"Yes." I fix my posture and scoot my chair closer to him. "At the end of every day, wherever you are, no matter who you meet on the road, write to me. In your voice. Not the voice you use in your books for everyone to read. Write in the voice that you only have for me. If you do…"

I want to say 'if you do love me,' but he hasn't gone that far yet, and I don't want to push too much. If he does as I ask though, maybe it means he does already.

I continue, "If you do care about me, and you do mean to come back, this is how I'll trust you."

Daniel takes my hand in his, raises it to his lips, and kisses my fingers gently.

"As you wish."

15

A week has passed and there's been no word from Daniel. Not a call or a text, not even a message through Instagram. Sure, I may have mentioned that we should keep it to letters moments before he left because I thought that would make it more meaningful, but did he really have to stick to it? Now I'm just getting impatient. What if he forgets to write at all? What if after a little bit of distance he's realized he doesn't actually want a relationship? No, stop it, Silvia. He promised he would, and there was no sign of lying in his voice when he said it.

Truth be told, it's been almost impossible to read *Stargazing* since he left. I've been on the last chapter all week. By the time I get through a paragraph, I get antsy! Here I am, reading his book, but I want to be reading the letters! It pisses me off more than anything and feels like the biggest goddamn tease!

I read a paragraph about this character Dillon fighting against all odds to be with Louise, but where's my Dillon now? I hate to say this because I know it's totally unwarranted, but it bothers me that he didn't even think to invite me along! Of course I'd never say that to him, and even if he did, I'd be apprehensive about such a major thing so fast. I'm just so annoyed!

Thank you for reading this and not judging me. It's nice just to be able to vent.

On Saturday, I watched Daniel's livestream of the book signing in the city. He talks briefly about the writing process of the book, and how it felt like he was totally re-inventing himself with this one. "It was a very strange task at first, transitioning from grounded, real-world storytelling, to something fantastical. But eventually I stepped back and realized, you know, the core is still romance. Something we've been doing for years. We as in, you all and I, together. The audience and myself. The romance is a universal story, and with that in mind, I just had to work out the plot details." At one point, someone asked him if the character of Louise was based on anyone, and who the "Auburn" in the dedication was. At the question, a need comes over me for him to tell everyone about me, but I know that's ridiculous. He tells the room, "Yes, there was someone who inspired the character, but… things change in the writing process. The person in the dedication was just someone I happened to pass by when I was still working on creating the character and the look stuck. Now I think… it's taken on a new meaning." He looks at the camera recording the live stream and gives a coy smile, as if he knows I'm watching.

My heart races a million miles a minute. He's talking about me! He's really talking about me in front of all these people! Will he say my name? Will he actually tell them about the girl in the bookstore?

I listen intently, hoping to pick up more subtle (Okay maybe not *that* subtle) hints he drops for me.

The person in the audience asks, "When do you think the next book in the series will be out?"

Seriously?! He just dropped major news about his personal life and you're just moving on?!

"I think I'm going to take a break between books in this series," Daniel says, the smile he had when he talked about me fades away and he's straight again. "This was a lot of fun, but I want to take my time with it. The story means a lot more to me, especially now, than I thought it would when I started writing." This time when he looks at the camera, it's not the same obvious smile, just a quick glance and a smirk.

Holy hell, I love this man.

Sunday comes and goes, and now on Monday, I rush home after work (helping out my parents at the dentistry) and check my mail. Praise the Lord, a letter arrived from Daniel.

I run up to the apartment with the stack of mail, run through the door without even taking my shoes off and blow past Aria without even a hello, and lock myself in my room. No one and nothing is going to ruin this moment for me.

I tear open the envelope and begin reading.

12/2/23

Dear Sil,

I've never really done this before, and don't re-

ally know what to say. I miss you. I hope you watched the livestream. Not ~~for me because I want you to watch me~~ because I wanted more views, but I was trying to talk to you through it. Did it work? Or was it too much? I didn't want to call you out directly. I didn't know how comfortable you would be with that with everyone watching. Anyway, I can't wait to hear back from you. Hope things are good at the store! I'll see you soon! (I hope!)

-Yours

Um... what the hell was that?

Sorry, I don't mean to be picky or anything but, come on... I'm not the only one that expected more from him right? Hope things are good at the store? Yours? Who the hell wrote this?

I storm out of my room, needing someone to complain to.

"Aria!" I knock on her door.

She's there almost immediately, looking concerned. "What? What is it?"

"Look at this!" I shove the letter in front of her face.

Aria takes the letter and read it in a whisper. "Okay? What's wrong?"

"Did you read it?!" I demand. "It's so dull!" I trudge over to the couch and fall on it. "It's like he didn't put any effort in!"

Aria stands there in the doorway to her room and re-reads the letter. After she finishes, she says, "maybe he was just busy. He probably wrote it really fast and sent it out so you didn't have to wait anymore."

I grumble, "Or maybe he stopped caring. It reads more like he's just checking in on a friend than writing to me, his *girlfriend.*"

"Ha ha, so it's official?" She sits down next to me.

"It *was.*"

"Well, he obviously cares, he says he was talking to you during his stream."

I only grumble something incoherent. To be honest, I don't even know what I was trying to say.

"If you're so butthurt why don't you just call him," Aria says, clearly annoyed at my attitude.

"I can't call him! We said letters only so it's more meaningful."

Aria rolls her eyes. "I don't know then. Write him back or something," she says as she stands to return to her room.

That's not a bad idea. I'll write to him. I'll show the writer what a real love letter looks like. A love letter filled with annoyance.

Daniel,

I received your letter, and I must say, I'm rather disappointed in you. When I asked you to write me in your own voice, I did not mean for you to dumb it down. I did watch your lives-

tream, and I was very touched by what you said. But when you follow it up with something like that, signed only "yours" you make me question how much of what you've said you actually meant. I waited all week for your letter and it felt so cold. I don't mean to be rude, but if you don't want me to feel like just some girl that will be waiting around for who knows how long for you to come back to her, then please put a little more effort in.

Sincerely,
Silvia.

There. It may not be romantic, but it's from the heart.

I read over it once to check for errors, then look around the apartment for envelopes and stamps.

"Aria, do we have any stationary stuff?"

She comes out of her room again and says, "I don't think so, but I just realized something."

I shoot her a glare, unintentionally, as my wrath is for Daniel, and she's only offered me support and advice.

Aria continues, "He's on the road right now, right?"

"Yeah? So?"

"So, how would you mail him anything? He won't be there when it arrives."

I… hold on…

Fuck. She's right. How did neither of us realize this?

"I'm calling him."

Daniel's phone rings twice, then he picks up. "Hey!" he says eagerly. "What happened to no calls?"

I could tell him what Aria told me, but no time. I have a score to settle. "What happened to romantic letters?"

His voice falters, then, "What are you talking about, Sil? Didn't you get them?"

"Yes, *Daniel*, I did. And I feel hurt! After all that waiting and you give me a few rushed lines? What am I supposed to do with that? A letter so generic it could be from anyone! Do you think that makes me feel like I mean anything to you?" I begin rattling on and on with my complaints, and he persistently tries to interject. Reluctantly, I let him speak.

"Did you read both letters?"

"Did I- what? Both?" I ask.

"Yes, I wrote two letters. The first one I wrote as soon as the event ended, but I was being rushed to dinner with my publisher and editor. I didn't know if I'd have any time before leaving for D.C. Then later, I was telling my editor about you and the letter, and what it said, and he said I should write a better one if I didn't want a call like this. Check your mail again, I only sent it out a few hours later."

I pause a moment, then tell him to hold on. There in the stack of mail, buried under the rest is another letter from Daniel.

207

Almost like reading my mind through the phone, or just guessing from my hesitation, he says, "Now let's stick to your rules. Letters only. Okay, baby?"

I feel like shit. I could almost throw up. In fact, I probably will. All the bitching about him and the letter I wrote. Holy hell, I gotta stop jumping to conclusions.

"Okay…" I say softly into the phone.

"All right, I miss you Sil. And keep watching the streams, I like talking about you."

He hangs up and I'm left there feeling like an idiot with the letter in my hand. I open it up slowly and begin to read.

12/2/23

My Dearest Sil,

I'm sorry for the last, rushed letter. I don't want you to think I'd be a bare minimum kind of guy. There hasn't been a moment since I've left your side that I haven't been obsessing over you. You've infected my mind and I never want you to stop. The instant I got on the train, I wished I'd asked you to come along. I'm sorry if that's forward of me, but I can't get enough of you. Enough of your cheek in my hand, or your hair, or ~~you're~~ your dazzling eyes that pierce through to my heart and melt me

*every time you look my way. Every bookstore I
go to on this trip, I'll be wishing was yours, and
every audience I have, I'll wish was only you.
I hope when you read this, you find honesty
in it. I know it could be easy to read this ~~and
see~~ as ~~the words of someone whos a just~~ just
another romantic line by someone whos done
this a million times. But I promise you, this is
the real me. This is the person you'll never find
in any of the "Daniel Cassidy" books. And these
are the words meant for no one but you. I'll be
back sooner than you know it, and I hope I can
prove to you then, if not through these letters,
just how much you mean to me.*

> *-Until I see you again,*
> *Daniel C.*

P.S.
*Realized you don't know where to send letters
back to me. I'll attach an address for my next
hotel after each letter.*

All is forgiven, Daniel.

16

Here we begin the segment of this love story in which Daniel and I put our love into written word:

Dear Daniel,

I'm sorry for that call. I hate to admit this, but I tend to overthink sometimes. I did see your stream, and the way you looked at me during those questions. It truly warmed my heart hearing you talk about the dedication, and how it's "taken on new meaning now" or something like that.

It's been hard for me to finish Stargazing. because of this, not knowing whether or not you wold would actually write. Thank you for putting my mind at ease. I think I'll be able to finish it tonight, and will be sure to let you know my thoughts!

It's funny you mentioned inviting me along on the tour. Just before reading your letter, I remembered I was about to invite myself along as you were leaving, but I was nervous about what you'd think. Next time though, I'd be more than happy to come along. Maybe I can help run your social media while I'm at it. I do have a bit of a history, working with my parents.

As for work, it's been a strange week. When I went in on monday, Eliza (my boss) gave me attitude because she didn't see me at church. She alwasys always asks me to go, and I do sometimes, but I never told her that I _would_ go this last sunday, even though she says I did as we were leaving after she almost caught us. I'm really just going to chalk it up to her still being stressed out about the holidays. She keeps droning on about the store closing, and this and that, but we've been doing as good as ever as far as I can tell.

Speaking od of holidays, do you know yet what your plan is for Christmas? I'm sure you'll be home in Iowa by then, but it really would be great to see you! Or even just, and not to ruin the surprise, send you a card to your place out there?

Whatever works out, I just hope I see you again soon.

Your dedication,
            Sil.

P.s.
I discovered what it was Aria and Richard were up to and I swear I wish I didn't. I cannot see her in the same light anymore, ha ha, and definitely not him.

12/9/23

My Dearest Sil,

I hate to admit, but I didn't think I'd actually get your letter. Not that I didn't think you'd write, though I'm sure it crosses your mind not to after reading that first letter from me, I just assumed the letter would get lost in the hotel mail room since I wasn't there yet. But I'm glad it didn't. It was great having it waiting for me when I showed up here in DC, especially with how the event went. I really don't mind not being in spotlights, and if I could avoid all the signings, I would. Honestly, I really didn't expect this kind of attention when I got into this gig. I thought it would just be a photoshoot every once in a while for a back matter or "about the author" page, and maybe if there was an event at all, it'd be JUST the signing. I didn't think I'd be giving full on lectures and questions/answer events on the books. If I have to be on stage, i can, but you saw how it went. At least i think you did. The audience was completely dead and that's so much worse than a loud audience. I had no idea what to talk about, especially when it seemed like no one cared. I was dying to get to the signing and be done so I could come back to the hotel and write to you.

I'm sorry to hear about your boss and the store. Is she usually like this around the holidays? I know it can be tough on broadway. ~~If she's talking about the store closing, do you really think she's exaggerating? Not to be a downer, but~~

As for Christmas, I don't know yet. My last event before the day is literally the 23rd, in Miami. I have a flight booked for home, but the chances of me actually making it, just with the time of the event that day, are almost null. I have a reservation at a hotel down here just in case.

But if I could, you know I'd want to spend christmas with you. I think I could spend one year away from the family. Besides, this is the perfect ending right? We meet, and I'm pulled away too soon, but I make it back to you for christmas ~~and we live happily ever after?~~ and the credits roll?

First chance i get though, I will be seeing you again. Don't you think for one second that while i'm traveling, you aren't constantly on my mind. Hell, this might be saying too much, but I;ve even been dreaming about you, What about? Well, you'll have to wait till i'm back to share.

Until I see you again,
Daniel C.

P.S.
Seems like we'll keep doing this. Took you long enough to figure it out. I'm surprised you didn't sooner since you read "Binds." But don't get any ideas ha ha

Dear Daniel,

You were always going to get a letter back from me, but to be fair, the first draft of the letter I wrote you wouldn't have liked. I had only read the first one you sent. But that's in the past.

I could kind of guess by how you acted and carried yourself when we first met that maybe you didn't love the spotlight as much as you give off through your ~~online~~ publicized image. It makes me think though, If we had met at one of your signings instead of how we did, would things have gone the same way? I hope so. I like to think things like this are - and forgive me, I read a lot of books - meant to be sometimes, even if it is super cheesy. Realistically though, I don't know. We may have exchanged a few words here or there, but I would have been way too nervous to try to really TALK to you. Let's just be happy with how it worked out in reality. Although, we would have to host you at Bookends for an event. Even though it might be a little crammed.

OH! Speaking of Bookends, it's been the weirdest week. Eliza hasn't shown up <u>once</u>. Not even to clear out the register for deposits. The most i've heard from her is short phone calls making sure I'm actually doing my job. So now I'm working full time there. ~~And on top of that, I haven't seen Harry since you met him. I know, I know, it's weird to talk about my ex, and I'm sorry. But he used to show up at least once a week, every week. I'm a little worried about him because of how poorly I treated him last time I saw him. Do you think I'm over thinking it?~~

I'm sorry. You don't need to be bothered with that kind of stuff.

On a lighter note! I think i've finally convinced my parents that you and I really are a thing! They still tease me about your books, but they've accepted it at least. So I hope you're okay with meeting them at some point. I'm not looking forward to it because it means time with my parents but, it will have to happen sooner or later. So when I say "lighter note" that was meant with a grain of salt.

Don't worry about Christmas. It's only my favorite time of year, but I won't try to guilt you.

Ha ha

But seriously, don't worry about it. I really do understand how busy you are, and everyone's stressing enough. But you have to send me your address for that weekend ahead of time so I can send you your present!

I finally finished Stargazing. after I sent out your last letter. Something about it felt so different from your other books. Not just because you took it into a new genre, but the emotional core felt strange. Not in a bad way though. By the end of the book, I couldn't really place it, but maybe it's because Dillon and Louise barely spent any time together for the bulk of the story. (sounds familiar doesn't it?) I think you really tapped into something with this was of developing their romance without any real interaction. What was the inspiration? Distance makes the heart grow fonder? My one criticism is with an ending like this, don't tell everyone there will be sequels until the audience has had time to read the book. It gave away the ending just a bit.

Now for as much as I loved the book, and I genuinely did, I'd rather not have that be us. It's been what, two weeks? and I think that's quite enough distance.

Your Dedication,
Sil

P.S.
Yes, we'll keep doing this. Don't worry, Aria didn't give me any ideas...

But maybe other parts of "Binds" did. We'll just have to see...

12/13/23

My Dearest Sil

I got your letter as soon as I checked into
the hotel. This week has, and is going to keep
being so busy, I wasn't sure if I'd even have
a chance to write to you. As if the signings
weren't enough, this week is all about speaking
at schools. Yes, I have a lecture at one of the
local colleges on the "creative writing process."
I don't know how the hell I'm going to pull this
off, and on days like this I really don't know
what the hell I'm doing.

Maybe I could just bail on this whole writing thing and you and I could take over the
Bookstore. Sounds like your boss is done with it
anyway. And something tells me that'd be your
dream, so why not? It seems like a peaceful
life. Much more at least than this sham I'm
living now. I don't know anything about retail
though, so if we did, you'd have to be the brains.

It's cool if you don't want to though...

I'll just have to open my own store and
compete with you, ha ha ha ha ha!

I'm glad you finished Stargazing, and
especially glad you liked it. Yes, I think it was

interesting trying to work that "romance at a distance" angle. And yes, it's all too familiar. Don't worry, for the sequels, I won't play that card again. They'll stick together, and grow together. But that's all I'll say to anyone about a sequel for now. I'll take your advice.

And I agree, two weeks HAS been plenty of distance for us. I'll fix that as soon as I can.

Until I see you again,
Daniel C.

P.S.
I'm looking forward to it.

Dear Daniel,

I didn't expect to get your letter so soon!

Hmmmm...I don't know if opening a bookstore together would be a great idea. I think it'd be hard to focus on anything if we worked together. Although to have you there would probably do wonders to sell our stock. And maybe you could write a book exclusive to the store. We could self-publish and print locally so everyone _had_ to buy through us.   It's genius, we'd make millions and never go out of business!

Looking towards this dream bookstore is better than what's really going on around here. I still haven't seen Eliza. I called her up and she blew me off. Okay, maybe not that harsh, but she was so dismissive. I'm honestly starting to think she might be serious about closing the store. Still a _wild_ overreaction, but these last few days have done nothing to support my case.

~~It's been the most dead that it's been of all~~ This is the most dead it's been all year. Yesterday we didn't have a single customer come in. I started promoting the place more online, tiktok and instagram, you know, but it takes time to build up a following and this place just isn't taking off. With time though, I think we'll do all right. It's just a slump, and I'll pull us out of it! (But an exclusive book would help!)

I was thinking about it last night, and this has to be the most writing I've ever done in my life as far as letters go. I remember when I was younger I tried being "pen pals" with Aria, even though she lived about five minutes away, but we probably only wrote one letter each and then gave up. This has definitely been an experience for me, and hey! maybe I'll even become a writer like you one day! I mean, I've been having ideas for the sequel to Stargazing. if you haven't worked out all the details yet. I'll give you a full write up when you get back. One thing I will say now though, maybe a little more of the... physical... romance in the next one? Just a little bit more. You did great in the beginning, ~~but it felt of this one,~~ but it felt like a tease that never really paid off. Like, I expected this big sensual moment at the end when they reunited, but instead we got a beautiful passionate kiss and open ending. It was fantastic, don't get me wrong, but who likes a tease? I'm not saying go full "Binds," and definitely not full "Habits," ew, but like, "Vanilla." That'd be a good level. Oh! Say that in at your next signing! Tell them the sequel will be spicier! I'm sure that'll generate interest.

Where is this next one, anyway? I'm looking forward to watching it. Hope I get a shout out...

I want to say, on a serious note, I don't think you know how much these letters mean to me. I've read and re-read each of yours about a dozen times each. They're all already crumpled up from me holding them close to my heart as I fall asleep. It's silly, I know, but our week together meant more to me, and felt more real, than anything I've known before. I don't know if you feel the same way, and I don't blame you if you don't, but I just had to say it.

In case you were wondering, I don't think I have any more doubts about your intentions, or interest in this relationship. I trust you Daniel.

Your Dedication,
Sil.

12/18/23

My Dearest Sil,

Your last letter must have been mailed
with such perfect timing that it got stuck in the
mail yesterday. I was hoping, that If I sent you
a letter sooner in the week, I'd hear back from
you sooner. Eventually we'll be writing so often
we might as well go back to texting. So, yesterday was pretty annoying knowing there was a
letter waiting but no one to deliver. I did almost
give in and call you, but resorted to watching
your posts about the store so I could hear your
voice again. I'd like to reshare it, but my agent
is extremely strict about what gets posted from
the "Daniel Cassidy" brand. If you never not
why I don't post that much, that's why. And
"Habits" fits into the reason too, but that's
obvious. I'll try to squeeze in a word about your
store this saturday at the event in miami. I
know it's not as good as holding an event right
in your store, but it's something. Right?

Now that I think about it, that might
be the only part of the miami event I'm looking forward to. Less than a week away from
Christmas, and I'm stuck down in florida. And

not even the good part of florida, fucking miami.
I HOPE, I PRAY, they ask me about the sequel.
It'll be off script but I'll be able to talk honestly
about the love interest for once. ~~Yes, being optimistic that things work out between us, the
inspiration for Louise will defin~~ I've never written something this from the heart before, and
I _Really_ want to! I don't want to keep righting
heartless, sappy romances(Yes, I know you love
the sap). It's like I said when we met, if I were
to write ~~something real to me,~~ a romance that
was real to me, it'd be more along the lines of
"When Harry Met Sally" but now I have someone that would really have it inspired.

So be sure to be watching this weekend's
event! You'll get your shoutout!

Until I see you again,
Daniel C.

Dear Daniel,

Merry Christmas! I hope this gets to you on time! I know NY to Florida might be tough in 3 days, but your letters to me seem to be making good time.

I'm sorry you can't be home this year, and especially sad, even if it's selfishly, that you can't be here. This week has been insane with holiday prepping, and I've spent way too much time with my family. Well, Lucas I won't complain about, I can't wait for you to meet him, but my brother Tyler broke up with his girlfriend Camille, who was by far the best girl he's ever had, and I guarantee he ended it for a stupid reason. We really connected during Thanksgiving, so I think I'll reach out to her to see how she's doing. I mention it because her and Lucas would have been my saving graces through all the family events, so now all the weight is on him. Another positive though is there is no Harry this year! To my surprise, my parents didn't invite him to ANYTHING. This is seriously a big deal for them. It took them way longer to move on from him than I did. The final piece for them will be meeting you. Maybe, if not Christmas, you can be here for new years? I don't spend the night with them, but at some point maybe we can stop by? My mom might have a heart attack meeting the guy that wrote "Habits," Lucas you HAVE to meet.

Are you doing anything down there, anyway? Any cool celebrity christmas parties in Miami? Just be sure you don't forget about me up here when all the girls are fawning over Daniel Cassidy. I think I have a much better Christmas present than they could give you.

I know things will probably get hectic for you in the next few days, but please don't forget to write back! And yes, I will be watching the event this saturday.

Your dedication,
Sil.

Dear Daniel,

I know I shouldn't have gotten my hopes up too high, but I have to be honest. I really was sad you weren't able to write be back sooner. I didn't expect anything on the 24th or 25th, but I hoped by yesterday I would have gotten something from you. Even, and I know we said letters only, but I thought Christmas would have been a special exception to give me a call.

I guess you're still stuck in Miami, or finally back on the road to your next event. This letter might not even get to you if that's the case

My letter writing is interrupted by a thud against my window. I turn and see flakes stuck to the glass as they fall outside. This storm has been coming down hard for the last three days, and in the dark, my first thought is a bird smacked into it, but that doesn't make any sense. Another thud follows and I realize it's a snowball. Some asshole is throwing snowballs at my window!

I hop off my bed and pull open the window, just as another snowball flies through and hits my ceiling, exploding into a short flurry in my bedroom. I look out, but can't see below the balcony. Shit, they're really going to make me do this?

I throw on my bathrobe and slippers, then walk out to the balcony, bend over the railing, and shout to the asshole with the snowballs, "Hey what the hell is wrong with you?!"

The warmest voice carries through the freezing, December storm. "Maybe I'm just a little crazy from being stuck in airports the last three days! Is it too late to say 'Merry Christmas?'"

Interlude:
Vanilla + Cherry

Released: March 10th, 2020

Synopsis: Vivian is in her final semester of college, but is unsure if she's ready to move on. She doesn't feel like she's gotten the full experience by always playing it safe… and innocent.

With just a few weeks until graduation, Vivian lets herself cut loose at a party, but goes too far, too fast, blacking out and waking up at a stranger's house, a Stripper named Cherry.

Cherry begins to lead Vivian on a road of self-discovery and lust she'd never before imagined. But things come to a head when Vivian discovers stripping is only a part-time thing for Cherry…

-Page count: 405

-Read: April 12th-16th, 2020

       Oct. 9th - 11th, 2020

       Feb. 14th - 21st, 2021

       July 3rd - 6th, 2022

Bookends

Sept. 20th - 22nd, 2023

-Rating (Goodreads average): 3.6/5 Stars

-Rating(Mine): 5/5 Stars

Review: There will never be a book better than this!

–Edit– Lisbon is. But first impressions are still important.

This last month, all anyone on booktok has been talking about is this guy Daniel Cassidy, so I finally came around and checked out this book. And holy HELL! For a guy to be writing this kind of steam? He's either a well read perv or incredibly talented, but either way, I'm not complaining.

On the surface, it feels like a high school boy's fantasy. Lesbian lovers, school girls and all that. But the book is written with such nuance that the (limited) sexual content takes a back seat and you can almost forget it was written by a guy. I also never thought I'd find myself so invested in a gay romance, but here we are. Well done Mr. Cassidy, you're making me question myself. Not sure how I feel about that.

I can't really do the "good v.s. bad" of this book. It'd be unfair because there is no bad. The rating for this book is pretty average, which is absolutely wild. As I said, everyone's talking about it. Maybe it's because of how steamy it is coming from a man and not being terrible. Either way. I love all the characters, I love the pacing, I love the twist(oh and it's juicy, but I won't spoil it), and the way Mr. Cassidy is able to trick the audience into believing this fantasy Vanilla(Vivian, that's just the nickname Cherry gives her when she takes her to dance on the pole with her. My bad, I said I wouldn't spoil it) is living, even though you're given all the info you need to realize her life is spiraling.

–Edit– On a reread, I'm realizing how similar the themes of this kind of build off of Runaway lover, but in a more linear way. And instead of jumping into a bad-but-redeemable person's life halfway through, we're able to see the full arc. Okay that's unfair. Vivian/Vanilla is never a "bad" person, just falls into traps. She's young, it's forgivable and there was never any malice in her actions.

Really, it's a book about discovery *and* self-control. It's very easy to lose control in times of massive change, but important to find balance before you fall too far off one end.

I can't help but recommend this book to absolutely everybody.

17

"What are you doing here?" I ask Daniel as he jogs down the hallway towards my apartment. He's so poorly dressed, looking like he's still in Miami with the sleeves rolled back on his jean jacket. Snow is stuck to his pants almost up to his knees, and his cheeks are a bright red from the cold. "You said you were going to be stuck in Miami!" I whisper-shout, half annoyed that he didn't tell me he was coming, but also completely overjoyed he's here.

Before he says anything, Daniel wraps his arms tightly around me and his freezing lips kiss mine. "I *was* stuck in Miami. And Baltimore, *and* Rochester. I got here in a rental car and it's gonna be a bitch to return it."

I kiss him back. "Why'd you fly into Rochester? There's an airport right here!"

"The storm, they had to reroute us. But do you really want to talk about planes, or do you want to get inside?" He kisses my cheek, then down my neck.

"Wait!" I push him off of me. "What about the tour? Isn't your next event this week?"

"Saturday," he says and kisses my neck again. "I'll fly out

Friday night for Houston." His hands run up my back, pulling me into him.

Fuck, Daniel, seriously right here in the hallway?

I glance through the apartment doorway, wanting to bring him inside, but right now is awful for what I think is on both of our minds.

"Hold on, Daniel," I say, as I realize we're slowly backing into the apartment. One of his hands slips through my robe, and I feel it against my side. It's so cold against my skin, making me shiver, but I love it. I don't want him to stop, but, "Daniel, wait!" I whisper. "Ari's here. She's with her boyfriend.

He stops kissing my neck, but leaves his hand in my robe, up against my back to hold me close.

"Why don't we get out of here then?"

Less than five minutes later we're in his car, driving to his place on the river. We don't talk in the car. Soft music plays, some of Wolf Alice's softer songs, and a few by other bands that fit the mood. Daniel's right hand is on my thigh, much higher than I let him put it on our first date. I lay my head on his arm and watch the snow fall around the car.

To be honest, I know all I've said before about sex, and right now, I don't care if it's a heat-of-the-moment thing. I don't care that we haven't openly called it "love" yet. I want him.

We pull up to a small cabin in the woods. The driveway is completely blocked by snow and we have to park on the side of the road. We step out and Daniel rushes around the car. Before I know what's happening, he has me swept up in his arms with a kiss and carries me through the snow. I laugh, and he asks, "Didn't think I'd make you walk through this did you?"

I reply, trying to sound coy, "I don't think I'd mind getting a little wet."

Even in the darkness, I can see him blush.

Daniel carries me all the way to the front door through the heavy snow and bitter wind. He places me down on the front porch and tells me to, "wait, just a moment," while he finds the key.

Snow falls in my fair, and down between my coat and my neck. It sends a shiver through me, but I love it. In these moments with Daniel, with this anticipation, I love everything I feel, everything I smell. I love how everything looks, the snow backlit by the moonlight, like a scene out of *Stars Through the Trees*. And I love the taste of Daniels's lips I still have on mine since he kissed me a minute ago.

"Got it." Daniel holds the key, having found it hidden under a flowerpot buried in snow. "How about we get a fire going?"

The house is absolutely freezing inside. Another reason to get close to Daniel. If he isn't able to get a fire going, body heat should suffice. Body heat and plenty of blankets, to be realistic. But thankfully, it doesn't take long for the cabin to warm up. It's more modern than it looks. Daniel tells me the house is winterized and has decent heating, but he "still prefers the fire."

I sit by the hearth while he fills the fire with fuel and makes us hot chocolate. He brings it over and takes a seat next to me.

Holy hell. This hot chocolate might be better than any book he's ever written. I nearly chug it, but he takes his time sipping, looking into my eyes.

"I need to tell you something," Daniel says. I shouldn't be taken off guard, but his voice toes the line so sharply between collected and stern. I almost choke on the hot chocolate.

Once I compose myself, I know exactly what he's going to say. This is what he was waiting for. What had to be said before we do it.

"Yes, Daniel?" I look at him with (hopefully, if I can get the look right) doe eyes.

He breathes deep. Everyone has a million people they've said the words to, but this look he has tells me Daniel is the exception. I hope I'm not getting false hopes, but I'll bet Daniel's never said it before.

"Sil, ever since I first saw you…"

Yes…?

"That very first moment, I mean, before I came into your store… I knew you were the only person I could say this to." He brushes a hand across my cheek and around my ear. It's warm from the mug he'd been holding and feels so comforting.

He continues, "Ever since I got into this life, I haven't been able to be myself. Living as this guy… Daniel Cassidy the novelist… I… I haven't been able to just… be honest with anyone. I always have to keep up this image that I can't handle anymore."

It might not be exactly, 'I love you,' and I feel bad for that being my first thought, but I think what he's saying means more. Celebrity pressure. Maybe they weren't that bad when he got into it, but *Habits* ruined his image. Playing it safe for the publisher's eyes had to have been a nightmare. I think back to seeing him in the cigar shop, a place no one, no fans like me, would see him in. And then there I was commenting on his smoking, a bad habit.

"Sil, I'm not-

I don't need to hear the rest. I should, but I know what it's going to be and Daniel, you've already got me. I interrupt him with a kiss and then say, "Daniel, I love you. Not for the books, I love who you are, and how I feel when I'm with you. I loved the letters you sent because I knew it was really you, writing for only me." I kiss him again, with my arms wrapped around his neck.

Daniel pulls back for a moment to breathe and say, "I- I love you too!"

FUCKING. FINALLY!

"I just- Sil-"

"Don't," I tell him between kisses. "You don't have to say anything. Just-"

He takes the hint.

I'm swept up again, and Daniel carries me into another room, dropping me on the bed.

I fall in slow motion onto the pillows. Daniel climbs on top of me and begins by kissing my neck. He's wasting no time with foreplay, and already pulling up my shirt. We both laugh as it gets caught around my neck, but it's not ruining the mood. Once it's off, I try to prop myself up to take off my bra, but Daniel is moving down from my neck, kissing my breasts, and down my stomach. With every inch lower he moves, I get more and more-

I'm sorry, but the details of this night, especially from this point on are between myself and Daniel. A lady doesn't kiss and tell.

Interlude
Binds

Released: Aug. 17th, 2020

Synopsis: Gabriella Hayes is a hard-hitting journalist willing to go to any length to get a story, but has a fatal flaw of letting her own biases get in the way of her pursuits.

Tipped off that a powerful politician is having an affair, Gabby throws herself into a world of bondage and hedonism to every juicy detail of the story. Slowly she finds herself unable, or unwilling, to get out and might just be a little too close to her latest target.

-Page count: 554
-Read: Sept. 17th - 28th, 2020
-Rating (Goodreads average): 4.1/5
-Rating(Mine): 4.5/5

Review(SPOILER): I guess I read smut now. This one has taken booktok by storm and it's not hard to see why. This book starts out hot and never cools down.

When we meet Gabriella, she's doing time as a stripper (the same club that Cherry works at. Such a cool connection!) We get hints right off the bat by the way she carries herself that she isn't doing this just for the story she's writing about the world of exotic dancing most people don't see. From my interpretation, the journalism is just a means to an end. I think she wants to push herself, and needs a socially acceptable way to validate her desires. I mean, her last few articles were all about sex workers or sex based organizations. I'd be a little worried if she ever did an "in-depth" story on drug addiction.

Senator Reed really caught me off guard. I went into this thinking, "Okay, obviously this is going to develop into a romance. They'll start their own affair and she'll be fooled into thinking he's a good guy." But wow, this one took risks. *SPOILER* The fact that he's never played as a good guy deep down, yet still captures the lust of Gabriella makes so much sense for her character. She doesn't care for romance, just the pleasure he, and the other guests of the resort can offer. Turns out this book isn't in any way romantic. She has no desire for his heart, she only wants what he can offer. It really is toxic, but equal to both parties. It seems like most people understood that this book doesn't necessarily promote these kinds of relationships, it's saying there are people like that out there, and this is where their needs are. Not everything is a fairy tale romance. Some people just want to be tied up, gagged, and get their rocks off. Do I need to try that kinda stuff? NOOooooo… probably not. Chapter 36? Didn't even know that was a thing until now. It's just fun reading for now.

But I'd be lying if I didn't say Mr. Cassidy hasn't piqued my interest.

Do I recommend this book? Yes, but anonymously.

18

I wish it was summer. I sit on Daniel's lap looking out onto the frozen river just outside the cabin. This place would be wonderful in the summer.

We're wrapped up in a thick blanket. His arm is wrapped around me, holding me tight, and his free hand traces up and down my bare thigh. We've been sitting like this since breakfast, kept warm by each other's body heat.

"Do you think you'll be around this summer?" I ask.

His arm squeezes tightly as if in reaction to the question, then loosens back to normal.

"I should be. Don't see why I wouldn't," he says.

I find my hand caressing his face and make its way into his hair.

"I just assumed you'd be going back home at some point," I say. "I don't want you to though... I know, it's so selfish."

His body shifts like he's about to sit up. "Sil, I-"

"Just tell me you want me," I cut him short. Ever since last night, this fear that the most I'd ever get from him had come and gone when our bodies were intertwined. Now I'd just be another fan he hooked up with. I know it's a terrible, silly idea.

"I want this, with you, Sil. I really do." With two fingers on my chin, he turns my head to face him more directly. "I just need you-"

He's cut off again by one of our phone's going off.

What the fuck... I guarantee this was going to be the most romantic shit I've heard in my entire life, better than anything from any of his books, and the stupid default iPhone alarm blares instead.

"Fuck! Sorry, Daniel," I blurt as if I caused it, and rush to my phone. I'm ready to throw it in the freezing cold river. "Let me just turn it off quick."

I want him to say, 'No, don't worry about it! They'll stop calling,' but he doesn't. Instead, he says, "Okay, it might be important."

Wrong answer Daniel, but, fine. I'm taking the blanket with me though.

When I check my phone, I see not just two missed calls from Ellie, but a series of texts from both Aria and my parents.

The first thing I do is call Ellie back. It's been over two weeks since I've heard from her. Just seeing her name pop up on my screen gives me comfort that she's not dead. I call her back and she picks up immediately.

She speaks slowly. Her tone is soft and collected, almost like she's reading off a script to get straight to the point.

"Good morning Silvia. If you're available this morning I need you to come into the store. I need help packing everything up. We need to be out by the end of the week."

I have no idea what to say. It's like listening to a recording because of how flat her delivery is. Is she waiting for me to respond? Is there more to say? Maybe a reason why she's doing this so suddenly?

Just as I find the words, she continues, "Whenever you're free. You'll still get paid for the next two weeks."

The call ends.

I feel naked. I *am* naked, but this… what is she talking about? How can she do this to me? She knows how much this means to me! That damn store is everything! She's lost it, that's what it is. She's old, and she's losing it. She's just quitting. She's quitting and she's not even thinking of me! What I need! I want to scream! No, I won't scream, I won't cry. I'll go down there and talk to her about it. Hell, if need be I'll buy the damn place from her!

"Everything okay?" Daniel asks, still sitting on the sofa.

"Fine! I'm fine!" I shout aggressively back as I grab my pants from the bedroom floor and pull them up. "I have to go. Ellie's being crazy."

Daniel jumps up, and I hear his bare feet pound against the old wood floor as he strides over to the bedroom. He stands in the doorway with the blanket wrapped around his waist. There's a concerned look in his eye that tells me he'll see through any excuse I'll try to pull.

"Sil, are you okay?" His voice is so gentle and warm.

I take a deep breath, not wanting to take my annoyance, borderline anger, out on him.

"Eliza is trying to close the bookstore."

His eyes wander across my face. He knows the slightest thing could set me off and is trying to be diplomatic.

This isn't his fault, but now that he's brought himself into the issue, the longer he takes to say something, the more I want to aim my emotions at him.

What he manages to say after making me wait a full 30 seconds is, "Do you want me to drive?"

* * *

I text Aria and my parents back in the car. They all want to make plans tonight. Aria is a maybe. She wants to go to the bars on Caroline Street. I really don't want to, but depending on how things go with Eliza, I might *have* to drink tonight. At least Daniel will be there. That might also be why she wants us to go out, so she can show off that she knows *the* Daniel Cassidy. My parents are in the same boat. Eliza called them because she couldn't get ahold of me sooner. Parents got a hold of Aria when I wasn't responding and she mentioned that I was "probably spending the night with Daniel." You know me so well, bestie. I have no interest in having dinner with my parents, but if they finally meet Daniel, maybe they'll get off my back about everything else. Just a Band-Aid I have to rip off.

Fine, we'll go to dinner with them, and take a rain check with Aria. But right now, I have to deal with Eliza.

We pull up along the sidewalk across from Bookends. Nyx is sitting outside her store as always, this time with what looks like a cup of tea.

Daniel turns the car off and unbuckles but I hold out my hand to stop him.

"I think I should be alone with her right now."

He looks at me with a smirk. "Sure you're all right?"

The smile is all I needed to lighten my spirit the littlest bit. "Yes. I'll be okay."

"Okay."

I smile back now. "Look, I'll see you tonight, okay? We'll try to make it a quick dinner then have some fun after."

"Just us?"

"Just us," I say with a small bite of my lip.

He leans in to kiss me. It's not a sensual kiss, not one that says he can't wait to take my clothes off. It's passionate and sweet. A kiss that simply says, "I love you."

Our lips part and he says, "I'll see you later. Hope it goes well."

Daniel pulls away after I cross the street. I can see Eliza through the storefront window, packing up books into boxes. When I open the door, I see the full extent of the damage. The high-value cabinet has been completely ransacked. Cardboard boxes stacked high crowd the front counter. Eliza's going row by row, purging everything from the shelf. If I hadn't known better, I wouldn't even be able to guess this was ever a bookstore at first glance.

"Eliza, what do you think you're doing?"

She's crouched down in front of the children's section, placing handful after handful of books into a box. Without looking up at me, she says, "There are more boxes in the office. Would you please start in the other room? Someone from the art gallery is going to be picking those up later."

"Ellie, you need to stop this. I don't know what's come over you, but this is ridiculous!"

Her head cocks towards me. She drops the books she's holding into the cardboard box next to her, then drops her arms on the edges, looking exhausted. "Excuse me?"

I flick open one of the boxes stacked next to the front counter. A tattered and beat-up hardcover of *The House at Pooh Corner* looks back up at me.

"I said this is ridiculous! I've barely heard from you all month and now all of a sudden you're giving up on everything?" I grab the book out of the box. It doesn't belong there. It belongs in the cabinet for some little kid to see, or for some woman to come by and be reminded of her childhood and buy it to share with *her* kids!

Before I can open the cabinet, Eliza is on her feet and grabs my arm. "Stop it, Silvia. I'm packing up, now help me. This isn't your store, it's mine. Now I'm saying it's time to pack up."

I refuse. I've devoted so much of myself to this store and I am *not* going to let her quit on it like this.

"What's gotten into you Ellie?" I pull my hand away from hers. The book falls to the floor but neither of us really notice. "Where've you been all month? You know I've been here every day running this place just fine while you disappeared. And you know it hasn't been as bad as you're always saying. People are still coming in! There's always someone browsing around here!"

"How much did you make last week?" she asks sternly.

"I... I don't know, but we were busy enough!"

"Four hundred, Silvia. Four hundred and thirteen dollars."

That's insane. I know we sold way more than that!

Eliza continues. "For the entire week. That was the lowest ever, but not much less than the week before."

I rush to think of something to say.

"I don't blame you, Silvy. I know how deeply you care about this place. But we've done our time. I'm satisfied with this store, and now it's time to move on."

This isn't happening.

"Ellie, I..."

I could ask my parents for a loan. Push some money into this store for better marketing, or renovation. Completely re-brand the place to get more people interested. By next summer, track season especially, this could be an all-new place.

Eliza must see what's going through my mind because she puts her hand on me again. This time gently, on my shoulder, then pulls me in for a hug.

Tears begin to well up in my eyes. One more word from her and I think I might burst and flood this room. I'm not even given a moment to process anything before everything crumbles further. Standing in the hallway to the office is the last person in the world I want to see.

"What the fuck are you doing here, Harry?" Eliza, twinges at the curse, and lets me go from the hug. I storm towards Harry with tears streaming from my eyes, and I taste them on my lips as I shout at him. "Why won't you just leave me alone?!"

He backs up against the hallway wall and holds his hands up in surrender like I'm about to stab him. Maybe I would if I'd had a knife on me. Him being here almost feels like *he's* to blame for all of this.

"I promise, it's important! We have to talk!" He says.

Yeah, sure. Important like all the other times he came in here, acting like he wanted to be "just friends" but never let either of us move on. Just like when he freaked the fuck out that I was seeing someone new.

"Get out of my life, Harry!" I shout back.

The next voice we hear is Eliza's and for God knows what reason, it's a condemnation of me!

"Silvy, it's all right! It's my fault. He was by and offered to help. I wasn't hearing from you all morning. I'm sorry, I should have told you he was here."

I want to shout at Eliza for this. Not telling me he was here, hiding in the back, and listening to everything we just went through is fucked up.

Harry cuts back in. "Silvia," he says, careful not to use a pet name or a nickname. "It's about your author friend, Daniel Cass-"

"I know his name, Harry. And he's not a 'friend.'"

"Whatever he is," he waves away my retort. "He's a liar. Daniel isn't-"

I throw my head up and shout, "Holy HELL, Harry! What the fuck is wrong with you?!" I turn and try to escape into the office, but one terrible thing led to another terrible thing, so why shouldn't I get one more punch in the gut while I'm here? My wall of methodically placed books has been torn down and turned into more of those soulless cardboard boxes. Every piece of evidence that I'd made this place my home, my escape from reality over the last few years I'd been working here has been erased.

Harry keeps talking whatever bullshit he has to say about Daniel, but I can't hear it. My heart and my soul are being ripped away from me today. I slowly back away from the office until I bump into Harry. I feel his arms moving behind me. He might try to touch me, make me listen to him, but I'm not ready to go to jail for murder. Almost ready, but I have a little bit of sense left.

"Silvia?" He asks. "Silvia, please listen to me."

I use every last fiber of my being to speak calmly and assertively. "Leave me alone, Harry."

I hear movement behind me from Eliza and Harry, but no words. If I had to guess, he's looking to her for a signal for what to do. I keep my eyes closed and wait for him to leave.

After a moment, I hear the front door open and close. A winter draft blows in and is the perfect cherry on top of how I'm feeling right now.

Eliza gives me a few minutes to collect myself before we get to work. I sit on the green couch in the office trying to figure out what's going to happen next. Selfishly, I hate that for me it means that I'll have to start working full-time for my parents. I know this is about more than just me though. I should be more considerate towards Eliza. This has been her home for what, fifty years maybe since she bought it with her late husband. And not just that, but Bookends is such an important part of this town!

Even when my tears are spent, I don't want to move.

Eliza walks in slowly and picks up a box marked "photography." It's a subtle hint that my time of self-pity is up.

I wipe my face one more time and then get up from the couch. "I've got it, Ellie," I say, taking the box from her. "Why don't you take a break now?"

She nods and takes my place on the couch.

The photography section only takes up a small portion of the shelves in the side room. I'd guess that 80% of them are horse books or photo albums of the horse racing track here in town. You'd think that anyone who actually lives here would be sick of all the stuff, but no. It's practically a law in Saratoga that if you're an artist, your work *has* to be about horses or you'll never make a penny. So, it's no surprise that someone from the art gallery wants these.

As I put the books away, one sticks out to me. "The Arts of Saratoga." What gets me right away isn't the lack of horses on the cover, but there isn't even a photograph. The design is a series of paintings themed around the town. It's not uncommon that a book is put in the wrong place by a customer who's decided last minute not to buy it, and photography is one of the arts featured in it(I notice as I read the back matter), but it's still the wrong place and shouldn't go with the rest of these books.

Out of curiosity, I flip through the pages. The first chapter is all landscapes. Congress Park is imagined in dozens of ways from acrylics to oil paintings to pencil sketches. Some are focused on the fountains, most on the carousel at various stages of it's life. One is a pencil sketch of a close-up of a child's excited laugh while riding the carousel that looks so realistic with its level of detail and use of motion blur, that it could almost pass for a black-and-white photo. It's truly amazing, the talent some people in the arts have.

I flip through a few more pages in the book. The next section shows sculptures that have been displayed around town, or crafted by local artists.

The section after that is portraits. "The Authentic People of Saratoga," the chapter is called. It sparks a memory for me of years ago, 2017 I think, when a photographer came into the store looking for Eliza. Then I see it, two pages past the introduction is a photograph of Eliza and Carl holding hands behind the counter, smiling at each other.

If only there were tears left to cry.

That should be enough of this book, but I feel compelled to keep looking. I need to find a new distraction, something happier in this book before I get back to work. I flip the pages over, past images of old men shouting at the race track(of course, there's no escaping it), and land on a piece that folds out like a Playboy magazine. The content isn't far off, and it's striking, to say the least.

The painting is of a familiar nude man, laying on wide, half-height steps. Steps that serve a more aesthetic purpose than functional. His head is lying back, eyes to the sky, and mouth hanging open. His left leg is bent strategically to hide his manhood. His left hand dangles off the edge of one of the steps, with the fingers spaced so it looks like there should be a cigarette between them. But the aspect that sticks out, no, screams at me, is that the man in the painting is undoubtedly Daniel Cassidy.

I look at the caption. The work is titled "Solace in Defeat," by Andrea Harlow. Below that is a short note, *Daniel Cassidy, Model, Skidmore University.*

Okay, so he did some nude modeling. He had to make a living somehow before the writing took off. It's fine, no big deal. At least it's art, right? Like, it's not like he was a porn star or anything.

I'm just surprised he didn't tell me. Sure, maybe he's embarrassed about it, but come on, Daniel, this picture is nothing to be embarrassed about. I might have to take this book home with me.

I will ask him about it though. I won't be mad when he admits to it, I just want to know why. Maybe it was research for some unpublished work. Maybe it was just a job. Either way, I'll come back to it later. Unless… are there more of him in here?

I turn the pages, one after another looking for his face, but in the "Authentic People of Saratoga" section, no one is appearing more than once.

Oh well, he can answer for himself later.

After putting the book to the side, I hear the front door open, and someone walks in.

"Helloooo?" an old voice asks. "I'm here from the gallery! You haven't closed yet, have you?"

I know this voice. I know I know it, but I can't quite place it.

"Back here!" I call and rise. "Almost done." I brush the dust of the old books off my hands and walk to the voice of the woman. When I see her face my blood starts to rise.

"I'm from the gallery." She repeats. No, 'nice to see you'

or even a 'good afternoon!' "Are the books ready?" asks the woman who called me 'incompetent' just before Thanksgiving.

Keep it together Silvia, she probably doesn't remember you.

With a fake smile, I say, "Good afternoon, ma'am. I'll have those for you in just a moment."

As I begin to step back, she says, "I can't believe this place is finally kicking it. Shame Saratoga's going this way."

There's something in her voice. I don't want to call it sincerity. After our last exchange, I don't want to believe she's capable of saying something nice about this place. She heard we were closing and came to pick up the scraps for cheap. However she said it, it has to be demeaning if she's using words like, 'kicking it.'

"If you'd like to browse while you wait, stuff on the shelves is still for sale." I hope if she's distracted in the other room, there won't be a chance to catch her condescension.

"Thank you, I think I will." She nods with a smile and fingers through the closest cardboard box.

Are your eyes rolling too?

It only takes a minute to finish boxing up the rest of the photography books. They take up two cardboard boxes. One large and one small.

There's something nagging at the back of my mind though, as I pack the books. I can't quite put my finger on it, but it's something about that painting. And not just that he was nude. Sure, that part was strange, but something in it was off. A detail in the hands, maybe? A cigarette that *was* there but edited out? A feature in his face that isn't really his?

"Will you need help with these?" I ask the woman from the gallery.

"No, my car's right out front. You can just put them next to the trunk."

Yes ma'am. I am your serv-

Okay, lighten up Silvia. She was a bitch last time, now she's just a customer. Give it a rest.

"Of course," I say. "Happy to."

As I turn again to grab the boxes, she calls for my attention.

"Oh! One other thing. This didn't have a price on it. Whatever it is, I'm happy to support this place one more time." She holds up a hardcover of "The House at Pooh Corner," then adds, "I'd love to share this with my granddaughter."

19

"Don't go out tonight." Nyx demands of me as I leave Bookends.

It catches me off guard, but somehow it's not the strangest thing she's ever said to me. I can't even count on one hand the number of times I've witnessed her grabbing people's attention with the most outlandish sayings just to try to get them to buy a crystal or sage so they can "ward off the bad energy." Honestly, though, I have to commend her for how often it works. She's a fantastic saleswoman.

"What is it this time, Nyx?" I ask, tying the belt of my coat tight. "Not the right moon sign tonight?"

As if I asked the question seriously, she responds, "It's just the right one. 'S why you shouldn't go out."

Down the road just past her, I can see Daniel's car turn onto Phila Street.

"If it's the right one then shouldn't I go out?" I wave down Daniel, doing my best to avoid eye contact with Nyx. "If you make me a potion maybe it'll be even better."

She rolls her eyes and stands from her chair. "Honey, you

don't need one. Do what you want, I couldn't care less."

The car pulls up next to me, and I go to open the door, but a thought hits me.

Just before the door to *Witch's Brew* closes behind Nyx, I ask, "Is Harry putting you up to this?"

She stops and turns, but her face is completely unreadable. In moments like this, she doesn't look like she's *trying* to be a witch. She is one. Nyx stands in the doorway to her shop of pseudo-magic cons, acting all mysterious, like something from a fairy tale inviting me to my doom. The tattoos on her arms look more like embroidering on a gothic black gown. Her hat isn't pointed, just wide-brimmed and black, but the way it's tilted back on her head you wouldn't even be able to tell. All that's left to complete the picture is that cat to walk around her legs, and for her to silently invite me in with the curl of her index finger.

Good thing I don't believe in witchcraft. She'd never help Harry with me, just wants to get one more sale before the end of the day.

"Take care, Nyx. I'll see you around." I get in the car and mentally prepare for dinner.

20

After only five minutes of being at my parents' house, I have come to the conclusion that I will be joining Aria for drinks tonight. Thank God she is always ready to go.

My parents meet us at the front door, waiting for us like kids at Christmas. Sally is the least excited to see us. I notice her pop her head up through the window to see who's here, then drop back out of sight. Nice to know you missed me!

"So, this is the writer guy?" My dad asks with his hand extended. When Daniel shakes, my dad continues jokingly, "Hope you're not putting my daughter on to any bad *Habits.*"

Daniel laughs politely and says, "I promise I won't, sir. My parents raised me right."

I try to signal to my dad to cut it out, but he goes on.

"Right, only write about it, never act on it, huh? Ha ha!" He slaps Daniel's shoulder playfully.

"Oh, cut it out, Stephen." My mom cuts in but without conviction. "Come on in you two. It's lovely to meet you, Danny."

"D'you drink, Dan?" My dad asks as we cross the threshold.

"No, Dad," I start, thinking *no more bad habits, right?*

But at the same time, Daniel answers as well. "I don't mind a Manhattan now and then."

Okay, right. The reform after *Habits* was just for PR. Well, he's still going to be DD tonight.

The Christmas decorations are still up around the house. The lights will probably be left up until January. This family is quick to put everything up and slow to take it down. Even the smell of the Christmas breakfast we had days ago is still lingering in the dining room where my dad and Daniel sit with their drinks, waiting for Mom to bring the food out.

I join her, offering to help set the table, but really I just want to listen in on my dad and Daniel's conversation. Not for my sake, don't worry I won't be like that. I just want to make sure my dad doesn't say anything that crosses the line or makes Daniel uncomfortable. My dad can't always read the room and Daniel is probably too polite to cut him off.

Between the commands my mom gives, she asks, "can you please turn the stove off? No, not those knives, the ones on the counter," I get bits and pieces of the conversation. Daniel is being questioned about his family in the area.

"Silvia said you're staying with your aunt while you're around, right? Who is she, I might know her. Audrey and I know just about everyone in town, but I don't know of any other Cassidy's."

I look in the dining room to listen for Daniel's response, realizing as my dad asks that we never actually talked about his family here.

Daniel looks back as if he felt my presence, but looks to my

262

dad to answer. "Richards. My Aunt lives over near Corinth."

My dad concentrates hard for a moment, then calls to my mom, "Hey Audrey, do we know anyone named Richards?" Then to Daniel, "What's her first name?"

Daniel almost answers, but I see the discomfort at the prying on his face. As he hesitantly opens his mouth, I step into the room and answer for him. "That's enough, Dad. Come on, if you're going to talk about him, talk about *him*. You don't need the whole family history."

Dad throws up his hands in surrender. "Fine, fine. Thought that was about *him*, but okay." He takes a sip of his drink, then the attention is back on Daniel like I'm not in the room. "But you're from Iowa, right? Or is it Heaven? Ha ha, you know, like *Field of Dreams*? You from around that part? Ever been to the field? Why don't you write something like that?"

"Dad, stop!"

"Good old, American feel-good drama. Not like that crap about perverts and druggies."

"Dad, that's enough!"

Daniel, "No, it's fine, Sil."

"Sil?" My Dad asks with a laugh. "That's a new one."

"Mr. Wright, I promise, those books, the stuff in them, it's not me. It's just entertainment, as much as I know Sil hates hearing me say. That's not the guy dating your daughter. I am. And stuff like in *Habits* and…" he takes a moment, calculating what he should and shouldn't say. "… *Binds*, isn't what I'm going to bring into our relationship."

Okay, Daniel. I know you want him to accept this relationship but let's not take *everything* from *Binds* off the table.

"Is that a promise?" My Dad asks sternly. He's leaned in, with his hand holding the bourbon glass dangling off the edge of the table. Daniel isn't Harry, and I think right now they both think that. Stephen Wright was comfortable with Harry. Daniel has yet to prove himself, and with the standard Harry set in my parents' eyes, he knows it won't be an easy task.

But the look in Daniel's eyes says *dammit, I'll try*. He takes a clean swig of the bourbon, keeping his gaze locked with my dad's. "If there's ever been something I've been honest about, this is it."

My dad leans back and swirls his drink. The rocks in his glass clink together and settle.

I look from one to the other, waiting for this unbearable dick-measuring of masculinity to end. Finally, I throw up my hands and escape to the kitchen. I know my dad approved after Daniel's big speech. He just *has* to make everyone work.

Once my foot hits the kitchen floor, my mom hands me a hot pan of lasagna. I almost drop it, it's so hot.

"Holy hell, Mom! You don't have a towel or something?"

"Calm down honey, it's not that hot," she dismisses.

I rush the pan into the dining room and place it on the table before my hands have the chance to catch on fire."

Daniel and my dad look at me while I shake my hands to cool them off, but all my dad can say is, "About time!"

The stress of the meeting has been enough to ruin my appetite. Thankfully, dinner is short and my dad goes easy on Daniel for the rest of the evening. My mom doesn't open up to him as much, but at least she doesn't hound him. Through it all, I'm in adoration of how collected Daniel stayed through my dad's barrage of questioning. The way he holds his ground and refuses to grovel like Harry would have done to earn his favor. A man like that makes me...

Before meeting Aria at the bars, I ask Daniel to pull the car off the road into a secluded spot. I need something to relieve my stress between whatever that shitshow was and an evening clubbing with Aria.

21

Regret pours out of me as soon as we arrive at the pin Aria sent me. The Cellar, which doesn't live up to its name as a three-story bar/club/lounge, is where I first met Harry. Aria should know better than to bring us here, but, you know, here we are. She's standing outside, flirting up the bouncer when we pull up.

Aria is wearing this exposing fur coat that lets her show off her breasts. It's a trick she's played since high school to get into bars, and why she still does it I'll never know. Like, you're allowed in. You're going to get free drinks anyway whether or not you show your tits. But I guess since I don't see Richard with her, she feels she has to ensure she gets the freebies.

My saving grace right now stopping me from telling Daniel to turn the car around and take me home is the pre-gaming I did during dinner. Two glasses of wine were more than enough.

"Silvy! Sil! Hey! Come on!" Aria sees me through the window of Daniel's car. Her use of 'Sil' sounds like blasphemy. Only Daniel can call me that.

I give her a wave of acknowledgment and a half smile.

"Do you want to get out?" Daniel asks. "I'll find parking

somewhere around here, but…" he looks around the street, "doesn't look like it'll be easy. Might have to find a spot a few blocks away."

"Try the movie theater," I tell him.

"Where all the homeless people hang out?"

"Well, the parking lot next to the park will be full. Always is."

"Daniel, it's Thursday. I think we'll be fine."

"That's a further walk, though."

A car honks behind us. I didn't even realize we'd been sitting in the middle of the street.

"Just hang out with your friend. I'll park and run over," he says, then takes my hand and kisses my fingers.

If it was between walking ten miles with Daniel or waiting 10 minutes with Aria, then right now I'd choose the ten miles. But this is Saratoga, at night, in the cold. I love my hometown, but I'd be lying if I said it was the safest place in the world.

"Okay," I say and open the car door. "But be quick, please."

"Might stop for a smoke first," he teases.

As I get out of the car, I come back at him, "What if I said I didn't like how it smells on you?"

"You be honest with me, and I'll be honest with you."

A voice in the back of my head, Harry's voice says, *he's a liar, Daniel isn't-*

Go away, Harry. I don't need to deal with your meddling.

"Just get back here quick, okay?"

"As you wish, Sil."

I shut the door and Daniel drives off.

267

Behind me, an ecstatic voice cries, "Tell! Me! Tell me it happened!"

I turn and see Aria with the biggest smile I've ever seen on her face.

"You fucked him, didn't you?"

"Can you keep your voice down?!" I plead.

Thank God it's not a weekend night. These streets would be packed with people, regardless of how bad living has gotten in Saratoga. But still, I don't need my sex life broadcast for the people who *are* still walking around.

Aria, thankfully, lowers her voice. "But you did, right? Oh my god. My bestie actually fucked a celebrity!"

"Can you stop? Please? He's not just a celebrity?" Fuck. Wrong word choice and Aria is about to run with it. "I mean- he's more than- he's not, I mean-"

A coy smile spreads across her face. "Okay... okay... so he's *more* than *just* a celebrity. I get it. Not something to be ashamed of, but you better tell me everything."

I whisper "Will you cut it out?! I don't hound you about your sex life and all the fucked up shit you do when I'm in the next room."

Aria is unphased by the retort. "Okay, my bad." She laughs, "Not every day your friend starts dating a celebrity. I just got excited is all."

"Aria, it's been almost a month."

"Come on. A month of being pen pals."

"Did you invite me out to drink or what? Can I get

hammered? Please?" I jerk my head in the bar's direction. "It's freezing out here, Aria."

"What about Daniel?" She looks over my shoulder in the direction he drove off. "Isn't he coming?"

"Yes! He's just parking!" I guide her over to the bouncer and hand the man my ID.

He doesn't ask for Aria's. Either he's already seen it or she's "flirted" her way in. Whichever reason, she winks at him as we walk in. The bouncer doesn't return the favor, but he smirks, then checks the couple coming in behind us.

Déjà vu hits me from two sides when we walk down the small flight of stairs that lead to the bar. The first is obvious. I think of the night Harry and I met. The feeling isn't as bad as I worried it would be when it first came over. Regardless of how the relationship ended, it wasn't a bad night. I'm glad I can hold onto a few good memories with him. The second side of the déjà vu is harder to pin down. It's like I'm experiencing it in someone else's stead.

Aria has me by the hand, leading me across the room. It's decently packed for the night, and honestly, looking around I feel like I'm going to like this place a lot better than last time. When Harry and I met, it was a bar, through and through. Now it's more of a lounge. The floor has well-spaced couches and coffee tables, and in the back corner there's a stage for a small band. A local jazz group is playing, something soothing. Not exactly my taste, and personally I believe jazz belongs in autumn and that's about it, but it's good for the mood. The patrons tonight don't look invested in the band, but the chatter is low and respectful.

Yeah, if Aria had brought me to *this* version of The Cellar sooner, I would have gone out with her more often.

"Excuse me! Hey! Mike!" Aria shouts at the bartender.

Mike checks us out, nods, and returns his attention to the glass he's pouring for some guy with his head held low.

"Mike!" Aria shouts again, eyes wide in annoyance.

The bartender hands the patron his drink, gives him a smile, and then gives Aria the attention she demands. "No free drinks tonight. Carl's noticing I'm picking favorites."

"At least I'm the favorite," Aria says, leaning over the counter, really showing off her cleavage for him. "Just the first round at least? Promise we'll pay for the rest."

Mike and I exchange a look. His says, *you got roped in too?*

Mine says, *I've been roped in the longest.*

Aria cuts off our unspoken conversation, putting a hand on his cheek to bring his eyes back on her. "Cactus waters?" she asks with pouting eyes.

Mike sighs, "One round. And I better still see you tomorrow night."

"Two rounds and you can see me tonight."

Sternly but with a smile, "*One.*"

Aria has gone fully puppy dog. "Okayyy. I might be busy later then."

"Babe, I'm working tonight anyway," he laughs and starts making the drinks. "You can't win this one."

Aria then turns to me. "Oh! Should we get Daniel a drink? What does he want?"

Mike pauses the pouring of the tequila bottle (wait hold the fuck on, tequila? Aria it is a THURSDAY night!).

"It's for her friend. He's famous."

Mike almost throws up her arm in feigned disbelief, but Aria settles him with a lip bite, and he grabs a third glass.

And here I stand, watching this exchange, wondering what the fuck happened to Richard. I just want my drink. Please. I don't want to be in this circle of sexual energy.

We take a seat on a couch by the wall on the opposite side of the room from the bar. The moment we sit, Aria downs one of the cactus waters, and takes a sip of the second.

"Daniel doesn't get any?" I ask.

"He can buy the next round. I just want Mike to know I can get it if I want." She waves at him and he laughs. "You gonna drink or what, Silvy?"

"Holy hell, Aria, I just sat down." I bring the glass to my lips and take the smallest of sips. I wish she had let me order my own drink. I wouldn't have ordered something with tequila. What happy memory ever starts with a glass of tequila?

Don't go out tonight. Nyx's voice says in the back of my head.

Let it go, Silvia. You've been through the worst. He's met your parents, and you don't have to worry about Aria making a bad impression anymore.

My heart tells me, though, something else is still lurking. Nyx wasn't talking about my parents. Holy hell, this is going to kill me. Where the fuck is Daniel?

"Hey! Silvy! You okay?"

271

I didn't even realize I was staring at the door.

"Huh? Oh, yeah. Just... hoping Daniel found a good spot."

Calm down, Silvia. You're getting hung up on the words of some delusional psycho. No, okay don't say that Silvia, that was mean.

But the painting. What the hell was wrong with the painting?

He's lying! Harry this time.

"Silvia!"

"What?!"

"Take a drink. You're weirding me out." Her second glass is half full already.

She's right though. It's just nerves.

I power through the sting of the tequila and try to catch up. Thank God Mike watered these the hell down.

"Better?" Aria asks.

I shudder with the alcohol. But yes, "Better. Fine."

"Good..." she pauses, reading me to make sure I'm actually fine. "Do you want to tell me what's up?"

The jazz group ends their number. The room claps politely for them. When the clapping dies down, the lead announces, "We're gonna take a hot break. This place only pays us in drinks and we play a lot better, and with a lot more energy when we're drunk. In the meantime, we've got an open mic, so please feel free." There is some light applause until the lead jumps back to the microphone. "Please, only if you don't suck though. Don't ruin this for everyone."

I watch them as they leave the stage and walk to the bar.

The lead pats the back of the guy that was sitting there with his head hung low.

"If you're not going to talk, then you lose your drinking privileges."

Aria, you don't know how good of an idea that is, but my arm doesn't agree, and brings the drink to my lips again. I drink the rest so fast I could put her to shame.

My face feels tingly. I probably should've eaten more at dinner.

Okay, I'm ready to talk now.

"When was the last time you saw Harry?"

She looks at me dumbfounded. "Harry? Everything going on now and you're thinking of Harry?"

A girl with a guitar takes to the stage and begins to play something to the applause of the house.

"What's going on, Aria?" I lean in. She knows something. Harry got to her when I kicked him out of the store. He must have!

"What do you... Nothing! I just thought you'd be over him now that you've got Daniel. You're not just using him to show off, are you?"

"What?"

"What?"

"No, Aria, no I just meant- I saw Harry today. He was trying to fuck with Daniel and I."

"Oh?" Instead of being annoyed at Harry with me, her tone shifts to intrigue, like this is some high school gossip.

Whatever. At least she's listening.

"He came into the store today and said Daniel was lying to me about something. Do you know anything about this?"

Aria pauses in thought. I want to believe that she doesn't know anything. That if she would she would share it. That she would have *already* shared it if she knew something.

"Aria?"

"He's just trying to mess with your head." Her tone shifted again. It's the voice of genuine care and concern. "He's mad you found someone else and he's lashing out."

A voice speaks up from the other side of the coffee table we sit at. "Sorry I took so long. Didn't want to show up empty-handed."

Aria and I look up to see Daniel walking over to us with three drinks in his hand. Two more cactus waters for us, and a beer for himself. He places ours down, then takes a seat in the armchair across from us.

"Everything okay?" He asks.

I open my mouth to say 'no,' but Aria speaks first. Playfully, she says, "Boy problems. Do you have anything to tell us? Any secrets you want to share?"

"Aria cut it out," I shove her off of me and grab my drink. The second glass goes down more easily.

Aria only continues to be a pest. "The dirtier the better."

Daniel looks confused. "I- I don't uh…"

"It's fine, Daniel. It was just something Harry said."

"Harry?" he asks, shocked but not shouting. "Your ex?"

I take a sip, shudder, then answer, "he came into the store today. Just trying to start shit, it doesn't matter."

As if I didn't just say 'It doesn't matter,' Daniel asks, "what was he saying?"

"Nothing, we kicked him out."

There is a pause between the three of us. Aria looks from Daniel to me, and back to Daniel like one of us is about to explode.

"You don't... have anything to tell me though, do you?"

The room erupts in applause, and we all look to the stage. I didn't even realize that girl played her song, but subconsciously I know she performed well.

The lead of the jazz band takes her place on stage, with a drink in his hand. "Don't get excited, I'm not back yet. I just want to introduce our next guest. He's got a very special message for a very special girl." More applause.

"Let's get out of here, Sil."

But I see who's coming to the stage next. I finish my drink (fuck, I don't feel good. This wasn't watered down as much as the last drink) then grab Aria's. I'll need it to get through whatever it is Harry is about to do.

"Do you have anything to tell me, D- Daniel?" My entire body shakes. Blood is rising in my face.

Don't go out tonight...

He's lying!..

"No! Sil, please," he stands up and holds out his hand for me to take.

Harry speaks into the microphone. "I don't think you fine people have noticed, but we have a celebrity here with us tonight. Can we all please give a round of applause to Mr. Daniel Cassidy?"

Bookends

A few people clap their hands slowly, but one random girl 'Wooool!'s. "Maybe you don't know him. That's fine. He's not a real celebrity, but I'm sure at least a few of your girls read his books."

Daniel takes my arm. He doesn't pull me but asks me again to leave. There's fear in his voice.

"Actually," Harry continues, "that's a lie. I'm sorry. I hate when guys lie like that. Not cool. Right, Daniel?"

The room turns to stare him down. If this were a movie, I'm sure a spotlight would look too.

"I'm sorry if you're a fan of his *writing*, but Daniel Cassidy... how do I put this? The guy doesn't fucking exist. That man, right there, holding that girl's arm, has been pretending to be some big-shot writer, but hasn't once actually touched a pen. Or computer. Whatever they use now."

Confusion takes over the room. I'm even a little confused. Aria and Daniel though, look terrified.

So you did know something, Aria.

"I can see the confusion. Look, that dude is just some studio, PR, fuckin' smoke show. He gets in front of the camera and does all the interviews, and you see his face on the back of the books, but it's some old dude writing all of them. But who wants to read dirty romance books by an old white dude? That about why they got you, Ian?"

There's chatter among the room. I think it's mostly still confused chatter; no one looks hostile or disappointed toward Daniel, except for me.

Still, Daniel asks me, "Can we please talk about this outside? I wanted to tell you."

276

22

All of the pieces start coming together. The painting, what he said at dinner with my parents, what Harry was saying. I look at his jean jacket, and see the poppy pinned to it. There was never any mention of his father being dead before I met him.

"I need you to tell me now, Da-, whatever your name is," I say through a shiver. The winter air feels 100 degrees colder now, and it freezes the tears to my face. From the moment I stood from the couch, I felt like I've been teetering on the side of a cliff, about to fall to my death. The alcohol is taking over my bloodstream. Everything left in my stomach is about to force itself back out, but I feel I have just enough control of my mind to demand this from him. "T- tell me… who you really are."

He sighs, "Can I please take you home first? It's too cold h-"

"*NOW*, Daniel!" The tears pour harder, freezing to numb my cheeks. "I'm not getting back in y- your FUCKING car, until you tell me what's going on. I saw you," I poke him hard in the chest, "in a fucking painting! Why the fuck are you in a painting, Daniel?"

"Okay, Sil," he puts his hands on my arm, probably an attempt to calm me down, but I throw them off.

"Don't f- fucking t- touch me!" I take a step back from him and almost fall over. The fall-and-save throws my brain around violently in my head. "Tell me your name. Your real name."

Daniel looks around as if for help, then, slowly.

"My name is Ian Richards. I've lived in Saratoga all my life and I've never written a single book. But I've always been as honest with you as I could. I've tried to tell you so many times…"

* * *

I am in love with a girl that can never see me. From a small table in a cigar shop, I saw her through the window of my Aunt's bookstore. I saw her auburn hair and the most beautiful eyes I'd ever seen, behind thin rimmed circular glasses. I wanted nothing more that day to go into that store and introduce myself as myself for the first time in years. I could finally drop the facade and figure out my purpose beyond being the face of someone else. But she wouldn't have me. There was another man who'd already claimed her. All I could do was feed the real author ideas. I told him he should have the lead be a girl with auburn hair, a light spread of freckles, and (find out Silvia's eye color). That was all I thought I contributed, but he saw my passion for this character and let me give the dedication.

It started in college. Not my college, I never went. I had a severe case of "lack of drive." I'd been from job to job, looking for whatever paid the bills. Eventually, I ended up at Skidmore College as a "general employee." Sometimes I'd help out with security, sometimes

I'd be a classroom aid if someone didn't show up for work. It was nice for a while, learned a few useful skills like sign language. But most of the work I got was modeling for the art department. When I saw the job description included nude work, I knew I should go by a different name just in case it came back to bite me in the ass. So, yes, I *am* Daniel Cassidy. But it was Dr. Phefferberger that made him big.

An old white guy with a name like that can sell history books until the sun explodes. But who would buy sappy or spicy romance novels from him? Even I was hesitant at first, but then I saw the contract. No more worrying about paying the bills when all I have to do is pose for the camera and attend a few events for each book? Why the hell not? I just couldn't let it slip that it was all a show, once the books really started taking off.

It was after "Lisbon" was released that I first saw her. I don't think she'd read the books yet, and she wouldn't have noticed me. After *Habits,* I was too ashamed to introduce myself. With all the other reviews, it was fair to assume she was disgusted by it too.

When she came out of the store that day a month ago, I decided it was finally time to make my move, and I made it by accidentally stealing her book. I swear, I tried to give it back to her that night, but she was gone so fast. Unfortunately, it was a Daniel Cassidy book she carried. Seeing her the next day, I went in determined to be upfront from the beginning. But you should have seen the way her eyes sparked when she saw Daniel Cassidy. I knew it was wrong, and this isn't a justification, but I didn't want to ruin that moment for her. When she got mad and thought I was treating her like some loose fan girl, I thought that was the end. Thankfully I bumped into my Aunt, Eliza May (formally Eliza Richards). She said she'd help clear things up.

I'd gained some ground back during our talk at the cigar shop. I'd hoped during our date I would have won her over enough so when I told her, it wouldn't even matter. I never found the right time, and then it was too late, and I was gone. I could tell her the truth over a phone call, text, or letter, so I sprinkled the truths in the letters. "You are my dedication." The moment I came home, all the truths would come out.

I learned though that Silvia didn't love Ian Richards. She loved Daniel Cassidy and his books.

It was the life I lived for so long, I might as well keep living it if it made her happy.

But the truth always comes out. It was only a matter of time.

* * *

"I need you to leave." I almost call him Daniel again, but the name feels like a curse and becomes stuck in my throat.

"Can I take you home first?" He reaches out, and I step away again.

"Leave me alone, I don't want to see you anymore," I say through the tears. I need Aria. I need her to save me right now.

"Sil, please."

"No! You do *not* get to call me that." I turn away and take my phone out to text Aria. I refuse to go back into the bar where

Harry is sure to be waiting to try and sweep me.

Behind me, Daniel, or Ian, I guess, tries to apologize. I can only ignore him.

-Please get out here. We need to leave.

"Silvia, listen to me. I wanted to be honest! I couldn't though, not legally at least. And you were so-"

"You can *not* put this on me!" I don't think I've ever moved so fast in my life to push him as I did. "I don't give a fuck about whatever contract you signed. If you told me up front I wouldn't have cared!"

"Do you really believe that? Silvia, you were in love with me before we even met. Tell yourself what you want, but we both know that's the truth."

"You can't say much better then! What did you 'love' me for? That I loved you too?"

"I actually got to know you, Silvia. I was taken by that girl I saw in the window, but fell in love with *you*. I knew it for sure on that first date when we sat on the pier. And it's not because I thought you were pretty, it's not because you liked the books. It's because I trusted you. I thought that I could tell you who I was and it wouldn't matter, or that if you only wanted Daniel, I could be happy living that for the rest of my life. I don't need Ian, all I need is you. I need the girl that can understand characters with all of their faults and have compassion for them. Because that's all I am. I am only faults, and lies, and a shell of a person... but for once in my life I want to be more than that. For you."

Caroline Street is exceptionally quiet. The wind is the loudest person outside. I feel like some sweet music should be playing, a romantic melody that swells as he gives his speech, but there's nothing.

To my right, Aria pushes through the door of The Cellar, with Harry in tow.

I expect a look of smug victory on Harry's face, but there's none. He looks heartbroken. Aria too. I can't look at either of them. I can't be around anyone. I can't go home with her after this betrayal.

"Silvia! Come back!" Aria calls after me as I walk up the street toward Broadway.

Interlude:
Habits

Released: Oct. 6th, 2020

Synopsis: Harold Zhegler is a bad man.

-Page count: 859

-Read: Oct. 12th – 28th, 2020

-Rating (Goodreads average): 2.5/5 Stars

-Rating(Mine): 5/5 Stars

Review: ~~One of Daniel Cassidy's more controversial books, or arguably,~~ Daniel Cassidy's MOST controversial book, is 100% unfairly criticized. This is one of his best books, and in fact, one of the greatest, most intimate, and honest books I've ever read. I don't mean honest in the way that other people are saying, where they think Daniel Cassidy is admitting that he did all of the obscene acts discussed in the book, but honest in the way that he didn't let anyone hold him back from the story that *he* wanted to tell. Everybody has demons, but this guy is a FICTION WRITER. Tolkien didn't actually go to

Middle-Earth and document its history to write "Lord of the Rings." People like the ones criticizing Daniel Cassidy for this book are the reason we get stuck with lowest-common-denominator stories that play it safe with tropes and an aggressive stance against anything that could be interesting because it could be perceived as "controversial." *Habits* shows that there are still writers that are willing to share something they truly believe in. And I thank you for that, Mr. Cassidy.

Habits is very reminiscent of William S. Burroughs' "Naked Lunch," in more ways than one. It retains those abstract depictions of events going on around the main character, really honing in on the idea of how deep he is in his addictions. This one though is about more than drug addiction, it almost feels like the main character (Harold Zhegler, I assume. The only mention of a name is on the almost non-existent back-cover synopsis) is the walking embodiment of all things evil and wrong with the world. He's violent and exploitative of other people's suffering, he takes every opportunity he can to poison his body with any and every toxic substance, and every sexual encounter feels like borderline rape. He really is the most vile, disgusting man in the world, but what's strangest about all of it is how there is this real pity I felt for Harold.

I think this is what people misunderstood about the book, and this is why context is so important. Daniel Cassidy said that Oscar Wild's "The Portrait of Dorian Gray" was a strong influence on the narrative. It's not Daniel's fault if y'all weren't paying attention. Sure, he didn't go in detail on how it was influential, but I think I figured it out.

In "Dorian Gray," the title character sells his soul so that a painting of him takes on all the physical damage his soul take through Dorian's evil acts, while the real man stays young and beautiful forever. The portrait, this beautiful piece of art was cursed to be a display of evil, by no choice of its own. This is Harold's place in the book. The actions he's making are not his own. He was forced into this horrible world, with these horrible needs, and will never be able to break away no matter how he tries because he is not in control. And this isn't a cop-out like, "well maybe he shouldn't have put himself in these situations to begin with." He's LITERALLY NOT IN CONTROL!

In fact, I don't even think Harold Zhegler is his name. Harold is the real person, the Dorian Gray of the story. The person we're following is just their cursed portrait.

I would ask that anyone who did not understand this, or didn't like the book on their first read, please try it again in this context. I understand the hesitancy not to, even I don't think I'll be able to pick it up again. It's definitely a disturbing read to say the least, and made me sick in multiple parts. But it never felt like it was there just to shock. It felt very real and necessary to the character's journey.

And if you were one of the people that bullied or harassed Daniel Cassidy for this, you can go fuck yourself.

23

This doesn't feel right. This isn't my bed. This feels like my room. The smell is familiar at least. All I know for certain is my head feels a million miles wide and crushed down to the size of a peanut. Every inch I move feels like a marathon. I should have stopped after the third, no, *before* the *first* hard cider.

"Keep resting, sweetie. It's a little early to wake up."

Another element I recognize for certain. The ring of Eliza's voice throws a shroud of embarrassment and shame over me.

From what I remember, I walked from The Cellar, up to the gas station to get a coffee while I waited for an Uber home. Instead of coffee, I get a pack of hard seltzers and no Uber.

"What time is it?" I ask.

"Almost three. In the a.m."

"What are you doing here?"

"I could ask you the same. This *is* my store, isn't it?"

I turn away from her. Her tone is so compassionate. I don't want her to see me cry. "There was a sign on your door. Said we're 'closed for good.'"

"Yes," Eliza sighs. "I saw you moved it to the middle of

the road."

"I need this place," I say quietly. "I don't know what I'm gonna do without it." I sniff back the runs in my nose. Only now do I realize I fell asleep with my glasses on. They lie next to my head all bent out of shape.

Eliza puts a hand on my shoulder. "Silvia, you were a blessing, coming to work here after Carl died. You gave me a few more great years and helped me move on, but I knew from then it was coming to an end. Now it's my turn to help you."

It's hard to look her in the eye, but I'll never forgive myself if I don't give her this moment.

"Bookends was never meant to be your future. This place isn't going to bring you anywhere, and the longer you hold on, the harder it's going to be to let go. You'll only ever fall back on the familiar, never reaching for something greater."

"But I don't know who I am without... without this place. Without *his* books."

"Is that why you didn't want to know the truth? Yes, he told me. And I know you're upset with me. But that was for *him* to tell, and *you* to ask. You loved him because you already knew him, Silvia."

"Yeah, that's what he said." I wipe away a tear. The brush of my hand against my face gives me a headache, but it doesn't bother me at this point.

"And do you think it's true?"

I take a deep breath, careful to plan out what to say next. "I…" I want to say 'I don't know,' but, I guess we all know that I do by now. "He helped me out so much. I never would have ended it with Harry without those books. I thought what I had was with him, getting through each day was all that was ever in the cards. I thought I deserved better with those stories."

Eliza laughs. "Isn't that the point?"

"It's false hope," I say stubbornly. "Maybe they should write more books about how boring and depressing life is! What good is escapism when we have to come back to this shitty life? 'Sorry, love's not gonna work out for you. He's gonna cheat, she's only in it for the money, someone's gonna ask for a divorce or fucking die.'"

Eliza's smile fades. I can't believe I just said that, and I wish I could kill myself. But she speaks gently, "Bad things happen every day. There's no stopping that. But the books you read shouldn't be escapism. It's something to strive for. Just because it's made up for a book doesn't mean it isn't real. If you want love, a real, lasting love like I have with Carl, yes, even in passing I'm still in love with him, then you have to work for it. Some people give up when they see others succeed. The idea of heroes like the ones in your books and movies scares them when they should take inspiration from them.

"That's what you have to do, Silvia. If you find strength and comfort in the books, good. But use it to accomplish great things, not as a weighted blanket."

My tears are not spent. I just no longer feel like crying.

"Thank you, Eliza... I'm sorry I broke into the store."

Her smile returns. "It's all right sweetie. I'm happy we mean so much to you." Eliza holds out her arms for a hug.

Holy hell, I needed this embrace.

"How'd you even know I was here?"

"That witchy girl next door called me. She lives in the back room and said she heard something." We end the hug and I swear, though it's hard to tell without my glasses, I can see the glisten of her watering eyes.

24

It looks like I have a lot of house cleaning to do. Eliza is right, I have to grow up. The hardest parts are hopefully over; Bookends and Daniel (I gotta stop using that fake name). The rest shouldn't be completely removed from my life, but I don't expect I'll flourish with resentment in my heart. So when I get back to the apartment I bring cardboard boxes with me.

Aria and Harry are waiting for me when I get in. I have every right to lose it at him for being there, but this doesn't feel like an ambush. Not after seeing that last look on his face last night before I ran off. Trust me, I'm not happy to see them, but I won't get into a shouting match either, I promise.

Harry is sitting up straight on the couch. Aria is on her computer. There are three coffee mugs on the table in the living room. Seems like they're really trying to make it a comfortable environment, waiting until I'm ready to make the first move.

"How did you know?" I ask, taking off my shoes by the door.

Harry perks his head up. "I had a feeling when I first saw him in the store. He looked like a guy I went to high school with."

Aria cuts in. "Richy thought so too when Daniel came to dinner."

"I got nervous the guy, Ian, was fucking with you, pretending to be Daniel and leading you on," Harry says. "I'll be the first to admit, I kinda went off a little. Started trying to get ahold of him, or find him, but after high school, he just dropped off the face of the Earth."

I place the flattened cardboard boxes on the counter and walk into the living room to pick up the coffee they made for me. For the rest of the conversation, I'll stay standing, leaning against the wall, a safe distance from them.

Harry continues, "I mentioned it first to Aria that I was suspicious."

"I didn't want you getting any anxiety over it," Aria interjects. "I thought it was an insane idea. But I mentioned Richy said he went to college with him. Or, not with him. But his girlfriend at the time was an art student at the same school, and one of her paintings of him got picked up for some town history book."

Going on as if not interrupted, Harry says, "Yeah, so I did some digging at the school and found out they were the same person."

I sip my coffee, listening intently. I never told Aria about the book I found, probably the same one, so this all sounds like the truth to me.

"He could have gone from nude modeling to writing, but that didn't seem like the guy I knew in high school."

"And you knew him well?" I ask. It's not supposed to be a

challenge, but it comes out that way.

"Well... no. No one really did. He was a quiet guy. Not really someone who stood out in a crowd even if you were looking for him. And I thought it would be hard to believe someone like him would end up, well, like this. So, I went a little further. Admittedly, at this point, it was mostly out of spite. I was just angry. I've accepted it's over between us, Silvia. I have. I had, I just wanted to be your friend. But when I saw him, it all just built up in me again, and I felt... I felt like I never mattered. I was some guy tossed to the side and found by your literal dream man, a celebrity. So I dug into the copyright claims of the books. Kinda like the guy that discovered Richard Bachman was Stephen King. And there it was. Some guy, 'Reggie Phefferberge, writing as Daniel Cassidy.' When I had all of that, I came straight to the bookstore to tell you, but you didn't want to listen, so I went to Aria. It wasn't too hard to convince her, so she let me in on your plans for last night. I know you were in love with him, Silvia, and I'm sorry I ruined that. I just wanted to protect you. I hope you can forgive me."

The coffee in my cup is cold. I don't usually drink cold coffee. Unless it's scolding hot, I don't want it. But this cup is okay. Not the best. A fair amount of the grounds have probably settled into a sludge at the bottom. Oh well, I've drunk most of it already. I wonder how long they've been waiting here. I'm sure they would have still been patient if I needed time alone in my room before this talk.

My eyes rise from the cup to look at Aria, then to Harry. How long has it been since he finished his speech? Best not to keep them waiting.

"Thank you, Harry. I'm sorry I treated you like this. If I-" I stop and rephrase myself. "I only believed what I wanted to. I guess it was... selfish, thinking you were still in love with me." I need to sit down. Self-centered-Silvia says that once I do, even if I sit on the opposite end of the couch from Harry, he'll take that as a cue to move closer. Thankfully, I'm trying to introduce myself to open-minded-Silvia, and her intuition is correct. Harry doesn't move. He sits there attentively like a friend would. "I wanted romance in my life. I didn't want it from you, but I liked being able to tell myself you were trying. With Dan-... Ian... I didn't need you anymore. That's no way to treat a friend."

I'm gonna regret this.

Holy hell, Silvia, shut up. No, you won't.

I hold out my hand for Harry.

His face lights up, he takes my hand, shakes, and says, "Friends."

A weight is lifted off me. I think I can smile again.

"This is nice," Aria whispers. "This is really good. I'm glad we worked this out... were you mad at me too? Because I didn't prepare a speech like that."

Harry and I laugh. "You're okay, Aria. Next time you have to end my relationship though, please don't do it publicly."

She nods her head at the boxes then. "So you're not moving out then? Cause that's what it looks like you're ready for."

"I thought about it. For a little while at least. Eliza and I talked and I thought I should start fresh. You know, just, restart my life. To start, a new-"

"Place?"

"Job," I correct. "But moving out would be a little rash. I do need a change of pace though."

The change of pace will begin in my bedroom. I look around the small room and am forced to ask myself, is there really nothing more I have to show for myself than the books on these walls? How many of these have I actually read? Will I ever read most of them a second time? How many are just for show? Here because someone else told me I needed to read it.

"Twilight" and "Heart of Darkness" stare me down from the top of a stack. Even though I said I'd get to it eventually, it is still untouched from when Daniel challenged me on it.

I take both books off the stack and see a paperback copy of "Lisbon," beat and torn all the way to hell and back.

How many times have I read "Lisbon?" "Twilight?" How often do I go back to these comfort books?

I remember the first time I read "Lisbon." It blew me to a whole new reality, I had to read it all over again immediately. The book never made me question my relationship with Harry, but as time went on, and I read it three more times, I began to understand it better. The book wasn't a grand victory for the woman in the story, it was a validation for the readers. It said, "It's okay to let go, it takes strength to move on." God, I loved this book. This is going to kill me, and probably ruin my love of Wolf Alice as well.

"Lisbon" is the first to go. I place the book in one of the cardboard boxes labeled "donate."

Maybe you're thinking, *Sil, you've got HUNDREDS of books!*

It'd be so much more worth it to trade them in!

What am I going to do with that? Relapse? Out of these hundreds, there are dozens upon dozens I haven't read. I think I'll be good. Besides, the library could use them better.

Next on the agenda: "Twilight" and "Heart of Darkness." Easy choice here. "Heart of Darkness" will go off to the side to keep, and I'll make it a priority to read. "Twilight?" Read it too many times. The series will go in the "donate" box.

As soon as it's dropped I regret it, and grab the series back out from the box. Baby steps, okay? We don't have to completely erase the past.

Three piles come out of this renovation; donate, comfort keeps, and to-be-read. Deciding which ones to put in "donate" or "comfort keeps" expected to be one of the hardest things Silvia Wright has ever done, but with every book put in the "donate" box, I feel a sense of relief, like the air is easier to breathe.

"Tale of Despereaux." Pages are falling out of the binding. I could get a new copy, but this one was *mine* as a child, and I want to read *this* copy to my kids. Keep. "When in Rome." Fantastic book, five out of five stars, highly recommend to everyone. But will I read it again? Probably not. Donate. "Thinner," by Richard Bachman, aka, Stephen King. Too on the nose. "Donate." Wait, no, shit that's a first edition hardcover. "The Dark Half," Stephen King's book about his pen name coming back to haunt him... donate.

Every thirty or so books I go through, I find a bookmark stuck between the pages. Sometimes the bookmark is one that came with the book. Sometimes it's a random sticky note.

Bookends

In one, a paperback of "The Book Thief" that Lucas passed down to me, the bookmark is a photo of us. We had to read the book in sixth grade. I was new to the school that year. It was only grades six through twelve, and Aria was the only kid I knew in elementary school who came with me to this new one. I don't know if I'd say if we were friends or not at that point. What I did have though, was Lucas. Even though he was a senior, he still treated me like I was on his level. Maybe it wasn't a major step down for him, he could never claim to be the most popular kid around the halls, but Lucas never treated it like it was a big deal. He was my older brother, and he'd always look out for me. He gave me his copy of "The Book Thief," and I printed out the photo of us to use as a bookmark to have a constant reminder that my first year of middle school was a good one because of him.

I look around my room. There are no pictures or reminders of my family. No group photo from any past Christmas, or framed portraits of Aria and I on a getaway together. Nothing, except the slowly disappearing stacks of books. When was the last time I called Lucas up? I bet you forgot I have two other brothers. It's okay, by the look of my room, I have, too. At Thanksgiving, I thought I made a new friend in Tyler's girlfriend Camille and I haven't talked to her once since then. Everything's been about Daniel.

It's time to get back to work. I search the stacks for the books. *Summer Snow*, *Runaway Lover*, *Vanilla + Cherry*, those are easy finds. Straight into the "donate" box with you. *Titles are Hard to Come Up With* and *Treasure of the Deep Desert*, those are harder, buried beneath a cacophony of other books I'll never read again. *Binds* and

Habits, the two problematic books of his fake career. I'm done arguing on your behalf. I find *Stars Through the Trees* and feel no emotion dropping that one into the "donate" box.

There. That's all of them, right?

Good. No more Daniel Cassidy, and no more Ian Richards in my life.

VVVVVPPP

Who's texting me now? I pull out my phone, and, surprise to no one, Daniel.

> *-can I call?*

Ignore it, Silvia. You don't owe him any more of your energy.

> *-I'm getting on my flight in a few*
> *-gotta be back on the road for the tour*
> *-at least until word gets out*

Good. He leaves and I don't have to make a fool of myself ending things. It's over. We're over. I don't need to talk to him. He doesn't deserve better than being ignored. I can just let it fizzle. Eventually, this whole thing will fade away and he'll never cross my mind again.

Never, unless word doesn't get out. Another Daniel Cassidy book will be written. I'll see the reviews of some new best-selling romantic tragedy or hear a quote from a signing event about how the girl with the auburn hair never let him apologize…

What the fuck am I talking about? *He* doesn't write the shit! He's just a puppet and that's just what it is, shit!

But, there was one book he had say in. I guess… there was one book of his I didn't put in the box.

Stargazing. lies unobscured on my nightstand. I've looked at it a hundred times since starting this cleaning out. That one, at least, was real.

Through the wall, I can hear the conversation Aria is having with Harry. They're trying to keep their voices down, and it's nothing important concerning Daniel or I. It's just Harry's voice that really catches my ear, the melancholy in his voice. It's the same voice he spoke in for those last few months of our relationship, and a period after the break-up. The period of time where I strung him along, too scared and unsure of myself to end it.

I'll do it right this time. If Daniel deserves anything, it's that much. And not over text or on the phone. I'd rush to the airport for some cheesy climax, but there's no way I'm getting there on time. And NO, that's not a 'there's no way I'm getting there on time' to set up a bait and switch. I'm 40 minutes away from the airport if he was smart and turned in his rental in Albany instead of Rochester, and he said he's getting on the plane in a few minutes. I won't call him to get him off the plane either, just to officially end it. That's just cruel. I'll have to wait until I see him in person again.

Interlude:
Stars Through the Trees

Released: July 12th, 2022

Synopsis: Harold and Lydia Zhegler always wanted to retire into a life of living out of an RV, with nothing tying them down in one place. After an accident with Lydia's job, Harold decides for them it's finally time to take to the road. With all their possessions left behind, Harold and Lydia can finally live out their dream, and take the time to look back on their lives. What parts were worth the heartache? Was any of it wasted? How will they make up for lost time, and is it possible to get any back?

-Page count: 201

-Read: July 19th, 2022

-Rating (Goodreads average):4.2/5 Stars

-Rating(Mine): 4.5/5 Stars

Review: After a wild year for Daniel Cassidy, and a long hiatus, "Stars Through the Trees" is being hailed as a well needed return-to-form.

Bookends

Every early review talked about how it is almost great enough to forgive the "strange" directions Daniel went in with his previous books this year. It's all about how it "feels like the *real*" Daniel Cassidy. Unfortunately, no one is talking about the quality of the book on its own. I'm glad it's getting good press, but this must have been what Stephen King felt like when he was writing Misery and the character of Annie Wilkes who is forcing the author she's a "fan" of to only write what *she* wants, not what is true to him.

I'm sure a big part of this novella did come out of the public response to "Binds" and "Habits," shown by the tameness of the content, but it still works incredibly well as a grounded character piece out of context.

Like the time we have left after we retire, this book is short. 201 pages doesn't tell an epic, but it's very fitting and doesn't try to force any filler. This is also one of those stories that you're not really sure of where it's going or what the point is until the very end. It works here and is able to keep your attention because of how short it is. I read this novella in just one evening.

– SPOILERS FROM HERE–

I'm still not sure how I feel about the ending. Whenever Daniel Cassidy's endings aren't traditionally happy, "love conquers all" type, they're at least optimistically ambiguous. When it's revealed that his wife is dead, and Harold has just been imagining her still there with him, it just left a slightly sour taste in my mouth. I understand the theme that love will always carry on, and he's learned to not be sad anymore because he too will die soon, and that means he'll be with her again, but the execution was off. Instead of it being a cute ending, I can only think of how sad it makes the whole story feel for me. The story as a whole is still phenomenal but… yeah. Wow. What a downer.

All in all, I still highly recommend this book. I wish the ending was a little more conventionally happy, but I'm happy to have romance back in Daniel Cassidy's stories.

25

Daniel spoke with a recognizable lower energy during his signing event in Houston. At the start of the event in Austin, it looked like he was about to pull through and put on a good show. For this one, he begins with a reading of the prologue.

"The last thing Dillon saw of Louise as her pod ejected from their ship were her sparkling sapphire eyes, and the tears that flowed from them," he reads in a low voice.

Someone, not even in the back, but close to the front row, shouts, "Speak up! Can't hear you!"

Daniel gives the woman a look with hardened eyes and keeps reading at the same volume.

Daniel's lack of energy spreads throughout the room. You can see on the audience's faces that they feel uncomfortable like an imposter wandered into the store where the event is being hosted in and was pulled to the stage. If only they knew, I guess.

What surprises me the most is I haven't yet seen anything on social media about his true identity. The patrons of the Cellar didn't seem all that responsive, but surely one of them had to be a fan, or at least knew about Daniel Cassidy books. But no, radio silence across the board.

When the prologue is finished, Daniel is slow to close the book, treating it like fine China. He doesn't even ask for questions, one of the event handlers has to announce that the Q&A has begun.

A woman in the front row is called on first, and she doesn't waste time with pleasantries. "Mr. Cassidy, are you feeling ill?"

A number of the raised hands drop.

"No, ma'am," Daniel says. "I'm fine, thank you." He then looks at the handler, who gives him an abrasive look. Then to the audience, "Yes, you, sir."

"Mr. Cassidy, you've said in previous interviews about the novel that the dedication *was* based on someone, but now, as you say, 'things changed.' It was noted that you bailed on an event in New Orleans this last week. Does this dedication have anything to do with that?"

"Ummm… I apologize for my absence. I had things to deal with at home. And furthermore, I don't understand what that has to do with the novel itself. It's just a dedication."

There is some chatter amongst the audience, and the man follows up his question. "Well, I'd say it's fair. If your personal life changes dramatically, a new love interest or something like that… well, you're a romance writer… I'd think that would have major implications on your work."

Daniel leans in slightly to the microphone. "They're just sappy love stories, don't look too deep into it."

At this, the crowd loses it. Some of them are up on their feet, shouting questions and accusations at him. One or two people even walk out. It's absolutely incredible to watch, like when a "Star Wars" nerd said a totally reasonable opinion, and the entire fanbase loses their absolute shit.

Through it all, Daniel retains his calm, low energy.

The handler steps in again and attempts to calm the audience down, then whispers something to Daniel. One can only assume it's a threat to get his shit together.

Daniel apparently ignores it and calls on another raised hand.

"Hi, Daniel. I'm just wondering, are you drunk? Not relapsing back into your old *habits* are you?" The question gets a few faint laughs from the audience.

"No, but I wish I was, and I plan to be later," Daniel says, for the first time with a smile.

The crowd again goes wild, but as I watch it all unfold, I know I should still be mad at him, but I admire his candor. Maybe I'm the only one who can, knowing the full extent of the situation and what *Habits* really put him through.

"All right, I'm sorry!" The handler steps in. "Thank you all for your time, but we have to wrap things up!"

The crowd becomes even louder, demanding answers to their questions and shouting their grievances at Daniel for ruining the magic of their reading experience. But through the crowd, Daniel sees one more hand rise.

"Yes, the woman in the back," he says in a demanding voice that quiets the room.

"Do you have any regrets with your work?"

It's impossible to read Daniel now, save for the truth in his eyes begging, pleading, tearing itself apart to escape. He thinks for a moment, searching for the right thing to say.

"All of it." He pauses, maybe expecting another round of shouting to begin, but it's like the audience knows there's more to come. "From the first book I put my name on, it's all been a mistake. I regret leaving home, and I regret not speaking up sooner. I regret lying to the people closest to me, to protect a career I don't deserve. I've always seen what was most important to me, standing right there on the other side of the window, and I regret being too scared to do something about it. I'm sorry, Silvia. More than anything, I regret breaking your heart, and knowing that it's really over."

There's nothing more I can say. The deed is done, and we can both hopefully have closure now.

I take my seat again, and the handler closes out the event. In a few hours I'll be back on a flight home, and tomorrow the final doors will be shut.

26

Bookends closed its doors for the last time on December 31st, 2023. All the stock that wasn't sold by the 29th was bought as a blind buy by a local author/collector (don't think it's a major coincidence that there's another author from Saratoga, they're like a dime a dozen in this town). When the store was finally emptied of all the boxes, Ellie and I had one last heart-to-heart on the green couch over a glass of champagne, a bittersweet send-off and celebration of things to come. I expected another flood of tears from both of us, but I think we've both come to terms with the fact that the story of Bookends has come to its close. At least, even though we acted like it was, this wasn't the end of mine and Ellie's relationship. I have finally run out of excuses to not go to church with her, especially now that I don't work weekends. And I won't lie, it feels good going again. Call this the epilogue if you will, or the first chapter in the next story.

I really expected this "change of pace" to happen much faster. Like I could just skip ahead to the "thriving" part of my character arc. Unfortunately, it's been eight months since Daniel and I broke up and I'm working full-time for my parents. And not even social media like I'd been doing before. At least, it's not my main role here. Next time you get your teeth cleaned at the Wright Dentistry & Oral Surgery, you can check in with me. In my parents' eyes, it's a good way to diversify my résumé. To be fair, it's never been the most impressive piece of paper.

It's not all a letdown though. There has been some good change. Like everyone else on New Year's, I decided a gym membership would be a good investment. Yeah, I know it's cliché, but you know what, I'm glad I did. For two, sometimes three days a week, I find an incredibly meditative state on the weight machines. I have no plans to become a bodybuilder or anything like that, but spending time in the gym has been unbelievably great for my stress! My only concern going into it was pervy or annoying gym bros. I asked Aria to start coming with me, to no avail, but God must be looking down on me and rewarding me for going back to church because a certain someone from recent memory has been my unofficial gym buddy.

After Camille and my brother Tyler broke up, I didn't think I'd see her again. Hell, I didn't think I'd see her at all after Thanksgiving, but we got talking, and turns out she basically lives at the gym. So along with a gym buddy, I sort of also have a personal trainer, which is great because I had no idea what I was doing when I first started here.

Camille isn't the only new person in my life. Don't get too excited, but I have gone on a date since the breakup. It didn't work out, but it wasn't horrible. He had an appointment for a teeth cleaning and on his way out dropped a cheesy pickup line. "I knew this place knew what they were doing when I saw how beautiful your smile was." Clint and I didn't have a terrible date, it was just one of those situations where we had fun but lacked real chemistry. We tried a second date, but we both knew it wasn't there. Hopefully, my date next weekend with Taylor goes better. We shall see. If anything, I'm just impressed with myself for not hiding away in my room 24/7 anymore.

Not quite "thriving," but doing better. Yeah, definitely doing-

What the fuck is this?

Why is Daniel's, I mean Ian's, face popping up on my phone?

Here I am, scrolling through TikTok looking for a trend to use for the dentistry and this post pops up for a new book.

This beautiful girl I follow with the cutest dimples I've ever seen and am incredibly jealous of, holds up a copy of a book, with a press image of Daniel (Ian! Holy hell, get it right Silvia) to the side.

"I really thought that after everything was exposed, that'd be the end of an era, but apparently, the guy behind Daniel Cassidy actually wrote his own novel! This is called 'Auburn Dedication," by Ian Richards, and I'm only three chapters in, but completely obsessed!"

I tune out the rest of what the girl is saying, and scroll through the comments.

Nope. lost all faith in this guy.

Why should we care? He's not a writer just a model

I'd give it a shot

I can't wait to read it!

Ehhh... this looks desperate

Does anyone know if this has anything to do with the girl at the texas signing for "Stargazing?"

> *Saw the early reviews. Self indulgent crap*
>
> *I loved ths one!*
>
> *I was there when he got exposed! Super awkward. This was before the* texas signing.
>
> *Pretty sure that guy modeled for me in college??*

So, Daniel (fuck it, I'm still calling him that) has a new book? Good for him. Could have been more subtle with the name. If this is an attempt to get back together, I'm not biting. Sorry, Daniel, I've come too far to give back into your schemes.

This is just sad, honestly. He went through all this work, something that probably cost tens of thousands in marketing, and for what? To impress me? No, thank you.

It's probably a massive failure anyway. I bet no one else is talking about it. I click the hashtag, #AuburnDedication, and am disappointed to see there probably hasn't been this much attention on one of his books since *Habits*.

Video after video has girls talking about either how great this new book is, or how desperate it reads, with very little middle ground. One post is a recording from the signing event in Texas. The person recording was in the front row, and it's impossible to see my face (thank God), but Daniel's face is clear as day. The pain in his eyes hits me as hard now as it did then.

It's just a ploy, Silvia. You've moved on. You'll see Taylor this weekend, and it'll be such a wonderful night that you won't even think about Daniel. In fact, I'm *done* thinking about him, right now.

Before closing the app, I hit the settings for the hashtag and click "Do not show posts like this." I've moved on.

* * *

Saturday takes its time arriving. I have a better feeling about this one than my date with Clint.

Taylor looks absolutely stunning, dressed up to the nines for some fancy restaurant she refuses to reveal. Aria teased that a "simple dinner date" for a first date was too plain. I disagree. I can't remember the last time I got to dress up like this for a night out. Even with Daniel, we never found the time for a fancy date.

We get in her car and the radio turns on.

A familiar soft yet plaintive keyboard, and the voice of the most incredible singer I've ever heard. I know this song, and it makes me want to smash the dashboard.

"How Can I Make It Okay?" by Wolf Alice. I have to change it.

"Not a fan of them?" Taylor asks.

"Not the right mood."

We both know there's more to it, but Taylor is nice enough not to pry. Instead, she steers the conversation into safe territory. Small talk. Work, family, the basics.

I do my best to engage in the conversation, it's easy to find natural dialogue about my brothers. Parents, less so. But the whole car ride, and into our date, all I can think about is Daniel.

At the end of the night, when she drops me off she says, "I don't know what's on your mind, but, I don't want you to worry

about tonight." Her smile is so kind as she speaks. "I'd still like to see you again, and if you want to talk, you know, I'm an open book."

"Thank you." I kiss her on the cheek. "I do. I do want to see you again. I think I just have some stuff to work out first."

As I lay in bed, I look up Ian Richards. In particular, his book tour. No, don't worry, I'm not going to crash another. I just want to know when he's going to be home again.

* * *

Lake George in the summer, truly is one of the places to be. All the peace of winter is gone, and every inch of every sidewalk and park is packed with tourists. I don't want it to end of course, that'd destroy the economy of this town. It only annoys me for the time because it's hard to see if Daniel is coming. What's easier to see is all the guys in swimsuits who think they're hot shit, giving me a smile and wink like that counts as a genuine attempt at flirting.

I check my phone constantly for texts from him. We said to meet at four, and it's only three-fifty, but I still feel annoyed he's not here yet. I just need to clear a few things up and get back home to get ready to go out with Aria tonight.

Right at four, I see him walk through the crowd toward me and sit down."

"I was worried you wouldn't actually come," he says.

"I told you I would. Think I'd lie?"

Daniel drops his head and laughs gently, "All right, I deserve that. Hope you didn't ask me here just to knock me."

Don't waste anyone's time, Silvia. Just get to the point. "I read your book last night."

He perks up, and when he looks into my eyes, his speak of joy. "What'd you think?"

"It's not your best work."

Daniel fixes his posture and looks out to the water. "Yeah, well... I guess I don't have a ton of experience in the field."

I wait a moment, wondering if he has anything else to say. When it's clear that's it, I add, "It wasn't your worst either. It was engaging having the point of view from the antagonist. But the flow could be a little better, and the dialogue needs a little more subtext. Everything was too direct. You left nothing to the imagination."

He looks at me again, this time from the corner of his eye. "I'll work on that. Any other critiques?"

"The protagonist."

Daniel turns his entire body to face me. "What was wrong with her?"

I turn to meet him. "Nothing. That's the problem. You painted her without any flaws. It makes it uninteresting for the reader. Unrelatable."

"What if that's the point? That's how the antagonist sees her."

"Good luck connecting with an audience."

"You're the only person it needs to connect with."

We've found ourselves closer together on the bench. His lips are almost on mine.

I pull back and stand up, walking over to the pier railing.

312

You came out here for answers, don't play around.

"Why'd you out yourself? I'm sure the publisher wasn't happy."

"Eh, for all I care, Daniel Cassidy is dead. Got hit by a bus or something, and you can't sue a dead man."

"Yeah, but they can sue you. Wasn't that a breach of contract or something?"

He nods. "Would have been. But Reggie, the writer I mean, we had a talk and he agreed. It was time to kill him off and let Ian Richards have his life back. The publisher won't argue with him."

"What about the sequel to 'Stargazing?'"

He stands and walks slowly towards me. "It had an open ending. The reader can work with that, right?"

No, stop it Daniel, I'm not playing this game. He draws closer and I step further back.

"You shouldn't have done that," I say, looking out toward the lake. "I didn't come out here to get back together with you."

"Then why are you here?"

"I…"

Why am I here?

I feel Daniel come up behind me, expecting him to wrap his arms around me like we're back on that first date in the cold November air. I could almost be there now.

"I didn't write that book to try and make it on my own." His hands fall on my arms and he spins me around. There in his eyes, the last place I'd ever expect to see it, is honesty. "I wrote it so you could finally know me. No more lies."

"But what about 'Runaway Lover?'"

"What about it?"

"The whole point about not rushing into those fantasy endings."

"Oh, Sil," he laughs. "*I* never said that."

<u>Epilogue:</u>
Stargazing Into Her Eyes

Released: Nov. 14, 2023

Synopsis: Love transcends light years. The U.S.S.S. Stevenson has been caught in a meteor storm. During the evacuation, Captain Dillon Perry was able to get his entire crew to safety, except for one. The love of his life, Louise Carmine's escape pod was sent hurtling into uncharted space.

Against all odds, Dillon commandeers a craft to go searching for her. He'll face off against terrifying creatures on terrifying worlds if only to look into her eyes one more time.

-Page count: 287

-Read: Nov. 21, 2023 - Dec. 10, 2023

-Rating (Goodreads average): 4/5 Stars

-Rating(Mine): 5/5 Stars

Review: It's been over a year since Daniel released a new book, and I don't think anyone expected a sci-fi adventure. But that's not what we're here to talk about.

I don't know if I can give an unbiased review of Daniel Cassidy's books anymore. Not since (plot twist) he asked me out! Me!

It has made the book extremely enjoyable, but also extremely hard to read. We all want to imagine ourselves in place of the characters we're reading about, but I'm on a whole new level now. The coincidence of Louise looking like me is insane! It's like this book was written just for me.

This is also the reason I struggled to get through it. At least twenty times per page I caught myself drifting off into a fantasy of Daniel and I, and I'd have to start the page over again. Every word the character Dillon professes to Louise sounds like Daniel whispering it in my ear.

This book got overall good reviews, but science fiction rarely seems pop off, especially with Daniel Cassidy's typical readers. Daniel said this was going to be a start to a series though, and I hope readers are okay with that.

One thing is for sure though, I will always love this man.

Acknowledgment

Wow.

I really did not see this happening. People usually save this for last, but I have to thank YOU the reader first. "Bookends" has been a very long, and at times very aggravating journey. The original Kindle publishing only sold about 10 copies over the year it was out, and most were to friends. I really didn't think I'd sell any, especially as a paperback. At times I wanted to quit, but you the reader let me know it was well worth it.

I'd also like to thank my close friends and family for being my beta readers for the original version. I apologize for all the spice that probably made it very awkward, knowing it was me writing it.

And thank you to my beta and ARC readers! This was honestly the most intimidating part of this process. Putting it out there was one thing. People might read it, they might not. But you actively wanted to read it. Your excitement for my success fueled my own!

Thank you to my team at Valenza Publishing! You took the biggest chance on me, and I won't let you down!

Thank you to my fiancé for sticking with me and encouraging me through this, as well as for all the help developing the story. The original concept was actually a joint effort so yes, I will be sharing the royalties with you in the form of better birthday and Christmas gifts. I love you more than the world.

And most importantly, I thank God for the life he's given me. I'm sorry again for the spicy original version of this book.

About the Author

Ella Madeline Hayes lives a peaceful, quiet life in Saratoga Springs with her wife. She's an avid reader of all things romance, fantasy, and science fiction.

Please leave a review on Amazon or Goodreads!

Follow us on social media!

Ella M. Hayes
@Ella.hayes.books - Instagram

Valenza Publishing
www.valenzapublishing.com
@valenzapublishing - Instagram/Facebook/Threads
@valenza_publishing - TikTok

And support indie authors by checking out these
incredible books!

"Fate's Tether" by Jade Nioma

"Love in the Air" by Jenny Rabe

"Goodwill's Secrets" by Christopher Mele

"Witness to the Revolution" by Kiersten Marcil

Milton Keynes UK
Ingram Content Group UK Ltd.
UKHW021045211024
449814UK00017B/307

9 798989 136889